CENTRAL OREGON WRITERS GUILD
2023 LITERARY COLLECTION

Copyright © 2023 by COWG

All rights reserved. This book or any portion thereof may not be reproduced or used in any manner whatsoever without the express written permission of the publisher except for the use of brief quotations in a book review.

Printed in the United States of America

Cover photograph by Amy Berlin

First Printing, 2023
ISBN 979-8-9866920-2-9

Central Oregon Writers Guild
www.CentralOregonWritersGuild.com

TABLE OF CONTENTS

Adventures in Cooking, *Suzan Hixson* — 9
    Fiction
Bessie Butte Riff, *Marina Richie* — 14
    Poetry
The Biker, *Karen Spears Zacharias* — 16
    Nonfiction
Tall, Dark, and Nihilistic, *Hannah Love* — 20
    Fiction
2B, *Irene Cooper* — 26
    Fiction
Will I Ever Understand Italians, *Christine Bell* — 27
    Nonfiction
Divorce Doggerel, *Arlite West* — 34
    Poetry
Setting Down His Stuff, *Ginny Contento* — 36
    Nonfiction
The Mystery of the Basement Boogies, *Minda DeBudge* — 39
    Fiction
Branding Time, *Cecelia Granger* — 43
    Poetry
Ian McPherson, *William Barry* — 45
    Fiction
Pastorale, *Andrew J. Smiley* — 55
    Nonfiction
Move It!, *Carol Barrett* — 61
    Poetry

A Friendly Rivalry, *Mary Krakow* — 62
    Nonfiction

Now I Know, *Gerald Reponen* — 64
    Nonfiction

The World Hinge, *Marc Wagner* — 73
    Fiction

About Prayer, *Donna D'Orio* — 76
    Poetry

Chasing Clouds, *Erik Frank* — 77
    Fiction

A Cup of Coffee, *Kendall Brown* — 86
    Nonfiction

Last Call, *Lynda Sather* — 92
    Fiction

The Waves, *Matthew Friday* — 96
    Poetry

3, 6, 9, The Goose Drank Wine, *Kiyomi Appleton Gaines* — 97
    Fiction

Distance, *Mike Cooper* — 102
    Nonfiction

The Ultimate Revenge, *Barbara Cole* — 105
    Fiction

Raised by Books, *Samantha Reynolds* — 109
    Poetry

Hunger and Motherhood, *Dani Nichols* — 111
    Nonfiction

Banning Books Playbook, *Kristine Thomas* — 116
    Fiction

The Beginning, *Jennifer Forbess* — 120
    Fiction

Two Sheds, *Pam Tucker* — 130
    Poetry

A Mother's Hand, *Maureen Heim* — 131
    Nonfiction

Passing Over, *Cameron Prow* — 134
    Fiction

Dad, Batman, and Cornbread, *Dan Murnan* — 138
    Nonfiction

Verde (excerpt), *Jeffrey Kramer* — 143
    Fiction

Mesquite Melody, *Ted Virts* — 152
    Poetry

Peace March 1969, *Janet Dart* — 153
    Nonfiction

The Critics, *Evelyn Moser* — 157
    Fiction

Door, *Joan Gordon* — 165
    Poetry

See No Evil, *Ted Haynes* — 167
    Nonfiction

The Price of Inequality, *Diane McClelland* — 176
    Nonfiction

Neighborly Conversations, *Anna Marie Garcia* — 179
    Fiction

Ridgeline, *Corbett Gottfried* — 184
    Poetry

Pasta Cortona, *Karista Bennett* — 186
    Nonfiction

Our House, *Eric Moser* — 193
    Fiction

Cheat Grass, *David Cook*   203
    Poetry

Amidst a Pandemic, *Kathryn Mattingly*   204
    Nonfiction

Cars: A Love Story, *Niki Rainwater*   209
    Nonfiction

What I Hunger For, *Nadra Mlynarczyk*   213
    Poetry

My Summer at Camp Riley, *Patti Lopez*   215
    Nonfiction

Shirley, *Bob Sizoo*   222
    Nonfiction

Silent Movie, *Pamela Mitchell*   227
    Poetry

A Place Called Normal, *Neal Lulofs*   229
    Fiction

My Mother's Hands, *Kore Koubourlis*   239
    Nonfiction

How to Have Everything, *Anastasia Lugo Mendez*   242
    Fiction

INTRODUCTION

The Central Oregon Writers Guild presents our 2023 Member Anthology. Now in its second year, we were humbled to receive triple the volume of submissions and want to thank all writers for their support, enthusiasm, and contributions to our literary community. Join us in celebrating this year's collection featuring unique voices in fiction, nonfiction, and poetry.

We would also like to thank this year's cover artist, Amy Berlin, and our editorial team for helping to shape our 2023 Member Anthology: Michael Cooper, Ginger Dehlinger, Kristin Dorsey, Denice Lewis, Kathryn Mattingly, and Trish Wilkinson.

Founded in 2002, the Guild is a nonprofit organization run entirely by volunteers. Our goal is to mutually support and advance the growth and success of our members, in all genres and skill levels, through monthly meetings, quarterly workshops, and annual events.

ADVENTURES IN COOKING
Fiction by *Suzan Hixson*

As you know, some people when they decide to make a dish will carefully review the recipe and check their cupboards and refrigerators. If they find that they are missing one or more ingredients, they will carefully write down the ingredient, and the amount needed, and then go to the store to obtain it.

But not me. My motto, given to me by my mother, is, "What you don't have you can well do without." I suppose it goes without saying that my mother grew up during the GREAT DEPRESSION. Those of you who follow my blog, "Adventures in Cooking," are familiar with my style, my joie de vivre, and my laissez-faire connection to instructions, including my inability to thoroughly read them.

You, Dear Readers, were with me through my ill-fated trip to the coast, where I put a pot of water on to boil and went off to find appropriate sea creatures as well as the appropriate seasonings to go with them. In my defense it was a BIG pot of water. How was I to know it would boil so quickly? At least, the over-flowing water put out the fire, so I'm still not quite sure just why the owner of the cabin was so irate. Luckily, thanks to this blog, I was able to write off most of the damages as business expenses. And I want to reiterate how very much I appreciate the GoFundMe campaign one of you started that paid for the lawyer, and for my bail. It turns out judges do not have much of a sense of humor.

And of course, on top of all that mess, I chose the wrong sea creature. How was I to know that unlike lobsters, one does not put clams alive (and of course unshelled) into boiling water? They are BOTH sea creatures, after all, and people eat them both. God knows why… I mean, have you LOOKED at them?

However, I was able to pull success from the jaws of defeat UNLIKE what my mother always said, "Suzan you could pull defeat from the jaws of success!" Always is perhaps too large a word… it wasn't ALWAYS, just often enough to stay stuck in my mind. Of course, research has shown that it takes twelve positive comments to negate one negative… comment that is.

Anyway, with the reduction of water, the shelling of clams and the addition of a great amount of cream, butter, and pepper (which as I have proven over and again makes ANY dish improve) I was able to deliver an excellent clam—not exactly chowder, but it WAS good. And some of my customers even asked for seconds, so there you go.

And that claim of food poisoning was thrown out.

And then of course you remember the time I mistakenly replaced the cinnamon with turmeric while making pumpkin bread. This is the same time that I did not have any butter in the house (I KNOW! Can you believe it?) and so I used coconut oil. Then I increased the amount of brown sugar and added additional ginger and allspice and really, it worked. I did not get any requests for that recipe, but no one died. And no need for bail.

And you shared my anguish when the oven caught fire as I was baking my first ever gluten-free chocolate Bundt cake. Smoke began billowing out every crack of the stove. I opened the windows, turned on the fan and pulled the cake out of the oven. I used a towel to waft the smoke away from the alarm, and eventually the alarm shut off. Eventually, I reopened the door. Since the fire was no longer in the oven, I stuck the cake back in and closed the door.

I suppose it says something that not one neighbor called the fire department. But with the cake back in the oven I decided that it was time I called the fire department. To heck with neighbors anyway. By this time, the stove's fan and the cabinets on either side were flaming. I retrieved the fire extinguisher from under the box of games in the broom closet, pulled the tab and bravely sprayed the flames. Or rather I tried to. You all remember, I'm sure, the photos the newspaper ran under the title, **Neighbors Claim She's a Menace**. However, since I own the house, they have not been able to force me out. Again, I want to thank those of you who set up and donated to the GoFundMe campaign that helped cover the cost rise of my insurance.

And the cake turned out great. It cooked within the specified time. And it tasted just fine. Although it was very, very dry and crumbly.

And so, to today's efforts. I know. It has been a long time since I've posted on this blog. Yet, I assure you, I have not lost my adventurous, yet practical perspective.

First, I rifled through my plastic bags filled with recipes that I am going to try, really, truly, sometime. I chose a recipe for Spinach and Bean Casserole. In this case, the "beans" are black-eyed peas, making it the perfect New Year's Day dish. Next I opened the Pandora App and after deliberation chose the Etta James station. The other possibility was, of course, The Good Lovelies station, but that was just a little too upbeat. With the music chosen I danced my way around the kitchen, throwing in my own dance steps while cutting onions and sautéing…. However, I'm getting ahead of myself.

I had pulled the peas out of the freezer yesterday, so they were almost completely defrosted. However, when I measured them, alas! I had only two cups, and I needed three! Did I go to the store? Please, Dear Reader, you know me better than that. Of course not. So, black bean, or kidney, or garbanzo? Hmm, kidney beans would add more color, but then the recipe also called for tomatoes, which are red, so then black beans! One decision made.

The recipe called for one onion, seeming to not realize that onions come in many different sizes. Is the onion I had too big? I could use green onions from the garden. Nonsense! I chopped the entire onion. Were two cups of onion too much? Impossible. More onion is always better.

I actually had most of the necessary ingredients, including the fennel seed which I reduced to powder. After briefly considering the use of my rubber mallet, or perhaps a hammer as the tool of choice, I reluctantly decided on a small blender. It worked, sure, but where was the adventure?

Well, this was boring, there must be something else I can do. What else was in the freezer? Digging through the pulled-out drawer, I discovered… yum! Some crumbly chocolate cake, complete with gluten. It looks like it's been attacked a few times as the freezer drawer was pulled out and pushed back in. I wonder how long it's been in here. Well, it is still very chocolatey. Oh, and here were some chocolate molasses cookies. Oh, oh! and some chocolate no-bake cookies. I was sensing a trend. Ah, but here was a find. Hot peppers from my garden, frozen now for at least 1-1/2 years. Still good, I was sure, and a good addition to my casserole.

All was well. Sautéing the onions, spinach, tomatoes, salt, peppers, and fennel together, but I realized there was no room for the peas. I got a stock pot out, added the sautéed mixture with the peas and put them back on the stove. Turning the stove down, I took the iron skillet over to the sink and cleaned it. I was away from the stove only a minute, I swear, however when I returned the smell of burned onion and tomatoes wafted up, and the bottom of the pot was decidedly blackened. I poured the pot's innards into the casserole dish, giving just a taste to be sure it didn't seem burned. It didn't, though I thought I could have put in more of the hot pepper, and maybe more fennel. Or perhaps the fennel powder was just too fine. I really should have tried the mallet.

The cooking in the oven went over without a glitch. No fire, no firemen, no lawyers, no angry letters to the editors or nasty notes left on my door. It was a relief, although, there was a part of me that felt a bit wistful.

At any rate, I want to thank each and every one of my readers. You have been with me through each adventure. I truly appreciate your suggestions of what and where I might next cook, although Bernie, I think there is no balloon company that would allow me an open-fire grill while flying over drought-stricken timber land. I especially want to thank Barbara Torte and Larry Sinder. I can always count on you to be there for me, starting donation campaigns and connecting me with lawyers.

Until next time, remember, the most exciting adventures happen off-trail. Although falling off a cliff while being chased by a bear and breaking both legs did set me back a while.

BESSIE BUTTE RIFFS WHILE HIKING
Poetry by *Marina Richie*

All the riches of the world—Bessie Butte
Millions of manzanita leaves coining the sky

Song of Fox Sparrow's arrival. Grace notes
perched on a speared branch

Two hands on weathered fallen juniper
I see the winged ant readying…

Woodpecker tattoos the burned tree—
'Beauty is in the eye of the beholder'

Ruffled in her brushy coat renewed by fire
Bessie Butte shrugs off the planted pines

When distant chainsaws rip, gnash, and roar
Courting sparrows cannot hear their own duet

Chainsaw lull, a raven circles
split-fingered flap on my worried brow

Violin bow across taut string of Cascades
vibratos uplifting volcanos past
the tipping point, all glaciers
will melt as my anger surges… at us

I am coast, I am ocean, I am Cascadia
I am, was, is, will always be slipping backwards on sand

Pause here. Rub frocked leaf-burst of bitterbrush
Resiny sap tanging tastebuds

I forget actors and movies
remember birds and flowers

An ashy scaled wish underfoot—
Western fence lizard plumes by

What is a stanza?
A beetle's round hole in a gray log

THE BIKER

Nonfiction by *Karen Spears Zacharias*

He doesn't ride a regular bike anymore, not since he had that heart attack. "Ah've only got 27 percent me heart working," he said. "It was when the virus started, two year ago Christmas. Ah thought Ah'd caught it."

His loss of breath didn't turn out to be the result of a global pandemic, but something equally as threatening.

"So, Ah's bought meself a' electric bike."

The Biker, who was walking the day we met, took a seat at the picnic bench, gingerly holding onto his cane's carved-ivory handle, yellowed with age. The cane once belonged to his dad, and his grand before that. "Ah mostly swing it," he said, as if to apologize for needing it. "Ah jes use it to steady myself."

He has the athletic build of a long-distance runner, trim with broad shoulders. His hair is thick and white as a puff of cotton. His sweater is of the finest navy wool and the scarf about his neck is a paisley silk. His shoes are orthopedics, thick-soled. They look out-of-place on such a well-dressed man. Deck shoes seemed more in keeping with The Biker's style.

"You American?" he inquired.

"Why do you ask?"

"Yer accent," he said.

"You think I have an accent?" I teased.

"Aye," he said. I laughed. He laughed, too, with the ease of a man comfortable in his own skin, and with his life.

"Ye here on holiday?"

It's the question I am asked the most since my arrival in Scotland. I get it. I'm of the age when pensioners spend that last quarter of life going on holiday. People, young and old alike, are gap-mouthed when I tell them, no, I'm not on holiday. I'm in Scotland for educational purposes. I see it in their eyes, hear it from their lips: The "But ye're mah granny's age" from the young ones; and the "What are ye daft?" from the older ones. The ones in the middle? They are both bemused and in a bit of awe, "Braw! Git for ye!"

"Ye're 'ere at Uni?"

"Yes. You ever been to America?"

"No, never. Ah got aunts and uncles in America and a few cousins. Mah father was Irish. He had sixteen siblings. One was adopted. That's the one that went to America."

There's something in his tone I can't quite make out. A hint of ruefulness? A sense of having missed out on an adventure never taken?

He stares off toward the River Ayr before, unprompted, he speaks again. "Mah father's father was a farmer in Baile Uí Dhufaigh. Ah hav' a young brother thar still. He's had a stroke. He smoked aboot 70 cigarettes a day. The doctor told him to give them up 'cause they weren't doing anything for 'em."

I ponder the politeness behind that approach for a minute. I suppose doing nothing for him is a less direct way of telling him cigarettes will kill him. Did the doctor really word it that way? Or was this a brother's avoidance of the inevitable?

My own mother's doctors weren't inclined toward such avoidances. They told her flat out that cigarettes were the cause of her cancer, and that she only had a few weeks, maybe a month or two to live. She'd wept as they told her, this strong-minded mother of mine. A nurse by trade, she'd made peace with other people's deaths. It was her own she sought to delay.

It had all happened so rapidly. One day Mama sat down at her computer and couldn't read the words. Her training taught her she was either having a stroke or something worse was happening. She called for my brother to carry her to the hospital, where a brain scan revealed six elongated tumors. The lung cancer she didn't know she had already metastasized. The morning after doctors sent her home from the hospital, she held my hand, and wept tears of deep regret. "I wish they had caught it before it went to the brain," she said. It was one of the few times in my life I'd witnessed my mother cry. The first was when I was nine, and Mama got the news that her husband, my father, had been killed in the American War in Vietnam.

Turning back to the Biker, I asked, "Did you grow up here?"

"Lived 'ere in Ayr all mah life," he said.

Ayr is a beach community of nearly 50,000, located on the Southwest coast of Scotland. Home to the Tam O'Shanter pub made famous by Robert Burns, or as he's called by the locals still, Rabbie. There's a statue of him on the town square, just feet from the stop where visitors can catch a bus to the Robert Burns Museum in Alloway, about six miles south. There's a promenade that follows along the Firth of Clyde through town, down past the beachfront shops, past the war memorial and along the Low Greens, which, as the plaque notes, was dedicated to the burgh of Ayr in 1205 by King William the Lion. Once in a great while, the Northern Lights are visible from the beach at night. The sunsets are also worth the wait.

Before he retired, and long before his heart attack, The Biker worked in telecommunications and traveled all over Scotland. His favorite place on his route was the charming village of Oban. Situated along the Bay of Oban, near the Hebrides, the town brands itself as Scotland's smallest resort. It boasts a population of about 8,500 villagers. It's only a bit over 100 road miles from Ayr but a train trip between the two towns lasts over five hours. It takes more time getting there than it takes to explore Oban.

On days The Biker rides his electric bike, he can get around most of Ayr in a matter of minutes. It takes longer if he pedals on his own strength. The Biker shares some insider information on best practices for getting around: "If ye are in the town, you know where Marks & Spencer is?"

He waits for me to say I do, before continuing. "If ye walk down to an orange bike tied to the outpost, go into the bike repair shop there. The'ves got bikes, you can take them for a week free."

The Biker's heart attack was followed by a bout with kidney stones and then a bout with shingles. To deal with the stones, they put in a stint.

"Ye know where they put it?" he asked.

I nodded that I did indeed know where they put such a stent.

He in return whistled at the memory of the pain of all that.

He got the walking stick after that surgery. "I'll be 72 in July. I never thought about getting old until a year ago. Ye never think about getting old."

"I think about it all the time," I said. "I have thought about it most of my life." That's the gift of losing a parent early in life. You recognize the brevity of it all.

"It's a waste of time," The Biker said of thinking about getting old.

He's probably right.

Too late now, though. I've arrived already.

TALL, DARK, AND NIHILISTIC
Fiction by *Hannah Love*

My senior year of high school, I dated the lead singer of a Portland garage band. He was tragic and brooding, obviously. Showered daily but styled his hair to make it seem like he didn't. He carried Camus's *The Stranger* in his back pocket like an accessory.

We met in early spring at a pizza parlor in Laurelhurst. He was looming over four other punk rock boys in ripped skinny jeans and scuffed Vans, arms crossed over a faded Ramones t-shirt. I watched him carefully as he lazed against the booth. He was looking down at his friends, brows arched in apathy bordering amusement. The boys beneath him were a bundle of tussling puppies, tusking their noses with plastic straws, armpit farting, clutching their bellies through waves of laughter. But he just stood there, watching over them like a patient teacher. He seemed so much older. I felt like a little kid in my frilly pink blouse. My lacy ballet flats dug at my heels. My long blonde ponytail buzzed. I wanted to rip it out.

I recognized one of the boys from school and pivoted so he wouldn't see me standing there. It was too late. He called me over. My legs were weak and uncertain, like I was standing on the edge of a diving board. Somehow, I moved forward.

"Take a seat," he said, "this is the band."

I nodded vacantly, still staring at the boy who towered behind the group. Soft emerald eyes shrouded by a tumble of black curls blinked back at me.

"That's Raymond, lead singer," my classmate said, jerking his head upward.

"It's just Ray, actually," the singer corrected, "but whatever, it doesn't really matter."

I watched his mouth move around his words. Budding stubble peppered his strong jaw. He pulled his lips into a cool smirk. I could feel him watching me.

My cheeks were burning, so I dragged my gaze to the tabletop, tried to focus on crumpled napkins and empty Coke bottles. The glossy surface was scattered with abandoned pizza crusts in plastic baskets. *The Stranger* was tucked against one, partially obscured by the checkered deli paper spilling from it. I pulled it towards me. The cover was a spinning kaleidoscope of black spears and piercing whitespace. I was dizzy.

"Cool book," I said.

Ray's smirk softened to a smile. "You should read it. We could talk about it sometime."

Naturally, I ran to Powell's and bought myself a copy as soon as I left the pizza shop. Armed with a yellow highlighter, I spent hours reading it front to back in my room.

"*The Stranger*, huh?" my dad said, leaning against the doorway. "That's pretty adult, Lizzy."

"It's Liz, Dad," I said, flipping the page as if my pending adulthood depended on finishing the chapter.

After dinner, I brought a white trash bag up to my room. Plastic whipped through the air as I yanked it open. I stuffed it with pink and frilly things until it was stretched and bloated. I picked up the book again, and under the gaze of stuffed animals neatly lining my bed, I mused over irony and flirted with the idea that everything could mean nothing at all.

The weeks after I met Ray smelled of rosemary and fresh bread. He worked at his family's food cart, La Fromagerie, in Alberta. The space was artsy but welcoming, a tiny house with a gabled roof glowing in satin string lights. I'd ditch my friends to meet him there after school, sliding into a wooden picnic table with *The Stranger*. I'd read the same lines over and over again, looking up only to collect glimpses of him: long arms passing someone a gourmet grilled cheese, a pen tucked behind his ear, the corner of his mouth as he chewed thoughtfully on the cap. I'd catch him looking at me too. He'd wink, and somehow it was as if I was falling and shooting up to the sky at the same time.

On his break one day, he sat across from me with a cup of black coffee. His olive shirt was dusted with flour. He rolled his sleeves and leaned forward, cupping his chin with his hands. I pretended not to notice him, hoping it seemed like I was concentrating hard on reading.

He playfully kicked my legs under the table. "Hey, Stranger," he said, grinning through the nickname we'd started calling each other.

"Hi there," I said, closing the book.

"Where are your friends? I thought they were gonna hang today."

"They went dress shopping instead." I sipped the coffee. Bitterness bloomed in the back of my throat.

"Dress shopping?" he asked, running a hand through his hair.

I looked down at the table. *The Stranger's* cover churned. I let my focus soften on it, zoning out, trying to make it spin the other way in my mind.

"Liz?"

I shook my head and took another sip of coffee. "Oh, just some dance."

It wasn't just *some dance*. I knew that. Even then. It was prom. The centerpiece of senior year. The final ball with my friends before we left for college. Our conversations about it held a frenzied gravity, as if prom was a wedding or a wake. The girls all had *committed* relationships and were curious about Ray. They pecked at me with questions at the bus stop. Why hadn't I brought him around? Was he even my boyfriend? Was he taking me to the dance? I wasn't sure about the answers. As they boarded the Red Line to the mall, I'd said, "We're not really into that kid stuff." They stared at me in wounded realization, as if they had just caught me cheating. Guilt leaked from me as the bus moaned away from the curb. My words lingered in the exhaust, a stinging, sticky cloud. As I sat on a rusted bench waiting for the train across town, something grainy, like quicksand, shifted in my chest.

I set the coffee down and looked back up at Ray.

"A dance?" he scoffed, picking up the cup. "Those things are silly."

I winced internally and nodded, my muscles stiff and screaming in disagreement. I brought a hand to the back of my neck and rubbed idly. "Ray," I paused, "what are we?"

He leaned back, crossing his arms. "What are we?" he echoed. "What is anyone? Two people having a good time, I guess. Do you really care that much?"

More sand slid down my chest. "No," I said, smiling weakly. "I guess I don't."

"Good. Labels are dumb. What I'd *really* like you to be," he went on, sliding a ticket across the table, "is a fan at our show tomorrow night. Can you come?"

I nodded silently, hurt and guilt eddying in my throat, eyes stinging with tears I wouldn't let fall until I was alone.

My friends ignored me at school the next day. When they saw me in the hall, they slammed their lockers shut and turned away.

"Come on, seriously?" I said to their backs.

They didn't respond, or maybe they didn't hear me. I wanted

to go to them, say I was sorry, but I didn't. I sank to the floor and pulled *The Stranger* from my bag. I tried to read, but the words were thick and blurry, dancing up and down the page.

I wore black to the show. I painted my eyes in silvery shadows and thick liner. I worked my lips over a smear of red until my pout was bloody and dangerous. I let my hair run loose down my back. I swayed in the crowd, arms stretched overhead. I watched my hands swirl in ribbons of blue and purple light. I ignored the sinkhole in my chest, pushed prom and dwindling adolescence from my mind. It didn't matter. Nothing mattered.

When Ray finished his set, he snaked his arm around my waist. We danced for a while, bodies fused, absorbing the light around us. I let my thumb run along the pages tucked in his back pocket. We left the club for a waterfront lined with blossoming cherry trees. Soft pink petals tiled the wet pavement. Lilac and vanilla drifted past us as we walked. He pulled his fake ID from his wallet and put it between his teeth, eyebrows arching in invitation. I reached for it, but he ducked and tagged me, jogging towards the corner store. Laughing, I chased after him, bounding over the sidewalk, splashing through puddles. The damp Portland dusk moved through me, cooling my cheeks. I leaned against a brick wall, catching my breath, while he bought us beer. We took turns swigging from a brown paper bag on the Steel Bridge, legs swinging in sync over the river. The city rumbled on above us, our faces flushed in Stella Artois, eyes brightened in the lights bouncing off the water.

"So. Prom," he said, passing the bottle to me.

"Honestly? It's absurd," I said, drinking deeply, swallowing the lie.

"I mean, yeah. But maybe it'd be fun to go."

"To, like, make fun of people?" I asked, chuckling. "Don't you think it's pointless?"

He shrugged. "I think I'd like to go. With you, I mean."

My mouth dried. I took another swig; beer fizzed over my tongue. "With me?" I coughed. "What does *that* mean, Stranger?" I handed him the bottle.

He took it and set it down tenderly. "Hmm, what does it mean? What does *it all* mean?" He tucked the curtain of blonde behind my ear. I couldn't feel anything but his hand. The shifting sand in my chest settled, solidifying into something else. Something harder, more sure. The honking and screeching above us evaporated; Portland floated in silence. Then he kissed me, and Camus slipped from his pocket—mask and meaningless spiraling into darkness, plunging through the stillness of the Willamette.

2B

Fiction by *Irene Cooper*

I am always losing my religion, Leo says to his seatmate, *just to see it pop 'round again.* He lays his hand upon the white fist on the retractable arm. *Catastrophe trots through this life, one right after another, kicking up the dust, and we can't breathe. But there, on the ground, something moves, something glints in the sun. We stoop, we pick it up. Pocket it for later.* The plane drops in altitude. Leo looks past the seatmate's capellini pomodoro, gone cold and gelatinous on the tray table, and out the sliver of window. South America rises like a page of crumpled newspaper in a gale. The sapphire of the shallowing Atlantic currents beneath them, crashing opalescent at the shore. Seatmate slaps the shade shut. Leo closes his eyes. The pilot rights and lands the aircraft. Passengers chirp into their phones and proceed to the terminal, retrieve luggage, or file claims for missing baggage, and are waved into taxis. It would be dinner time soon, every bird asleep. *So much beauty in the arrival, in the departure, but of course, it is difficult to remain astonished at every middling moment of the disaster.*

WILL I EVER UNDERSTAND ITALIANS?

Nonfiction by *Christine Bell*

It was late Friday night. I had flown back to Milan from a week-long business event in Portugal. I was exhausted and anxious to get home to Cernobbio and into my bed. I speed-walked to my little Nissan Micra in the parking lot. If I drove quickly, I could be home before midnight.

All week, I had woken up early each morning to prepare for the day's meetings. I was responsible for keeping my team of forty people focused, making sure each session accomplished its goals, that our evening activities were fun. I put every ounce of myself into making it a successful event. But these week-long meetings always wrung me dry.

Now, I just wanted to crawl under the covers, close my eyes and sleep. I couldn't wait to wake up to Jacob and Zoey's not-so-quiet whispers as they tip-toed into my room and stood by my pillow peering at my face. As soon as my eyes opened, my children would urge me to get up and make them chocolate chip pancakes and play Zingo with them. That would be a nice change from the alarm clock waking me up all week.

I hit the highway, staying in the fast lane, and went as swiftly as my little car could carry me. I was close to home when a car behind me started flashing its headlights at me. It was pretty standard for Italians to flash their headlights. It meant: "I'm coming in fast, bitch, so move over. And hurry it up, because I really don't want to have to touch my brake pedal." I was already flooring it, going way over the speed limit, and I wasn't in the mood for dealing with Italian drivers. Did this idiot really need to go even faster than we were already driving?

My husband, John, and I always rolled our eyes at this headlight flashing. It felt rude and aggressive, but we were used to it after having lived in Italy for five years. Italians are proud of their fast cars, and they don't want anyone in their paths when they are trying to drive like Mario Andretti. We always just flicked on our blinker and moved over, even as we muttered to each other about it.

On this particular night, I simply wanted to get home, and the flashing headlights irritated me. Wasn't I going fast enough already? As I watched in my rearview mirror, the car kept coming, the headlights getting bigger and more menacing as the car came closer. I thought this guy might run right over the top of my car and keep going. He pulled up to my bumper, just a few feet away, even as we were still going close to 90 miles per hour.

I really had no choice. I moved over to the next lane, but I was pissed. And without thinking, when the car started to pass me, I lifted up my left hand, and gave him the bird, the good old-fashioned middle finger.

This did NOT go over well. The car slowed down, staying even with me on the road, driver to driver. I ignored him and kept staring straight ahead at the dark road in front of me, though I could sense him right next to me.

He veered into my lane, inches from my side mirror. My reflexes kicked in, and I swung the wheel hard to the right to avoid his car smashing into mine. My tires hit the gravel still going at Mach speed. I worried I'd crash, but I didn't. I regained control of the car and got back on the highway. Every inch of my being was in a heightened awareness; my skin tingling, my heart racing, my hands shaking as I gripped the steering wheel.

He steered toward me again. I thought I would crash and die because of this crazy bastard. My hands gripped the wheel. I looked through my side window to see if I could see who this person was, but it was dark, and I just saw the silhouette of a man. Even though he couldn't hear me, I screamed: "You fucker! What the hell are you doing?"

I was in shock and didn't know what to do. I had to get home. But he wasn't done yet. He pulled his car behind me, inches from my bumper, tailing me. His headlights were like evil eyes, with menacing eyebrows. Tiny lightbulbs arched up over the main headlight, glaring at me ominously.

Was he trying to make me have an accident? Was he going to try to kill me? It was close to midnight, and there weren't many cars on the road. There certainly was nowhere I could jump out of my car and run to in the middle of the highway. My four-cylinder, putt-putt car was no match for a Mercedes. I couldn't outrun this monster car; I just needed to keep going, never stop. I kept the pedal on the floor. He stayed steadily behind me.

When I saw the toll booth ahead, I worried about stopping. Would he hit me from behind, jump out of his car, and run up to my window? The toll booths were all unmanned, automated pay machines. I couldn't get help. I had a choice; either stop and pay or crash through the gate. I got my credit card ready, moved like lightning through the process, my foot already on the pedal as soon as the gate started to lift, my eyes checking the rearview mirror.

But he wasn't behind me anymore.

I picked up speed again, and suddenly he was behind me again. I wondered if this was how my life would end. Was this my fate? To be killed on the highway by a madman driver? But I didn't have time to dwell on that. I tried to think calmly. Maybe he would leave me be when I exited the highway.

But no. The headlights followed behind at the exit. I was in a complete panic now. What if he followed me all the way to my house and then killed me or beat me up? No one would be on my tiny street at this hour to protect me. Nothing was open at this hour. It was pitch dark. I decided to call the police.

As I drove down the highway off-ramp, I dialed from my cell phone. When a man answered, I spoke very quickly. "Someone's following me. They're trying to push me off the road … No, he got off the highway where I exited. He's right behind me. I'm scared he's going to follow me home and hurt me. Please, you have to help me."

"Instead of driving home, just drive to the police station. You know where it is?" he asked. I did know where it was; it was a couple hundred feet from my house.

"*Va bene*, but someone has to be waiting outside when I get there." The station had a big fence around it, and if no one was outside when I pulled up, who knew what would happen before I could ring the police buzzer? He agreed, and we hung up.

I drove down the long off-ramp and headed toward the police station. As I sped along, about half a mile from my house, I saw a welcome sight. A man in a *Carabinieri* military police uniform waved me over. The military police had set up a road-block and were randomly pulling cars over. Usually I dreaded a potential pull-over, but tonight, the familiar sight caused me great joy. I pulled myself into the checkpoint along the side of the road with huge relief. I would be safe now. Thank God.

Then, to my complete horror, the crazy man in the Mercedes pulled in behind me. I couldn't believe it. What was he thinking? A *Carabinieri* officer came over to my car. I was hysterical as I tried to explain what was going on. My words tripped over each other as I told him what had happened. "You have to protect me. That man in the car behind me. He tried to push me off the road. He's been following me for miles and miles. He is going to follow me home and I don't live far from here."

"*Calmasi*," the officer, an older overweight man, told me. This did NOT calm me down.

"You don't understand. That guy might try to kill me."

"Just sit here a minute. I'll be right back." He walked to the car behind me and stood talking to the man. I couldn't see the man at all through his windshield in the dark, and with his frightening headlights still glaring at me.

A few minutes later the *Carabinieri* returned to my window, leaning down to speak to me. "He says you flipped him off." This was said in an accusatory tone as if I had done something wrong. As if a simple gesture justified attempted murder on the man's part.

"What?" I was astounded. "Yeah, I did flip him off—he was flashing his lights at me. Who cares? That doesn't mean he has the right to try to kill me."

"But you shouldn't have flipped him off. Then he wouldn't be so upset. Why don't you both get out of your cars, and you can apologize to each other?"

"Apologize? Let him see my face? No way!" If I apologized, then the man would know who I was and would try to get me another time. "You have to keep him here when I leave so I can get home safely."

"He's not going to try to hurt you. You're fine. Just get out, and you guys can make it all right."

Clearly, as a man himself, he had no idea how threatened I felt. I had never felt such direct and imminent fear for my life, ever. I had traveled all over Europe by myself as a teenager, hitchhiked in Sicily, letting random strangers pick me up in their cars to take me to my next destination. But this was different. This man had tried to push me off the road. I couldn't stop shaking. Adrenaline coursed through my body and all I wanted was to get away from this threat—to hide and never be found.

"No. No!" I yelled. "I'm not doing that. I am terrified of him. I am NOT getting out of my car. You absolutely must keep him here. Please! I'm begging you. He tried to run me off the road. He's been following me for a long time. He's crazy!"

Finally, the officer acquiesced—my terror had gotten through to him. "Okay, okay. I'll keep him here. You go on home. Everything's going to be fine."

"*Grazie.*" I rolled up my windows quickly, glanced at my rearview mirror again, and pulled back onto the road. It was only two more turns to my street. I was home in two minutes, looking through my rearview mirror the entire time to make sure I wasn't being followed. I squeezed the car into a parking spot, jumped out, and ran through the safety of my condominium gate, watching the entire time to make sure the evil Mercedes didn't come around the corner.

Once I got through that gate, I sighed with relief. I had made it. Everyone was asleep when I came into the house, so I couldn't share my terror with anyone. Instead, I had to sneak into bed next to John. I tried to calm my breathing as I lay there, remembering the events of the past thirty minutes. I had a hard time sleeping. That comfortable bed I had been looking forward to didn't have the power to counteract the Mercedes of Terror.

A few days later, I recounted the story to my Italian friend, Laura. When I finished, I expected her to mirror my outrage. I was waiting for her to say, "I can't believe he did that. It sounds terrible." But she didn't say anything like that. She shook her head at me instead, and then, as if she was chastising a child who didn't know better, she said, "But you flipped him off." I looked at her, my eyes wide.

That was exactly what the *Carabinieri* had said. "You shouldn't have given him the finger. That's very bad."

She was disappointed with *me*. I sat there in stunned silence. Then I sputtered, trying to defend myself, "But … but he tried to run me off the road."

She just shook her head. "You shouldn't have flipped him off."

As I took in her reaction, I realized that something wasn't right. I had felt justified in flipping off the man. But I was learning that giving someone the finger in Italy is a much more egregious action than in the U.S. How was it possible that after living in Italy for close to ten years by that time, I was still learning about the differences between our two countries? Shouldn't I have figured this out by now? If my friend, who was a perfectly reasonable human being, thought that flipping someone off was a reason to try to run someone off the road, then I still had a lot to learn about Italy.

DIVORCE DOGGEREL
Poetry by *Arlite West*

Force force yourself up
despite the huge boulder
dropping hard in your stomach
when your feet hit the floor.

Each week has 3 Thursdays
to drag trash barrels out
to the curb late at night-
it's your job now.

You hurt when the neighbors
neglect you—no invites;
fearing you, a divorcee,
on the prowl for their mates.

You tell your friends
you're managing fine
because you'll burst into tears
at their pitying eyes.

Solo at the movies
or in church pew alone,
with no one to talk with
about film or sermon tone.

Pile up the pillows
on that now too-big bed
for something to hug
though you're feeling half dead.

Turn on the radio
your first homecoming choice—
fill up the empty house
with a substitute voice.

Invent new ways to bear
holidays all alone,
spending your birthday
trying to get a new loan.

Try hard to ignore
the gossipy news:
he's dating a colleague
who's divorcing, too.

Take a culinary course
to enhance your meals,
knowing full well
that time wounds all heels!

SETTING DOWN HIS STUFF
Nonfiction by *Ginny Contento*

"I think that's the last of it. Could you carry this last box down to the car for me?" he asks.

He has back problems. Since we first met over six-and-a-half years ago, I've always carried his stuff. Off the table I lift up a box with the small pile of expensive suits laying over it, suits that hardly got worn during these last five.

We walk towards the front door of the apartment. He stops and knocks on my son's door before entering.

"See ya, buddy," I hear him say. "Hey, you take care of yourself."

"Yeah, you too," my thirteen-year old son says from inside the room.

Coming back out into the hallway, he gently closes the door. He looks straight at me. I'm not looking back.

The elevator whispers as it carries us down. He interrupts, asking, "Are you okay with what I said to him? I mean, I just don't know what you're supposed to say."

I'm studying a spot where the paint got chipped off the metal elevator cab door, leaving a deep scratch. The elevator comes to its gentle stop. The door slides sideways.

"How the hell should I know?" I say, leaning in to swing open the second door made of heavy wood, with more force than I had intended. My vision blurs and my throat is starting to harden and ache. Blinking helps to steady my focus.

We pass through the small lobby and out to the enclosed garage. None of the neighbors are down here. Nobody is unloading groceries from a car trunk or dumping out their recyclables. The silence echoes. It's just us.

He unlocks and opens the passenger side door for me, the only space left in our one family car, otherwise full to the brim with his belongings.

In the meetings with Karen, the mediator we had hired, I told him to go ahead, please take the car. In fact, take anything, just please go *away*. And take all the reasons why you can't find a job while I'm working two—or why you refuse to take a class or volunteer somewhere—or for Christ's sake, even help around the house. And take all those reasons why you'll only take pills, and more and more and more of them. The medicine cabinet can't even hold all the different bottles anymore.

And the denial, the broken promises, all the lies?—to me, to the doctors? to yourself? *Please, oh please, take all of those, too.*

I place the box on the front seat. On top of it I fold the suits that he never wore as a lawyer. I gently close the car door.

I'm done.

"So, I guess that's it," he says standing there. He tries hugging me one last time. I reciprocate his inexhaustible politeness with a perfunctory pat on his back. I pull away from his embrace.

His gaze searches mine. Looking straight at the car, I say, "Hey, you take care." My lips are pursed, and I'm blinking more quickly. The ivy over there is in need of trimming. And who forgot to roll up the hose?

I step aside as the car backs up and halts. The decrepit garage door grinds away, slowly rolling itself up. These last seconds seem to lag on for more than they should. I'm counting each breath. But then the car lurches forward and glides out into the late summer glare, disappearing, its soft hum trailing far behind. Somewhere nearby a large dog barks a few times. In the distance a gardener is wielding a leaf blower. Wind chimes next door tinkle a breezy lullaby.

Standing there, staring into the blurry brightness, I hear myself saying out loud with a sudden knowing that startles me, "*I WILL NEVER SEE HIM AGAIN.*"

And in fact, my soon-to-be ex-husband, eight months later, will be found dead in a motel room off some freeway outside of Tucson, Arizona.

I walk towards the lobby door and push the button that shuts the garage door. I watch it grind its way down to its final stop. All is still. My fingertips wipe off my cheeks and then rub the wet mascara onto my jeans.

Now I can see better.

In the elevator, going back upstairs, I realize that this is the deep sigh that I've been waiting to exhale for years now.

It's over.

At long last, my son and I can start looking forward to the rest of our lives.

THE MYSTERY OF THE BASEMENT BOOGIES
Fiction by *Minda DeBudge*

"Don't be silly, Jeremy, there's no such things as basement boogies." Crossing my arms, I frowned at my cousin.

"Yes, there is." He looked serious.

"Ok, what are they, because I don't believe you."

"It's a mystery." He nodded toward the basement door.

"I've been down there lots of times with Grandma and I've never seen one."

"They don't come out when grown-ups are around." Peeking around the corner, he walked to the basement door and opened it.

"You have to stay down there with the door shut, then you'll see."

I knew I shouldn't trust him, especially after he locked me in our shed at my 10th birthday party a month ago. Still, I was curious. I leaned through the doorway into the dark. My bare arms tingled; the damp air gave me goose bumps. The smell of old books and stored vegetables stung my nose. I could taste the dust; it made my throat dry and itchy. At first, it seemed pitch black, but after about a minute I could see the two small, dingy windows near the ceiling. The glass was dirty, only a little light came in making the sheets on the furniture look ghostly. I slipped through the door.

"You're just going to shut the door for a minute, right?"

"Geeze, Wendy, you're such a wuss." He rolled his eyes.

I inched my way to the stairs.

"Chicken." He flapped his arms like wings.

"I'm not a chicken!" Scowling, I stomped down the stairs. I

plopped down on the last step and covered my face with my hands to keep the dust out. The door slammed, making me jump. I sat up straight; I wasn't about to give Jeremy the satisfaction of calling me "chicken" again. I sure hoped there were no such things as basement boogies.

Glancing around, I shivered, the basement really did creep me out. I looked up, barely able to see the pull string on the ceiling bulbs. I jumped up and grabbed for it but couldn't reach it.

"Dang it," I whispered. "At least he didn't lock the door." I rubbed my arms. How long is he going to make me sit down here? The kitchen door flew open banging the wall, startling me.

"See anything yet?" He sounded snarky. Keeping my back to him, I tried to sound bored.

"No, am I supposed to?"

"I forgot to tell you something," he whispered.

"What?" I jerked around glaring at him.

"They only come out when the door's locked!" He slammed the door and the deadbolt clicked into place. I leaped over the first three steps and raced to the top, stirring up dust. I yanked on the doorknob. No use.

"Grandma!" I yelled, "Jeremy's locked me in the basement!"

Looking through the keyhole, I saw Jeremy's eye staring back.

"Too bad little cousin. She's in the garden and can't hear you."

I felt the blood race to my head, my heart boomed, and my stomach rolled. Black spots winked in and out of my eyesight. I rattled the doorknob.

"Leeeeeet meeeeee ouuuut!" I screeched, becoming light-headed. I slid to the floor and begged.

"Please, open the door, please, please." Tears stung my eyes. I heard muffled laughter and creaky footsteps move away. My heart was pounding, and I couldn't breathe, the air felt heavy and stale.

"Oh no," I whined and twisted the knob, knowing nothing would happen. I was stuck huddling at the base of the door. I didn't want to see the boogies, but I was stiff with fear. From where I was sitting, I could see out over the room. Nothing in the basement moved except the dust in the air. I shivered. The air was becoming colder and the light dimmer. The tank top and shorts I was wearing left my arms and legs exposed, and I shivered again. Desperately my eyes darted over the clutter, searching for something ... was that, a quilt? I had to get it. I crept down the squeaky staircase. Slowly I went over to a plastic bag and yanked out an old quilt. I wrapped the musty blanket around me and sneezed. I froze, glancing around quickly to see if anything was after me. Everything was eerily still. I backed up and sat on the step, my eyes wandered over Grandma's murky basement.

Frankenfurnace sat in the corner. I called it that because it looked like Frankenstein's head. It had two black air vents in the same place as two eyes would be. A crooked piece of metal was riveted over the right "eye" vent, just like stiches. In the middle of its green body there was a soot-covered grate yawning like a monstrous mouth. Silver damper handles stuck out on both sides of the furnace resembling neck bolts. Hissing, popping, and groaning sounds came from it constantly. It sounded like it took a deep breath, rumble, bumped and turned on, letting out a loud, hissing noise. Fire jumped to life behind the mouth grate. I jumped and my insides quivered. I jerked the quilt over my head, just my eyes peering out through a small gap in the fabric.

I could see the root cellar door was closed; the other door was open a crack. Movement caught my eye, and I squinted a little. I could see the corner of a bed, and something was ... moving! The boogies! My stomach lurched and I bolted up the stairs, leaving the quilt behind. My heart thumped in my ears. I flew at the kitchen door, pounding so hard I bruised my hands. I pushed myself into the corner between the staircase and the door. A loud bump came from the furnace. I slid down the wall, moaning. Holding my breath, I waited, but nothing seemed to be following me. I took a deep breath and looked up at the rafters, cobwebs fluttered, keeping time with the swaying light bulbs. I watched them slow and become still. I peeked through the rails of the staircase trying to see through the haze. The bed's gossamer lace bedspread had stopped moving. I stared at it a minute and realized that the air from the furnace had made it move, causing it to look wraithlike.

"Oh, boy," saying it out loud made me feel better. My cousin got me good this time. I was mad. What was I thinking letting that jerk talk me into coming down here? I trudged down the stairs and flopped on the last step. I snuggled into the quilt and watched the shadows crawl toward me. Just like I thought, no mystery. No boogies, just me scaring myself. I'd solved the mystery of the basement boogies. I shook my head, I'd get even with Jeremy, somehow.

A small shaft of yellow light slithered down the stairs. Jeremy's head popped around the corner. Grandma was standing behind him with one hand on her hip and the other pinching his ear.

"Sorry!" he yowled. I scrambled upstairs, quilt in tow. As I squeezed between him and Grandma, I whispered, "You better watch out, they're waiting for you." Jeremy's eyes grew wide, as hissing sounds came out of the basement.

BRANDING TIME
Poetry by *Cecilia Granger*

Brown dust clouds the azure sky
As sweat and dirt and meadow muffins fly.
The calf screams in a key
Unknown to you and me,
While ropes and hands and brazened metal
Grapple for purchase on what will be peddled
At market. The auctioneer will take bids
From ranchers and butchers and fathers with kids
And purveyors of fine beef on the hoof—
Some who are greedy, and some who are tough.
The calf, so frightened and blinded by pain,
Tries to tear free once more again,
But reddened iron and brute strength prevails,
And I stand entranced behind the rails,
Wondering what it's like
To be branded.

The stench of sizzling skin assaults my senses,
As apathetic cowboys lean on fences.
When all is done, the calves are led away.
The caller leaves to call another day.
My thoughts are shattered by a final squeal,
And once I again I ponder how it feels
To be branded.

And I'm grateful, as away I ride,
That the mark on me is deep inside.
Oh, yes, I have been purchased,
But do I live like I am branded?

IAN MCPHERSON
Fiction by *William Barry*

One very clear, very crisp, and very dark night, Ian McPherson sat on his front stoop, sucking on his pipe, and gazing up at the stars. He was blowing smoke rings at Cygnus and occasionally tilting his head to the right or left to make the rings curl around the swan's long neck.

The night was still and he was thinking about his life. Ian was a potato farmer, had been, so it seemed, almost from birth. He was the son of a potato farmer and he had inherited the family plot from his parents, both now long dead. He was an only child and a lonely man, though about the latter he could usually pretend to himself otherwise. Pretending, in general, worked pretty well for Ian.

As he sat on his stoop, gently exhaling his smoke signals into the universe, Ian thought about how curious it was that he had really never gone anywhere in his life. He once had a chance to go to Dublin—the opportunity was tempting for many reasons (a girl had been involved)—but he refused because the crop had to come in. Ian was a worrier.

"But at least I've got my potatoes. They've stood by me. Who knows where I'd be if I'd tossed it all for the big city."

Ian spoke these words cheerfully and to the stars. He took a long drag on his pipe and picked out the Big Dipper and Cassiopeia, slowly circling, always stuck on the North Star. Aye. There they were.

And he exhaled.

The night was now perfectly still.

"Ian. Ian McPherson."

Ian jumped. The voice that broke the stillness was deep and quiet and it startled and frightened poor Ian McPherson.

"Who ... Who's there?" he asked nervously. He peered hard at the hedge in front of his little cottage. The voice came from there, from somewhere in that dense, dark thicket. He could see nothing. There was no moon.

"Ian McPherson," the hedge called again. The words came slowly, and the accented syllables were drawn out. "Eeeean McPhaiiiirson."

"Who's there?" Ian said, with a little more strength and courage. He got up on to his creaky tired legs and edged cautiously towards the hedge. "Who's there?"

"Ian. Ian McPherson. What about your potatoes?"

What do you mean what about my potatoes? was the first panicked thought that came to Ian's mind, but he didn't say this.

"Who are you? Where are you?" Ian cocked his head to the right and leaned towards the hedge, careful not to get too close. He reached with his right hand into the darkness and shook the branches quickly and anxiously. He gripped his pipe tightly in his left. He couldn't quite pinpoint the voice.

"Who's there?" Ian spoke these words a little more aggressively—or maybe it was a little more defensively.

"Who's here?" said the whisper. "Why, Ian, it's you," the voice said.

And that was all. Well, except for the fact that Ian dropped his pipe, stumbled backwards, and fell on his behind. He fumbled his way toward the scattered bits of tobacco glowing on the ground, and quickly found the smooth burnished wood of his pipe. He picked it up, and, with hands shaking, cleaned the dirt from it. And then he sat there, expecting more, but there was nothing. The voice never whispered again. It blew away, one might say, with the gentle breeze.

The next morning, after a restless night's sleep, Ian poked around the hedge, but could find nothing. Every evening, for days afterward, Ian sat on his stoop half hoping, half not, that he'd hear the voice again. He'd peer at the stars (and sometimes at the hedge), try to have the same thoughts as he did that evening of the voice, draw on his pipe deeply (or sometimes not smoke at all), all in an effort to find that right combination of gestures, words, and thoughts that might magically conjure the voice.

"What?" Ian might start one evening.

"Did you say something?" he'd say on another.

"Is that you again?" he'd whisper into the blackness of the night.

But Ian just heard things in his head. There was nothing there. The voice in the hedge never came again. Ever. Maybe it was just in his head, maybe it was in his subconscious. Maybe it was his ghost traveling back in time. Maybe it was his dream-self from his youth traveling forward in time. Maybe, maybe, maybe.

***

About a month after the night of the voice, however, and well after Ian McPherson had given up waiting for it, something did come to Ian's village. Ian was in his field, on his knees, bent over, repairing potato mounds. He happened to look up and caught a glimpse of movement on the crest of a low hill in the distance. It was a small caravan of station wagons, small trucks, and old jalopies slowly making its way down into the village. Ian figured this was a troupe of actors, come to his village to put on a play. He'd seen many come over the years. Their visits were always fun.

That evening, word went around the village that the troupe would put on a play the next day in the village commons and that a grand feast would be held after the performance. Ian was asked to bring to the meal his favorite potato dish. He was not much of a cook, but that was fine. He often marveled at God's genius: not only had God given the Irish the great gift of the potato, but he had also seen fit to endow his gift with a sublime flavor that could stand on its own. Staring blankly at the potatoes on his kitchen table and feeling a little intimidated by the task of preparing a "potato dish," Ian found solace in praising the generosity of God. Ian brought boiled potatoes and some salt to the feast.

Ian showed up at the play about ten minutes before it began. He found a seat towards the back and read the program. The play was written by the troupe itself and was called "The Seamstress and the Songstress." It told the story of two sisters, one quite beautiful with the voice of an angel—she was the songstress—and her younger, much less attractive sister who sewed the beautiful clothes for her older sister—she was the seamstress—clothes that made the songstress look even prettier. The play was a meditation on what brought happiness in life—art and beauty or labor and creativity? Like any good play it kept its answer a little uncertain and ambiguous for the audience. In the end, both young girls seemed to find happiness. "The Seamstress and the Songstress" was a story about acceptance of truth and beauty and everything else.

Ian thought the play funny and joyful. He especially loved the duet, with the younger sister sewing at her machine and the older singing only the notes, no words, to her song in that choppy way singers sometimes sing. The duet ended with both girls laughing and giving each other a hug.

After the play, Ian hung back a bit, smiling, watching, occasionally gesturing a hello with his hat clutched in his right hand as people walked by to get in line for dinner. The troupe joined the village for the feast—this was part of their pay for the performance—and the two communities sat down together to share stories and make new friends.

When Ian had gotten his food, there were no more seats at the four long tables set up on the commons, so he sat down with his back to a tree, crossed his legs, and began eating. He set a mug of ale beside his leg.

"Ian. Ian McPherson," the tree whispered.

Well, now, Ian had long since given up on hearing the hedge-voice again, but he'd not forgotten the experience. With the trauma of that earlier visitation still fresh, this tree-whisper so startled Ian that he threw his arms in the air, his left hand still holding the plate and his right his fork and tried—unsuccessfully—to turn around while still sitting with his back to the tree. Potatoes sprayed everywhere and he knocked over his mug.

"Oh dear, I'm so sorry to have startled you, Ian. I thought you saw me sitting here."

"No, no. It's not your fault. I didn't realize the tree was already taken. I'll move."

Queer, isn't it, that Ian still hadn't appreciated the strange fact that this woman knew his name? Ian was grateful enough that he hadn't leaned up against a talking tree.

"You don't recognize me, do you? It's me. Claire O'Malley." She said her name a little hopefully. "Do you remember? Years ago? Last time we were in this village?"

Of course, Ian remembered. He had often thought of Claire over the years, or rather he had often thought about not thinking about her—which is really the same as thinking about her all the time. She was the first girl he had kissed (she was the only girl he had ever kissed). He had kissed her only once, on a little bridge over a little stream, on a path in the woods not far from the village. At night. And when he kissed her, his whole body shook, and he conceived in that fleeting instant the most profound question that he would ever ask: "How could something so beautiful come to a place so small and to someone so insignificant as me?"

So, yes, Ian remembered Claire O'Malley. She was the girl he had kissed and who'd asked him to come to Dublin with her.

"Claire O'Malley?" Ian said uncertainly. "I think I remember you …"

"Ohhhh, I sure remember you." She smiled broadly, and twenty-five years disappeared for Ian.

Most of the time people live their lives like they're driving along a dirt road with deep ruts in it. The sides of the road rise up sharply and oppressively and discouragingly if you're looking for adventure. If you're looking for security, however, they rise up protectively and reassuringly. Ian mostly found reassurance on his life road.

Occasionally the road rises and you hit a piece of solid rock (granite, let's say, the hard rock of truth) that has no ruts and no protective walls. It extends for about twenty-five feet before dropping back into the rutted road. For those twenty-five feet—in your life, it can be only a few seconds—you can peer out around you and see the possibilities of the world and of your life in that world. Most people miss the granite entirely because they're going too fast or not paying attention or worried only about the little bumps on the main road to notice the world that is not the main road. A few others notice the granite and the view, but their minds are so rutted that they just decide to push forward and to get off the granite as fast as possible and back into their comfortable ruts.

This was Ian, especially years ago when Claire first asked him to go to Dublin. He said then he was worried about the crop, but what he was really worried about was the sharp and violent turn he would have to make on the granite.

So, when Claire said, "Ohhhhh, I sure remember you" and smiled, Ian was back on that slab of granite again—only the second time in his life. And for some inexplicable reason (maybe it was the voice in the hedge, maybe it was because he had been on that piece of granite once before and had sworn somewhere in his soul, many levels down—beneath his pretend love of potatoes, beneath his pretend satisfaction with gazing at the stars while sucking on his pipe, beneath all his little happy—but pretend—reassurances—that he would turn if he ever found himself on that piece of granite again), he turned.

"Oh, Claire. What am I saying? Of course, I remember you. I've thought about you so often over the years."

This was good. He needed to confess something to Claire to keep himself from pretending any more about her and to keep her from disappointment and slowly walking away, a little hurt and a little puzzled. He had accomplished what he needed to with this brief confession. Now, maybe, some light conversation to move things forward, and he would be on his way.

But Ian was unfamiliar with anything besides ruts and driving along at about 30 mph. He should have applied the brakes, gently. Instead, he panicked and hit the accelerator.

"I mean, Claire, I've thought about you so much," he blurted. "And that kiss on the bridge and your breath and your hug. I've thought about that kiss so much. You know, it was at night. Why am I telling you that? I'm sure you know it was at night. I mean, if you remember it at all. Even if you remember it, I guess I shouldn't assume you remember it was at night. I think about it most at night, when I'm lying in bed … well … I've got to tell you: it was a fine kiss!"

Very new and rough terrain for poor Ian McPherson.

Claire smiled upon the wreckage, and helped Ian out of the car.

"Yes, I remember. It was a wonderful kiss. And it was at night. How have you been, Ian?"

Gratefully, Ian said, "Oh, I'm doing great. Going to be a good harvest this year. We've gotten a lot of rain, all at the right time. Some of the mounds took a beating, but still, it'll be a rich harvest of potatoes."

"Do you have a family?" asked Claire.

This question tells you all you need to know about Claire O'Malley. It was innocent enough, a natural question, but would give her critical information for their future. She was an expert at driving on new terrain, pushing forward, charting a path. Her life had been about turning off the road and avoiding the ruts. Claire had joined the theater troupe as a kid, having run away from a mean father and a meaner mother. Claire had stayed with the same troupe all these years (she was their costumer and had written some of the plays, including the "The Seamstress and the Songstress") and had become a leader among the actors and stagehands, directors, and assistant directors.

For her part, Claire had never married, though she had had many boyfriends. It wasn't that Claire didn't want to marry. Having been deprived of a home at a young age, she was desperate for a family. But none of the boys seemed quite right. None except Ian. She always kept him in her heart, even though—Ian would have been surprised to learn—she feared him a little.

Ian and Claire had a lovely conversation. She told of places she and the troupe had visited and some of the plays she had put on. Ian mostly sat and listened, laughing occasionally, and thinking that he had little to share about his own life. The most interesting thing that had ever happened to him was Claire's visit years ago (and now her return) and then the voice in the hedge weeks ago. He worried that regaling Claire about her visit wouldn't impress her very much, and telling her of the voice in the hedge might scare her away.

But fortunately Ian was desperate to say something to Claire—because, yes, simple as it sounds, he was in love—and fortunately he had led such a drab life that the only things he could say were about Claire and about this strange voice, both of which, to his great surprise, when he told her of them in just a few minutes, would bind them together forever (you'll see). Fortunately, too, Claire was persistent—because she was in love—and a careful and patient listener. Still, none of this came easily.

"So, Ian, oh my. I've been doing all the talking. Tell me about your life. Has it been a good life?"

"Oh, aye. It's been good. The land has been good to me. Did you try the boiled potatoes? Those were mine."

"They were very tasty," Claire said. "Ian, do you ever get tired of potatoes?"

Ian suddenly felt very exposed.

"Potatoes are God's greatest gift to the Irish," Ian said firmly, tamping down all his doubts.

Claire had her answer.

"Yes, they are a treasure. So, you've farmed most of your life here and it sounds like it's been a wonderful life …"

Ian McPherson could feel Claire O'Malley begin to drift away for a second time, and he was right. For she had begun to despair. She had kept away from Ian for a quarter century. Now, with their lives beyond their halfway point, with her realizing the truth about them that she had tried to ignore for years, now with her having been encouraged only a few weeks earlier by a strange and mysterious voice whispering in the wind, "Where are you?", she had come back to Ian's village to try one more time. But she just couldn't seem to break through, and now she was about to give up, and Ian knew it, and Ian was desperate. He had nowhere to go, except the truth.

Ian took a deep breath, looked up into the sky—for it was dark now. He spotted Venus low on the horizon and noticed his old friend Cygnus flying directly above him, and so Ian McPherson began to tell Claire O'Malley of the only two true treasures in his life that he possessed.

"I once met a girl who I kissed on a bridge not far from here, and I've heard a voice in my front hedge, whispering to me, 'it's you.'"

PASTORALE
Nonfiction by *Andrew J. Smiley*

I've spent most of my life chasing something. Someone's attention, an ideal, a girl, a degree ... even a grounded bird or two. Since I was very young, I've had a strong compulsion to pursue and catch things that tickle my fancy—or my peripheral vision. Objects like the shiny bauble winking at the bottom of a wishing fountain at the mall, a brightly colored action figure, a confused chick in the barnyard, or some scurrying insect or reptile—as long as I thought it wasn't likely to take its stinging revenge on me. I don't really know what I'm going to do with it once I catch it, I just know I *want* it. I want to keep it from escaping and vanishing. I want to know about it, to examine it, to have it stashed in reserve in case I get bored. Because boredom is the ultimate gateway drug.

It all comes full circle with frogs, though.

See, frogs *can* be caught, and if you have a sense of what you're doing and don't mind getting a little mucky in the process, they will provide some quality entertainment for the effort. Many a folksy tradition regarding the length and quality of their legs and leaps can be found in the annals of Americana—Mark Twain himself popularized the still-running frog jumping tournament in Calaveras County, CA. I still maintain that these bug-eyed pond minions are some of the most amusing creatures tumbled out of the bottom of creation's barrel, even though they are voracious carnivores and occasional cannibals, depending on the conditions and the species. They are even gender-fluid at times of extreme circumstances.

But I digress. My childhood is inseparable from the frogs and other creeping things populating and tantalizing it, and when I think of a yardstick to measure what childhood *ought* to be, my thoughts turn to northern New England.

Easton, Maine, is a bucolic little town; at least it was in the mid-to-late 1980s when my family lived there. In many ways it was quite the Pleasantville existence. We lived in a grand old Victorian fixer-upper overlooking the single-broken-line state highway that sliced through town and fed the local business enterprises: Campbell's General Store, town fire department, livestock auction and feedlot, truck stop and diesel-drenched maintenance yard, even a school or two. Pretty standard, really.

A river (called the Prestile Stream in those days) ran through Easton, whose surface froze quite reliably in the deep, protracted winters—enough to guarantee an ice-skating zone in the recreation area above the dam, and downstream there were sure to be a few good spots to chip away at the black glass with rocks until the ominous crackling started the clock before you would inevitably fall in. Which I did, on more than one occasion. Chasing a thrill.

We lived in our New England mansion—I like to say mansion, but it was more of an aging monument to colonial aspirations—at the top of the hill at the only four-way junction in town. My combined elementary and middle school were about a half mile up the main road, past the dam overflow that always had some weird aquatic insect life to scoop up in Gerber food jars before getting to the first classes of the day.

Our backyard sloped down about an acre of untamable lawn into the garden which grew as many rocks as vegetables. My sister and I later learned that our suspicions about this phenomenon were actually valid; each year's cycle of freeze and thaw did indeed force stone and sediment upward, so we were actually growing rocks alongside the pumpkins, tomatoes, and corn. Beyond the garden and the ancient oak swing-tree, an ATV path wound along northward past the backyards and the truck scrambles of our neighbors and past the ghosts in the cemetery three plots down. It was on this very trail that I would one day come face to face with the country bumpkin version of the headless horseman—a plaid-clad farmer in an ancient GMC flatbed chasing me off from where I had been poking at a pile of bovine entrails left at the bottom of his property. I still maintain that his head was bobbing around detached from his neck as I dove for the trees and he roared by in a cloud of dust and profanity.

Again, I digress. Chasing a point, it seems.

Most of the topography in that glorious "back forty" was untended woodland and fields gone to seed—exquisite territory for an imagination fed by fiction classics and the afternoon cartoon block. Video games were coming, but they did not have hold on me just yet—obsessing over *Teenage Mutant Ninja Turtles* and nursing a crush on *Chip & Dale: Rescue Rangers'* Gadget Hackwrench was about as edgy as I could be in those years.

Trouble was on the way in my looming pre-teens, but I was still fairly unspoiled, just like those northern Maine backwoods. Except for the ticks and the horseflies. No paradise is without its serpents. In every open field there was the possibility of ticks strong enough to urge the tucking of jeans into shoes.

About a mile or so—as measured by the unreliable canvas of adolescent memory—down that winding, weedy, bumpkin-haunted track, there was a brushy break in the trees where a lane had been cleared for industrial power lines installed some decades before. A dozen or two meters off the trail, well-screened from view by brambles and blackberry brush and burdocks (oh sweet mercy—the monstrosities of those burdocks—it is a known fact that the diabolical microhooks of burdock husks tangled in one's hair inspired the invention of Velcro) there was a pond, of sorts. I say "pond" because at the time I was unaware of its actual source, and since it contained multitudes of lily pads, cat-tail reeds, and water striders, it seemed to tick all the boxes of a pond's essential elements.

I loved this place. It was chock full of greater bullfrogs, stick-shelled damselfly nymphs, and a number of very industrious water spiders thriving among the reedy verges. That and the hordes of horseflies in the sticky summers—named so for the power with which they could bite. Those things packed the equivalent wallop of a horse's tombstone-sized front teeth. I named this playground "Secret Springs" because *surely* no one else knew of such a froggy Avalon to while away afternoons that needed roaming and adventure.

The irony was that it was neither *secret* (everybody knew it was there; nobody cared but me) nor a *spring* (in reality it was a graywater outflow from some municipal concern in the town and likely the reservoir of a number of undetermined fecal-tainted runoffs).

I would wander out to the ol' Secret Springs pretty often in the warmer months to catch things; though, miraculously, tetanus and Lyme disease were not among them. This was still when the great outdoors was relatively wild and usually the worst you had to fear was a moose in rutting season (which you *should* fear). People hadn't soured that part of the land yet—at least, not all of it. I would wade thigh-deep in the silky "mud" and catch frogs by the dozen sometimes, lugging home a wastebasket half-filled with water and a riot of panicked amphibians. Most of them would escape overnight and have instinct lead them back to moisture, and a few inevitably died of shock (which I still feel guilty about). But I felt incredibly rich to have a ready supply of frogs at hand to chase around the yard or just watch sitting sullenly in my improvised washtub terrarium.

I even managed to harvest some frogspawn a time or two, bringing back double-handfuls of the pale yellow jelly in which the clear eggs with their tadpole nuclei were suspended. Now this was the REAL treasure—these glutinous masses seemed to hold the very secrets of life itself. If you were careful, you could push individual frog eggs out of the clutch like popping a grape out of its skin. There was a certain satisfaction to this—something akin to working your way through the snaps of a remnant of bubble wrap—and though this was decades before ASMR became a thing (thank you, Bob Ross—you are an afroed angel sent to this earth), I imagine freeing frog eggs could probably be some version of a YouTube "Most Satisfying" video. I even managed to get a functioning group of tadpoles and then froglets one year.

Good times. A good catch, even.

For me, frogs are a metaphor. They're generally treated very badly by little boys (and certain science teachers and research firms), and I have spent most of my life repenting for my ignorant abuse of these croakers, but I love them still. I harmed frogs sometimes, out of curiosity or as an outlet for my bad temper, or even some devilish black humor a time or two. This still bothers me, even though I have left behind the tail of my youth and its petty behaviors. Frogs are my peculiar treasure. They are my spirit animal. They are a symbol of my joy, my excesses, and my journey through the changing states of this life.

They're an indicator species; this means they are some of the first to be affected by climate changes or pollution in their environment, but they indicate something else to me. They are a symbol of transformation, able to bridge the gap between one state and another and endure terrible hardships and thrive despite their natural fragility. They also indicate the persistent wheeling of the year; I wait to catch their high, piping voices reaching out in the nights growing warmer in late spring.

I'm always chasing something. Sometimes I catch what I'm after. Sometimes I go raving crazy and try to catch more than I need, more than is necessary or even good sense, just to say I *could*. Sometimes there was nothing to catch, and I felt that void quite keenly. And I wondered what happened.

These days, it's enough to catch something every so often. The irregularity of it makes each time a unique treasure, easier to recall with more clarity. The frenzied scramblings of a childhood driven by an urgency to see everything is now tempered by having seen and caught a lot—and being stung or snarled or dirtied by the effort at times.

That's good enough for me.

MOVE IT!
Poetry by *Carol Barrett*

Convenient location. I've been warned: the car will be towed
unless I can prove some school business to justify parking
here. But I no longer have a child in school. Paying taxes
to support education won't help—courthouse four blocks
over. Perhaps I could build a quaint shelter for kids waiting
for the bus near my home. *Might we discuss that?* Or,
how about a school warming station with shiny new boots
and fluffy socks for downpour days? Surely I can figure something
to prevent a humiliating tow charge. The price tag, not minor.
But the way they get you—it's so damned inconvenient.

A FRIENDLY RIVALRY

Nonfiction by *Mary Krakow*

In Central Oregon you have to choose: are you a Beaver or are you a Duck? With football season upon us, even those who don't follow the sport claim allegiance to one or the other. Markets mine this frenzy by offering products displaying team logos ranging from car accessories to clothing. You can even find chips, sodas, and candy bars packaged in team colors. For the uninitiated, Oregon State Beaver fans prefer orange and black while those of the Duck persuasion go for University of Oregon's green and yellow.

The Beaver vs. Duck rivalry is alive and well at Metolius Elementary. Nestled between farm fields and single-family houses, the school serves about 300 students from Metolius and nearby Madras. A microcosm of Central Oregon, its staff and students stand behind one team or the other. I can't tell you how many times I have been asked by my kindergarten students, "Are you for Ducks or Beavers?" My standard response is "Go Beavs," as I hoist my fist in the air.

I wasn't always so strongly aligned with my alma mater. My first year at Metolius changed that. The third-grade teacher, now retired, was a die-hard Duck fan who schooled me in the finer points of the feud. In classic Hatfield and McCoy fashion, he used guerilla tactics and caught me off guard. He led a parade of quacking third graders through my classroom to assert Duck dominance. In retaliation a Beaver Nation poster mysteriously appeared the next day on his classroom door.

In my thirteen years at Metolius Elementary, I loyally sided with fellow OSU supporters. We photoshopped pictures showing

Webfoots in Beaver apparel; they plastered Duck posters on our classroom doors. We gifted them with Beaver-themed items at the Christmas exchange; they kidnapped a stuffed Benny mascot and demanded ransom. Through it all, the rivalry lived on in good-natured fun.

Whether you cheer for the Beavers or the Ducks, wear your colors proudly.

NOW I KNOW
Nonfiction by *Gerald Reponen*

Over a period of forty years, my wife Ruth and I had lived either on the East Coast or the West. During this time period we had made annual trips from one coast to the other. In doing so we had traveled on every major highway across the country. We did not have the time to do a lot of exploring on the many interesting places along the way.

When I turned sixty-five, I decided to buy a nineteen-foot self-contained motor home. In retirement we would now have time to explore many of the out of the way places we had noted in our travels. Larger motor homes had length restrictions on where they could go. With this smaller unit we would be able to visit any place that a pickup truck could go. This opened up an entirely new world of locations to visit.

In late August 1994 we visited Sumpter, Oregon. We took our two granddaughters for the ride on the train through the gold fields. Unfortunately, Ruth fell on the tracks and broke her left arm. Her arm was now in a sling across her chest and immobile, but this did not deter us from our new life of adventures we wanted to undertake.

In September, she felt it would be easier to travel in the motor home with the ever-changing scenery than to put up with the daily tasks at home. We left from Burns to explore the places we had not seen before. We decided to drive across the country on state highways and sometimes gravel roads as we explored this great country.

We entered southwest Minnesota to explore the state we were born and raised in. We were traveling east from Huron, South Dakota on US Highway 14. As we entered the state, we were on Buffalo Ridge looking for the Hole in the Mountain County Park. A local farmer had died and donated his eighty-acre farm to become a recreation area for the adjacent city of Lake Benton, population around 2,000 people.

We pulled off onto a dirt road which was adjacent to the highway. There was a large A-frame building and then the open parkland. Tent campers were along this dirt road, and we found room to park between tents. The park land was all to our south with a two-hundred-foot-wide strip of grassland before it sloped up into a forest of trees. After dinner we decided to walk up an open area to the top of the hill. This was apparently the access area where a ski tow rope would pull skiers up through the woods to the top of the hill. They had made an open area about fifty feet wide for the tow rope allowing skiers to ski down the hill on a gentle slope.

It was twilight as we started up the slope to see what was on the top of the hill. In the flat prairie country, a hill can be used for skiing if only two hundred feet high. The forest was well groomed with just grass under the well-spaced trees and no brush, just open forest land.

When we were almost at the top, we stopped as a beautiful large white tail buck deer was running through the forest. When he got to the open area of the slope, he suddenly stopped, turned, and looked at us. He was about three hundred feet away. It was such a beautiful sight we stood speechless and watched him. Suddenly he started walking towards us.

Oh, oh! I told Ruth, I think we have trouble coming our way. We were only about twenty feet from the open top of the hill. There was a small four foot square building which I assumed contained supplies for the ski tow. I told Ruth to walk up next to the building and I would keep my eye on the buck.

The buck just kept walking directly towards me with head held high. He stopped about twenty feet away and just stared at me. Suddenly he put his head down and charged at me. I hollered at Ruth what was happening and told her to get behind the shack. As I backed up, I bumped into a ski tow post. I was able to step behind it just as the deer hit the post with his forehead.

I was now standing on one side of this small four-inch by four-inch post looking directly into its eyes. My hands were on the top of the post and his horns wrapped around the sides of it. It had a beautiful rack of six points on each side.

Now what do I do I thought. My first thought was to grab a horn in each hand and twist his head sideways. Wrong! I knew his neck muscles would just throw me to the ground and then stomp me with his front hooves. I knew I was dead. We stood locked like this for a few minutes although it seemed like an hour. My mind was racing on what options, if any, I had.

Looking into those black eyes was like a bottomless black hole. There was no indication of what might be in the mind of this buck. It was the scariest scene I could ever imagine. What will it do next? I called to Ruth and asked her if she could find any type of stick or branch. But I thought it was hopeless as the forest was well groomed and there was nothing loose anywhere. She called back that she could get a post out of the building. There was a glimmer of hope!

I told her to bring it the fifteen feet to me and throw it at my feet. Rather a ridiculous request as her left arm was in a sling and useless. However, she did courageously step around the building and dragged it towards me. She attempted to throw it at me, and it was now about eight feet away. This was not good, as I knew when I turned to retrieve it, the buck would rear up and stomp me before I could reach the post.

I reassured her the buck was not after her, only me. Courageously she stepped forward and picked up the post. This time she was able to get it within three or four feet of me. Now I had to think through how I would be able to be fast enough to pick up the post and try to defend myself.

There is nothing worse than staring into those black bottomless eyes. There was no way to know what might be going through this wild animal's brain. I thanked Ruth for her courage and said I had an idea of what to do. I said to just stay behind the building regardless of what happened. It was not a goodbye comment, I had hope.

I moved my body an inch in either direction and the deer would shift its head and legs. So, I thought my only course would be to fake I was moving in one direction and then quickly jump from behind the safety of the post in the opposite direction. Then try to pick up the post Ruth had thrown towards me.

I faked flinching an inch or so to the right and then quickly to the left. The deer was slightly behind me, so as he moved to my left, I took a step and grabbed the post and held it in both hands at head level. I hollered at the buck that I now had a rack bigger than his and shook it towards him. The buck stood frozen, not knowing what to do. My ploy had worked, I now had something with which to protect myself.

During all of this time twilight had ended and it was now pitch black where I could see nothing more than a few feet away. I told Ruth to start walking towards the east across the grassy top area. It was about fifty feet wide, and it was at least a quarter of a mile to the east to the other main downhill ski area. My prayer was to hold off the buck while moving backwards across the top of the hill. I told Ruth just to go as fast as she could walk near the tree line so she could get behind a tree if necessary. Also to keep talking as I would be walking backwards and could only follow her voice in the blackness. Not to worry about me, a very difficult task I knew.

No longer could I see where the buck was nor what it was doing. It was a clear cold night and all I could rely on was what I heard. With her voice directly behind me, I knew I was near the tree line and could slowly follow her voice. The buck would snort and then I could hear the stomping of its hooves as he ran towards me. All I could do was to hold the post in front of me, brace myself and holler as loud as I could. Slowly I would back up and hear the thumping of his hooves. Then it would stop six to eight feet away and snort. All I could see was a white V of hair on its chest when it stopped. Steam would come from its nostrils which I could also see but it did not get closer.

For the next hour I was backing up slowly without knowing where I was going. Listening to the buck, I could hear him snort and then charge at me. But each time he stopped just short of me. After about an hour of this just repeating and repeating, I knew I must be getting close to the downhill slope. I kept calling Ruth so I could hear the direction I needed to go. The area on top was narrow and somehow I managed to stay in the grassy area while walking backwards with no direction. I knew God was with me and guiding me how to walk backwards in total blackness.

When I heard Ruth call that she was now heading down the hill, I knew I had a chance to live. Up until this point all I had was my faith in God and the voice of my wife to guide me so I would know the direction to go backwards.

Every time the buck would charge, it would snort, stomp its hooves and then I could hear it coming. I was yelling at the top of my voice continually. Suddenly I would hear the stomp stop and I could barely see the white V of hair on its chest. For more than an hour this is what we experienced.

Heading down hill on the three-hundred-foot-wide slope, I could suddenly sense I would be able to see soon. I started to see the image of the buck as the two lights at the bottom of the hill showed up on his white V hair formation. Halfway down the slope I knew I would live. I could start to see the grass on the hillside and even glanced back towards the A-frame building and the two tall floodlights.

About two hundred feet from the building the buck suddenly stopped and stood and watched me. By the building were a dozen people all fascinated by what they were seeing. But not a single person made a sound nor made any attempt to save me from the buck attack. They just marveled at what a show we had put on as the two of us struggled to come down the hill with the buck attacking periodically.

Once at the bottom of the hill, I started walking down the dirt road towards our RV. There were tents on both sides of the road, but I saw no people along the road. The buck walked parallel to the hill off to my left about two hundred feet away. Once we got next to the RV, I knew I could soon relax. We quickly stepped inside and then it struck us what had happened. I was very weak, sweaty, and needed a glass of wine. We were alive!!

The next morning, we left the area and there was no sign of the deer around. No one inquired about our experience. I had been very upset the evening before when all of the people just watched us as the deer would charge and then stop prior to engaging me. I would have thought they would come up the slope to help but they just stood and watched us try to survive. Once we approached them, they said we put on a good show for them. We were very disgusted with the Minnesota people who watched us almost perish before their eyes.

We were very happy to leave and headed towards Yellowstone National Park. The drive was a beautiful one with all of nature's beauty on display. As we entered the north entrance to Yellowstone we headed for Mammoth campground. There were elk all around the area. As we pulled into our campsite, there were three female elk adjacent to it. We had no bulls nearby that we could see. This made us less apprehensive after our experience in Minnesota but still not trusting the wild animals.

We sat outside at the picnic table enjoying a glass of wine when suddenly the elk approached us. We were still concerned with our safety and went inside immediately. The next morning as we drove the loop to leave the campground, there was a large bull elk lying in the middle of the road. I pulled off to the side about one hundred fifty feet short of the bull and shut the engine off. A park ranger pulled up near the rear of our vehicle and also stopped but on the road.

It was a cool morning and as the bull breathed steam would come from its nostrils. To the right off the side of the road was a herd of about a dozen cow elk. Apparently, this was the harem the bull was watching closely and safeguarding.

A few minutes later the bull stood up and stretched his body out. Steam kept coming out of his nostrils as he stood in the cold morning air. Suddenly, he turned and looked at us. We were shocked when he put his head down and charged the one hundred fifty feet towards us.

He smashed his horns into the right front fender. Then he started smashing the front of the vehicle and his horns were on the windshield. Ruth screamed as she was sure it was coming through the windshield. We were absolutely stunned as it kept ramming the front of our vehicle for several minutes.

After several minutes the bull seemed satisfied. It turned and walked across the road to near where all the cows were standing and watching. He stood off about fifty feet from the road and turned to watch us.

The Ranger pulled up next to us and told us to follow her to the gate to fill out the accident report. As we followed her the bull walked adjacent to us watching and walking alongside about fifty feet away.

When I stopped at the gate, I had a feeling of apprehension getting out of the vehicle to walk to the gate. However, I was fortunate as the bull just stood and watched me. Steam kept pouring out of its nostrils with each breath.

The Ranger told us she had never seen anything like that before with the elk. She had no idea why it had attacked our motor home. We left the campground, and the elk did not follow us any further. After this experience we had no idea of what we might encounter on the rest of our journey back to Oregon.

We had arrived safely home with some exciting stories to tell our sons. Our beautiful motor home only had 4,000 miles and now it looked like a wreck. When it was repaired it needed a new grill, headlights and hood which were all damaged. It took time to repair it and cost $3,000 to make the vehicle look like new again. We would be ready for the next adventure in retirement.

Over the next two weeks I did a lot of thinking. What could have been the reason for two separate attacks in different parts of the country? One day the answer came to me. It was fall rut season and both attacks had happened by male animals. Why would they attack us like this? I then realized I knew the answer. I had used musk deodorant for many years and never thought of this. But with the deer actions I knew it was focused on Me. I realized what had happened and discontinued the use of musk deodorant from that date on. I did not want this frightening experience repeated.

I told my four sons what I was sure was the reason for the attacks. I told them when they go deer and elk hunting to hang some musk deodorant in a tree nearby. One of my sons took this to heart and brought a tube with him on his elk hunt.

Early in the morning in the dark he forgot and left the tube in his tent. He went to set up his watch for any passing bull elk. After the morning of sitting watching two trails, no animals came by. He went back to his camp. Much to his dismay, a bull elk had smelled the deodorant and came in and trashed his campsite. They all decided that they would forgo this experience in their future hunts. Lesson learned. Now I know!

THE WORLD HINGE
Fiction by *Marc Wagner*

The circle of standing stones vanished into a 360-degree panorama of amber light. It was almost too bright to look at. Liam visored his eyes.

Unfolding all around him was a landscape of rolling hills that rippled with grass and bracken and small patches of gorse. Gone were the bleak and bare winter fields he had trekked through to get here.

A breeze found his mouth. It tasted of salt and mist. He turned. Behind him lay a pewter sea, murmuring. Everything was different. The hills on three sides were crisscrossed by meandering footpaths, and from each path grew things that looked like ivory arches, or maybe birch trees without leaves. The arches entwined themselves at intervals every hundred yards or so like steepled porticos over the paths.

In the distance, tall people walked the pathways. They strolled arm in arm, trailed by forest animals and children who darted among the fading tendrils of the walkers' cloaks. The walkers did not walk so much as glide. They strolled in long slow strides and made astonishing progress for their pace. They advanced in a kind of flickering motion. Like figures in an old-fashion film, they disappeared and reappeared at successive arches along the pathways without appearing to have traversed the distances in between.

Liam's breath stopped each time a walker flickered from one arch to the next. His eyes strained at the vacant spaces they left behind. Then his breath halted altogether when he saw what lay beyond the walkers. It had been too big to notice at first, like some innocuous rack of clouds. Now it was all Liam could see.

On the horizon stood a city, a city made entirely of trees. The trees were the size of skyscrapers, world-spanning trees that braided and branched until they merged into a canopy that seemed to reach beyond the sky and entwine itself with the stars. Unfamiliar constellations peeked through the canopy's upper reaches. Pale nebulae hovered among the boughs. In the lower recesses, suspension bridges swayed across leagues of empty space where temples hung in the air and rotated. Spiral roads winked with distant lights and entire townships climbed, helix upon helix, around trunks the size of Devil's Tower in Wyoming.

The scent of clover and resinous trees drifted from the city, a waft of pure Northernness. It gathered in Liam's nostrils and overflowed into pinpricks of pleasure that lifted the small hairs on the back of his neck.

For the first time, he could hear it, a deep and resonant chord, a subsonic tone that quivered from the lowest registers of stone and bone up to the most full-throated vibration of human voices and onward to the highest bell-like sheen of birds and whistling things: a perfect fifth, a stack of perfect fifths arranged just so. The voice of a planet, the voice of two planets aligned. It was everything Liam had imagined and everything he had failed to imagine, a megalithic chime that shivered through the warp and weft of things, through molten rivers and groaning glaciers and twisted roots and a billion-billion trembling leaves.

The music of the spheres.

The polyphony was like the blast of a pipe organ. It shuddered through the open hinge between the worlds and shook the grains of dirt at Liam's feet.

He took a hesitant step toward the curved wall of images. A feeling of looseness struck him behind the knees. He took another step, then another, then two more steps until the barrier of light touched him and a shower-tingle of pleasure raced across his skin. The looseness in his knees became buoyant as if he were wading into a warm and sonorous ocean.

He took another step.

And the step took him.

ABOUT PRAYER

Poetry by *Donna D'Orio*

Sometimes the old repeated prayers
ask to be laid down.

In your weariness, dig deep enough for the resilience
to climb to the ancient trickle,
to the gurgling song of the tinaja that invites your
prayer,

and rest there.

Your prayer, so old you no longer remember its first
emergence, will be tended well–
held and unwound by the narrows,

watched over by the scraggly sentinel

whose roots still cling
to its place of germination.

It is safe there.

You don't even have to beg. Your prayer is welcome, wanted.

CHASING CLOUDS
Fiction by *Erik Frank*

My older brother Gavin wrote a report about Renaissance men in the sixth grade. It changed the course of our lives forever.

The principles of possession mystified me, but there was little doubt a Renaissance man hijacked Gavin's brain overnight. Without delay he reset his allowance priorities around science magazines and musty art history books he unearthed at thrift shops. No more candy for him. And no more comics for me after he finished with them.

He lobbied our parents brashly for an early birthday present—a paint set with an easel and palette. I was shocked when they agreed; and swooned in secret with the implications it held for my birthday. After one day and six half-finished *Mona Lisa*s, Gavin announced he would "answer henceforth" only to his painter name, Gavino, because he "needed a re-birth to create his masterpiece." Whatever that meant.

He remodeled dinner into a recitation of Renaissance painters and their esoterica. Each intro included a fraudulent pause for objections before Gavino wormholed us directly into 16th century Belgium. We became involuntary experts in that dullest of art history topics—Flemish portrait painting. I believe now my parents indulged him because he furnished them with fantasies of an "artist in the family."

My brother idolized Leonardo Da Vinci the most, but not for his paintings. It was a fascination with flight. He wallpapered every square inch of his bedroom with pictures he found in the science magazines, even the ceiling. The mosaic of strange flying-car prototypes, mini-rocket ships, and jetpacks mesmerized my eyeballs whenever I stepped into his domain.

Fresh sets of sketches materialized on his door every morning as well. They advertised fantastical machines, full of fire and glory. It was easy to imagine one of those contraptions thwop-thwopping Captain Gavino, age 12, to and from school. Or the arcade. He polished the chops of his future CEO-self on me while I was trapped in the shower—extolling the virtues of each machine's purpose, and the great need for immediate production. His repeated invitations to be his assistant-private-in-charge of landing pad operations flattered me, but I was unimpressed with the job description.

One morning not long after summer vacation started, Gavin woke me through the walls with a spicy Italian cantata. Gavin's gifts excluded singing like Pavarotti, but he tried anyway. He interrupted knocks on my door with the news that I was officially hired for a job on his "big project."

"Are you sure I'm the right person, Gavino?" He didn't see how my face curled in delight when I said his name.

"Peter, now Peteri." Gavin tested my willingness to be re-named by him daily. "Don't be absurd. I've been interviewing you since you were born. I know you're my person." Reading comics—in bed, on the couch, on the lawn—was my single agenda item for the morning. Our parents had left early to attend some starchy seminar with a famous British gardener; they told us we could fill the day as we wanted. I suspect now it was probably a test.

"Dad tells me jobs earn money," I said. "What's the pay?"

He threw the bedroom door open. Maybe at my temerity for asking. Or to show off his outfit. Gavin was never above a little showmanship when it mattered. He was in a baggy, beet-red corduroy jacket, sleeves rolled up, over his favorite Space Invaders t-shirt, a pair of cargo shorts, tall white socks, and hi-tops; but it was impossible to look away from the bright green, three-pointed hat on his head. The feather in it was so large it had to be ostrich. Da Vinci blurred into Don Quixote in my doorway.

"Where'd you get that hat?" I snickered.

He grunted. "I bought it from the theater teacher at the high school."

"Do I have to dress like you?"

Gavin pursed his lips and squinted at me with all the serious bones in his body. "No. I have something else in mind. Your pay will be determined by your attitude." Pay uncertain at best. Forget benefits. "Now get out of bed. And get dressed. We'll talk about the job over breakfast."

It was pointless to resist. I knew the tiny tortures Gavin usually subjected me to all summer would multiply by a factor of a billion if I didn't help. Besides, to be honest, adventures with Gavin were sometimes highlight-reel material. On the flip side, grounded for a month with no TV was just as likely.

I trudged downstairs to find Gavin in the kitchen cooking eggs and bacon, giant ostrich feather in sync with the shaking skillet. I rubbed my eyes to be sure I saw what I saw.

"Push the button on the toaster," Gavin said.

I complied, while taking in the scene around the kitchen. Mom's new bath towels and a few paper airplanes were piled by the door to the garage. Duct tape, packing tape, Scotch tape, and a giant tube of crazy glue sat on a chair at the kitchen table; two extension cords and a hose draped over the back.

"Thanks. Grab a seat. Breakfast is almost ready."

I found a sweet Lego model on top of a set of drawings on the table. "Project *CloudChaser1* – Phase 1" was scrawled across the top of the pages. It looked like a glider. My brother never lacked for ambition. "You're gonna need a good base for today."

"Gavino, what does that mean?" My spidey-sense tingled like I was about to get a rash when he delivered breakfast only to me.

"Well. I had to do some recalculating after talking with my science teacher. And make some sacrifices for the mission. You're gonna be the pilot of *CloudChaser1*. I think you're the perfect weight, but we need to check."

He slid our parents' scale out from the pantry closet. "We'll weigh you after breakfast so I can make final calculations."

I was in it now. No turning back with Gavin's breakfast sitting in front of me. I accepted my fate and ate like it might be my last meal as a nine-year-old.

***

"Get on the scale. Ooh yeah. I thought so." The way he stared at my hair, I knew he was considering shaving it off. "We need you lighter. Go change into this." Gavin whipped out his old, solid gold wrestling singlet from the freezer. A big "CC1" in bold, black electrical tape was fixed across the front.

My name was on the back.

I snatched the singlet from him, and for the first time, wondered how long this plan had been in the works. The icy feel of it in my hand foreshadowed a fair chance of looking like Charlie Brown before the day was done.

"Why was it in the freezer?" My gross dissatisfaction with wiggling into a frozen singlet was unequivocal in my tone. His string bean shape and my slightly rounder form meant his hand-me-downs didn't always fit well either.

"Because the freezer shrinks things. Like Shrinky Dinks. Remember? Smaller is lighter, duh. Go put it on." As I stomped to the bathroom Gavin half-sung, "I said you didn't have to dress like me!"

Squeezing into an undersized, frozen wrestling singlet was like dipping yourself into a giant Wendy's Frosty. Worse, Gavin clearly washed it, but threw it in the freezer before it was dry. Flocks of crunchy ice crystals shocked me, like a game of Operation gone haywire, no matter what position I stood in. And there were bulges in unacceptable places to a nine-year-old.

"Get back on the scale." I stepped on, hoping I made the weight he wanted. There was no way he was shaving my head.

"A perfect 59.2 pounds. I think you're gonna be a great pilot." Gavin gushed with generosity after being proved right, as a general rule. "But we gotta hustle. Jed and Toby are meeting us at the school at 10:30. Go change. Then pack that singlet in a bag with ice and put it in this cooler. Meet me in the garage when you're done."

***

Stepping into the garage turned my grouchiness into wonder. A life-size version of the Lego model from the kitchen table sat before me. There were no words. *CloudChaser1* was the most beautiful thing I had ever seen.

I wasn't even mad Gavin used my Big Wheel seat for the cockpit without asking. The four hockey stick-bath towel wings, shaped like long feathers, were pinned back for transport, Gavin explained. I inspected the lashings that kept the hockey sticks together and the Duct-tape covering the towels. Everything was trampoline-tight.

"How'd you do this? And how did I not know?"

"You were on a need to know basis only. Jed and Toby and I put it together at Toby's house. His parents are never home, and his dad has all those tools in the garage."

The steering system consisted of two foot pedals connected by rope to a rudder. Press the left pedal to go right, and the right pedal to go left. "Easy," Gavin said. Even a rookie pilot like me could handle it. Slick wagon wheels up front and two wider ones in back lent *CloudChaser1* a drag racer look, like the ones at the car show on the Fourth of July. Gavin bragged about the family-sized tub of Vaseline he used to grease the axles—for "maximum speed." But grumbled about the three showers it took to wash the excess away.

I saw Gavin's first real grin of the morning when he pointed to the armada of paper airplanes swaying in the breeze under a tree branch in the front yard. They were strung with fishing line in rows of black, white, and red. The plan was to attach them to the broomstick fixed above and behind the Big Wheel seat. The armada would chase *CloudChaser1* as they all moved through the sky.

"We should get goin'," Gavin said. Together we pushed *CloudChaser1* out of the garage and attached it to Gavin's bike with rope. He loaded all the extra items into the kid trailer hooked up to my bike, pulled up his socks, and straightened the ostrich-feather hat. We set off slowly to meet Jed and Toby at the school.

On the way, Gavin explained the plan was beautiful in its simplicity: they would pedal as fast as they could while towing me in *CloudChaser1* across the parking lot. "You'll probably catch air on our first run," he said. No doubt in his mind.

The runway was measured and marked by the time we got there. Gavin called Jed and Toby over to *CloudChaser1*. "As you already know, our goal is to achieve 2.3 seconds of flight time. We'll do this by pedaling at twelve miles per hour for a sustained twenty seconds. You two feeling strong?"

"Red Leader standing by," Jed said.

Toby followed form. "Copy that Gold Leader."

"Good. Let's get the speedometers attached and working on the bikes, and then lock and load *CloudChaser1* in. I'll prep the wings and do final inspection."

"Gavin, what should I do?"

"Get in your jumpsuit and safety gear, and get your head in the game. Don't forget the goggles. Then get the armada ready to go." I forgot about the frozen singlet. Charlie Brown whispered something in my ear, but I ignored it. I would probably look ridiculous; but my name *was* on the back of the singlet. Gavin said I *was the pilot of CloudChaser1. We were chasing clouds.*

Sometimes true pride can be earned on the wings of a little genuine discomfort.

Gavin called us together after we finished our tasks. We each put a hand on top of his. "I wanna remind everyone today is just the first part. We may fail. We may succeed. Doesn't matter. Renaissance Men are undeterred. We are always learning. And we always get better. Let's do this. Leonardo on three!"

They strapped me in to *CloudChaser1*. We pulled up to the runway start line. At the signal from Gavin, we took off. Faster than I expected. I gripped the handle bar and made sure the rudder was straight as an arrow.

I heard Toby yell. "Ten MPH!"

Then Jed. "Twelve MPH!"

I glanced up at the black, white, and red armada, soaring in the wind, chasing *CloudChaser1*, just like Gavin imagined it would. More than anything I wanted Gavin to see what I saw.

He yelled instead. "We have to glide left!" *Left?* No one mentioned gliding left during the pre-flight meeting. Then I saw it. We were running out of runway and *CloudChaser1* was still on the ground.

"Prepare to glide left," Gavin yelled. "Ready. Three. Two. One. Left." And I pressed the left pedal. Which made *CloudChaser1* go right. Everything scrambled after that.

***

Gavin, Jed, Toby, and our parents were standing over me when I woke up, still strapped into the Big Wheel seat.

"Honey, can you hear me?" I heard our mother say.

"Yeah."

"Are you ok?"

"I think so. But my wrist hurts pretty bad."

"Yeah, we're going to the ER. Can you stand?"

"I think so. How'd you get here?"

My mother undid the buckles. My father helped me up.

"We came home early from gardening class. The paper airplanes caught our attention."

"What happened?"

"I think I miscalculated," Gavin admitted. The plans were in his hands. Everyone stared at him. "I misplaced a decimal point." The "Gavino the unstoppable" tone he adopted months ago was missing from his voice.

"Which one?" Toby asked.

"Peter's weight. He was only able to weigh 5.92 pounds, not 59.2, in order for *CloudChaser1* to get off the ground."

We all groaned. Even our parents.

"Jed, Toby. Go home and tell your parents what happened. I'll be calling your mothers later to make sure," our mother said.

Our father pointed at Gavin and me wordlessly, and then the car. They tidied up the scene while we watched from inside the back of the car. I looked over at my older brother. We both knew we were in deep doodoo.

"Gavin, I hit the wrong—"

He put his hand on my shoulder and smiled. "Hey, it's still Gavino," as he pointed at himself. "And I know. We'll fix that as soon as we're not grounded anymore."

I looked down at the "CC1" taped to my chest. "Can I keep the singlet?"

"Of course. You're gonna need it for Phase Two."

A CUP OF COFFEE
Nonfiction by *Kendall Brown*

Like specific music, coffee shops have the power to define and transport me back to different periods in my life.

I didn't truly start drinking coffee until I met my boyfriend, now husband, in 2015, but I have always felt a profound sense of peace when inside a coffee shop. It all began predictably at Starbucks.

Back in middle school, I yearned to hold a Starbucks cup, despite feeling uncomfortable inside their stores. I would order their hot chocolate, even though it tasted terrible. I walked around with that branded cup throughout the day, long after I had finished the disappointing drink.

By high school, I had evolved. My beverage of choice became a "lite" caramel Frappuccino (the "lite" indicating that I had made the "healthy" choice of skipping the whipped cream on my coffee milkshake). I would spend hours chatting with my friends, sharing our most intimate stories.

However, a cruel twist of fate awaited me in college: the only coffee option available on campus was the dreaded Peet's. I felt betrayed. If I wanted to enjoy a Starbucks Frappuccino, I had to walk 20 minutes away and couldn't even use my meal points! Didn't the powers that be realize that a Peet's frappe was terrible? I logged countless miles trekking up and down Bancroft Avenue, hoping to reach the promised land, only to find no available seating. Berkeley was a crowded place, and gone were the days of occupying a table with friends for hours of gossip. I was alone and without a coffee refuge.

Fortunately, I eventually discovered the unofficial coffee shop of my college campus: Cafe Strada. Strada had a lovely indoor/outdoor ambiance with charming string lights. It was the go-to spot for graduate student instructors to meet students who had questions outside of office hours. Despite its appeal, I never quite felt comfortable at Strada. For one, they only accepted cash, which I always seemed to forget until after my drink had been made. Moreover, I had a panic attack when I realized they didn't serve Frappuccino-type drinks.

Back in high school, I once visited a non-chain coffee shop and ordered a caramel macchiato (my hot drink equivalent of a caramel Frappuccino). I was horrified when they brought out a beverage that did not closely resemble the dessert-like drink I had grown accustomed to. It was tiny and tasted … bad. The barista informed me that what Starbucks called a macchiato was not a real macchiato. How could Starbucks openly deceive me like this? That incident marked the beginning of the end for me and Starbucks.

I attempted to love Strada for its ambiance, but it never truly felt like home. I then gave Cafe Milano a try, another coffee shop with a fantastic layout, but it still didn't feel like my place.

I also explored The Musical Offering Cafe and Elmwood Cafe (RIP). It saddens me when places I used to love close down. I know I'm not alone in this, but it feels personal every time I search for a place and see the words "Permanently closed." It's as if the universe is erasing my memories by removing the existence of those places. It feels like being told I can never revisit those moments in my life. All that remains are my memories. It's like a small death.

I graduated from college a semester early without intending to and ended up getting a job in Berkeley. I continued living with my friends while they finished their senior year. I felt very sad and spent all my lunches at Artís Coffee, a pretentious and unwelcoming place. Peet's was my only other alternative. Since I didn't know how to properly feed myself, I foolishly attempted to subsist on coffee alone. This was my misguided attempt at dieting to lose the 20 pounds I gained while studying abroad, where my meals consisted solely of bread and wine.

After college, I moved to Portland, OR, without knowing anyone, and spent over three years building a life for myself there. My first home in Portland happened to be near Bipartisan Cafe. After ten months in the corporate world, I quit my job without having another lined up. Every morning, I would go to this cafe to work on my resume while enjoying bagels with cream cheese (not exactly helping with my post-study abroad diet). Afterward, I would take a walk up Mount Tabor and feel less alone in the world.

Sound Grounds Coffee (RIP) was the closest I ever came to replicating my high school Starbucks experience. Every Saturday, before an AA meeting, I would meet up with my girlfriends to catch up. I no longer keep in touch with them, which makes me sad. I miss those simple times, even though they didn't feel simple back then. The years I spent in AA, from age 22 to 24, comprised one of the most painful periods of my life. I think after the AA meeting moved we tried to move our coffee dates to Broken Robot Coffee, but it wasn't the same.

Although Kornblatt's Delicatessen (RIP) wasn't strictly a coffee shop, it deserves an honorable mention because it's where my husband and I fell in love. We spent many weekend mornings devouring corned beef hash and bagel sandwiches while enjoying a constant stream of drip coffee from our favorite waitress.

After years of dating a coffee addict, my mornings soon felt incomplete without this bitter beverage. We embraced the label of coffee snobs. We procured a gooseneck kettle, set it to the proper water temperature, and left it to rest for the precise amount of time in our French Press. Our bean budget and preference blossomed from Costco bulk savings to artisanal $20 bags. We moved to Bend and set out to taste-test each offering.

If you're a coffee lover, Bend is a great place to be. However, if you enjoy waking up early and having coffee, you might be out of luck. Bend is a sleepy, slow-paced vacation town, so most coffee shops don't open until 7 a.m. (which, in my opinion, is a crime). Recently, my husband and I found ourselves at the emergency vet at 5:30 a.m. because our dog had some cheat grass in her ear. While she was sedated, we needed to pass the time and wanted to grab some coffee. Unfortunately, nothing was open except for Dutch Bros and Starbucks.

Dutch Bros, however, doesn't serve coffee. They serve what I can only describe as sugar water to the masses. We stopped there last summer on our way to an early morning hike and when we asked for drip coffee, we were told they didn't serve it! Instead, the barista offered an Americano that was poured out of a dispenser. I don't understand how they can call that an Americano. Maybe Dutch Bros is not aware of what an Americano is supposed to be or how it's prepared. Per Google, "An Americano is a type of coffee drink made by diluting an espresso with hot water, giving it a similar strength to, but a different flavor from, traditionally brewed coffee." The barista drowned this "Americano" in what I can only describe as "scoops" of cream, which was quite terrifying.

She handed over our drinks and asked how much we'd like to tip. I feel personally attacked by Square readers. If you're filling a cup from a dispenser, shouldn't Dutch Bros be responsible for paying a fair wage? I'll tip when I receive deserving service or when a drink is made with more effort than simply pressing a button on a machine.

We were inspired to visit Dutch Bros in the first place because we met a couple on our honeymoon who raved about a coconut tea drink from their secret menu (my husband loves coconuts). Unfortunately, we forgot the name of the drink when we arrived at Dutch Bros, and most of their secret menu items contained coconut. However, none of the drinks sounded appealing. They were primarily tropical, rainbow-colored, sugary concoctions. Unlike my former self, I no longer enjoy drinking my calories, especially not 500+ to start my day!

Now, back to my search for coffee before 7 a.m. Luckily, by now it was 6:30 a.m., and we noticed that a coffee spot called Still Vibrato had just opened. Still Vibrato is located on the bottom floor of a new apartment building on the west side of Bend, near Safeway. I expected them to serve someone else's coffee (like how Spoken Moto serves Megaphone Coffee), but I was pleasantly surprised to find that they use proprietary beans. The atmosphere was light, airy, and inviting, with Andrew Bird and Beirut playing in the background. The barista was incredibly pleasant, which is a rarity in coffee shops. And the Americanos were the most delicious we've ever had (apologies to Thump). We didn't want them to end. We were delighted to have stumbled upon this gem.

Kudos to Still Vibrato for opening (marginally) early (though not by "real" city standards) and for serving a scrumptious Americano without any pretentiousness or alienating hipster elitism!

In the end, what makes a coffee shop feel like home? Why didn't the spots I ventured to in Berkeley ever feel right? As inviting as these coffee shops were, I have come to realize that what truly makes a coffee shop feel like home is the people. I never loved Starbucks; I loved spending quality time with my friends. It was never about the coffee. It's about feeling a sense of connection. I used to think coffee was the thread weaving through my twenties, but it was the small groups, the intimate connections. Coffee shops are the container, but people are the substance.

As a remote worker, I have tried to find "my" coffee spot where I feel most comfortable. It feels good to leave the house and force myself to wear pants. Yet, when I look around and see silent zombies staring at their screens, I feel a deep sadness and loneliness. We are so disconnected. Quality beans can't replace quality connections.

What matters are the people and the stories that unfold over a cup of joe. While coffee shops provide the backdrop to my life, it is the friends, both old and new, who make those coffee shop moments truly meaningful.

LAST CAST

Fiction by *Lynda Sather*

"Last cast!" my date called as the tide turned, threatening to leave the skiff stranded on the rocky beach and us with it. Trout fishing on a beautiful, isolated river accessible only at high tide was his idea of a perfect first date—and it was.

After ten more last casts, we wrestled the heavy skiff across the barnacle-encrusted rocks to the ebbing tidewater and shoved off. It may not have been the typical first date dinner at a fancy restaurant, but fishing, just the two of us, turned into a forty-year romance.

We fished rivers and lakes throughout Alaska, reluctantly sharing the riverbank with hungry bears during salmon season or finding our string of pike left to cool in the water—stolen, sight unseen, by stealthy martins.

In Mexico, we chased the same school of fleeing tuna as a pod of hungry porpoises, the sea around us churning with the flash and splash of predator and prey.

While trolling for marlin in Panama, wily dolphins stole the bait right off our hooks.

On a clear, sunny day in Belize, our skiff capsized a mile from shore in rough water on our way to fish the reef.

Off Admiralty Island in Alaska, a pod of orcas surrounded our small skiff, their breaching scaring me so badly I bit teeth marks in my rubber rain gear.

Never, in all those years, was the last cast really the last cast, but rather, the prelude to a series of last casts.

In all that time, in all those places, we always, *always*, ate what we caught. In our early years, we ate tasteless grayling because we couldn't afford meat. Later, we filled our freezer with salmon, halibut, cod, trout, char, you name it. In New Zealand, we feasted on brown trout roasted over an open fire. In Tahiti, we picnicked on tropical fish we'd speared, washed down with milk from fresh coconuts. In Mexico, we cleaned bonitos and sailfish in the shower of our budget pensione because they were too large for the tiny sink. In nicer hotels, the restaurant chef would happily turn our catch into a scrumptious meal seasoned with cilantro and slices of mango: some for us, some for the other guests.

All this to say, my husband was *not* a catch-and-release fisherman.

Four decades after that first "last cast," I checked my husband out of the memory care home and took him on an expensive charter trip to catch steelhead in Idaho, a bid to relive old times, I suppose. On the long drive there, he jabbered incoherently about past fishing exploits and how great a meal of fresh steelhead would taste. At least, I like to think that's what he said. We spent the night in a nearby hotel, where he obsessively checked and rechecked his tackle box filled with rusty hooks, dented bobbers, and lures collected from around the world: the life-like barbed mouse for fishing in the marsh, lethal eight-inch lures from Mexico, pink and green plastic squid, tiny mosquito flies and ugly horsefly-looking things. Glancing over at his hunched form, I thought of an old pirate rummaging through his treasure chest of jewels, unwilling to part with a single diamond or plastic bauble.

The next morning, we found the charter operator waiting on the banks of the Snake River. Aspen leaves on the riverbank were just beginning to turn gold and the water sparkled as sun burned off the fog. Sunny and cool, it was a perfect day for fishing.

The charter operator coached us on the proper technique for catching steelhead, casting downriver into the riffles, and then reeling just fast enough against the current so the heavy lure bumped against the rocky bottom but didn't snag, or at least not often. My husband either didn't heed or couldn't comprehend the advice. He spent the morning casting and reeling, casting, and reeling, by rote and muscle memory. He didn't speak but seemed happy.

As the day wore on, discouragement set in.

Please, I prayed to the river gods, please let him hook into a fish. It's been so long; it would mean so much to him. Please, just one steelhead to take back.

I saw when the fish struck his line. The tug on the end of the pole, the zing as the strong fish took line and ran. Twice my husband brought the big fish close to the boat, only to have it spook at the metal hull and bolt, heavy monofilament spooling off the reel at warp speed.

Finally, the guide was able to reach over the side of the boat with his long-handled net and scoop the exhausted fish aboard.

"Quick, get a picture," the guide said. "Before I release it."

"What?" I asked.

"Take a picture," he said impatiently.

"But why throw it back?" I asked, confused. "It's over twenty inches."

"Wild fish have their fins intact," he said brusquely. "We can only keep hatchery fish with clipped fins."

My husband stood in the stern, struggling to hold the heavy, slippery fish while I took a quick photo. Then the guide took the fish, leaned over the side of the skiff, and let it go.

My husband's eyes, which earlier were the color of a turquoise river on a sunny day, turned dull, like the bright tropical fish whose iridescent scales turn muddy two minutes after being pulled from the water.

There was no announcement, no call for the last cast. My husband just set his pole down and turned his back to the river. After all those years of last casts which weren't, I wasn't prepared when this one was.

THE WAVES
Poetry by *Matthew James Friday*

To me the sea is a continual miracle (Walt Whitman)

The rolling and rushing of waves
breaking with a constant roar, a rage
of entropy and the music of the grave.

On the beach there's arrayed
storm-wrenched tree trunks rolled
by the rolling and rushing of waves.

The threat to consume is displayed
in constant promise and petering-out
of the waves, the waves, the waves.

The theatrical sky is part of the play,
directing the wind to act as lover
to the rolling and rushing of waves.

The medicine of the sea is displayed
in the vibrating pain that is relieved
by the rolling and rushing of waves.

At night there roars a shocking rave,
a fear of what is unseen, unknown,
the rolling and rushing of waves
of entropy and the music of the grave.

3, 6, 9, THE GOOSE DRANK WINE
Fiction by *Kiyomi Appleton Gaines*

> *Three, six, nine*
> *The Goose drank wine*
> *The Monkey chewed tobacco on the streetcar line*
> *The line broke*
> *The Monkey got choked*
> *And they all went to Heaven in a little rowboat*
> —*The Clapping Song, Lincoln Chase*

Sun Wukong had come a long way. He was finally near the end of his journey though. He spit tobacco juices discreetly into a small plastic cup as he gazed out of the streetcar. Here again, and perhaps here at last. He unfastened his top shirt button, his one concession to the heat. He wore a three-piece beige suit with collarless shirt and matching short-brimmed fedora. The streetcar stopped and the young driver leaned back, "This your stop, man."

Sun Wunkong stood, gripping the wooden seat for stability. He was not a young man anymore, and the driver was already coming back to offer an arm. He was not too proud to take it. The driver handed him down to the street.

"Thank you, young man." He extended his magical staff to walking stick length and leaned on it.

"Enjoy your visit." The young one returned to his post.

The streetcar trundled off. Sun Wukong waited for traffic to pass, and crossed Canal Street into the French Quarter. He marveled at how much had changed and how much hadn't. At the corner, he plucked the tobacco from his cheek and deposited it, and his cup, into a trash can.

"A filthy habit," she would say.

He continued down Royal, one of his favorite walks. The music slid over him in ways beyond what his old ears could hear. He took in the art displayed at the back of the cathedral. It was vibrant and bright, full of remembered joy and hope, great swirls of untamed colors, all mixing at the edges. He continued, easing between the tourists and the locals, taking in the place that felt like an old friend. Old gods never died, someone said. Yet inevitably, he thought, they ended up here, in the antechamber to whatever came Next. The scent of human exertion, effluvia, errata mingled with the heady jasmine, stilled the monkey mind, anchored him. It wasn't his first visit, but he thought it might be his last. Eventually, he turned down Ursulines, directed more by the feeling of his feet than his mind. He knew the way. He would never forget the way.

They had ducked in to escape a sudden rain and been drawn by the music pouring out into the street, so much younger then. They had come here often, met by plan, over the years. The place had changed, aged, and mellowed as they had and so remained, if not "the same," then ever "as good as." This street was quieter, walked mostly by locals, living and not, who all greeted him with a nod or friendly drawl of, "Alright."

As he neared, he thought he should have brought flowers, and felt a momentary sinking. It was too late now, and she wouldn't expect it, but it would have been a nice gesture. Would she think him rash? He was that, even steadied by age, but she was as steady as the seasons in her routines. He shook the thought off. Flowers were funerary.

He came to the tiny gap between buildings, through a wrought-iron gate. It was a place that didn't exist on any map, a place only half the city's denizens could even see, let alone find. He walked down the narrow, cobbled alleyway, and a figure appeared.

"I have an appointment," he said. That wasn't the right word. "Er, a reservation."

The young woman smiled at him, and bowed, "Of course, sifu, we've been expecting you. Mother Hulda is already here."

She turned into the narrow doorway, gathered up a menu, a rolled napkin bundle, and led the way. Inside, the restaurant was a warren of small spaces between spaces. It was dark, but he made out familiar faces and new ones as well. There were writers, street performers, artists, and of course, musicians. There were other old gods, statesmen, and ordinary faces, too. He nodded to a few as he passed.

He saw her before she noticed him. Hulda staring into nothing, her fingers trailing absently at the stem of her wine glass. It would be eiswein, he knew. He asked how she could drink it after sputtering on a taste once in their early days. She laughed and told him it was like all the beauty, happiness, and sweetness of wintertime condensed into flavor. It was her favorite.

She was beautiful, and his heart warmed to see her. When she noticed him, her expression softened and brightened, and she stood. They fell together in embrace, laughing and talking at once. How was the journey? You look well. Can you believe how much has changed? And how much is the same? How long has it been? It's been too long. As they settled into their chairs, he set his hat on a hook, contracted his staff down to the size of a toothpick, and tucked it behind his ear. The young woman set the menu and bundle of silverware in front of him with a smile.

"You look well." Hulda smiled.

"And you." He shook the napkin out across his lap. "The trip was longer this time."

"Slower."

"We're older. I think this might be the last time."

She tilted her head.

"I don't know," he said, "it feels different."

"They don't need us as much as they used to."

"Everything is so big and fast and complicated now."

"It's different, and it's the same. Lives were always complicated. And simple."

"It's more connected now." He shaped his hands, fingers meshed and touching at the tips. "Net work. Everything is net work, and no fish."

She smiled and sipped her wine. "It's good for them to go find their own ways, new ways of doing things."

He nodded and scratched behind his ear, "Mmm. They tell the stories wrong now anyway."

"They need different things."

"Food, adventure." He shrugged. "What's different?"

"Companionship. They're so lonely, you know. I worry about them, but what can we do?"

"Mmm. They go their own way, what can we do?" He paused, stuttered, "An-and-that is the most important thing. Companionship. To be close to the people we're … well, close to …?"

The server returned; they ordered their food.

They talked about the old and the good. Hulda had a second glass of wine and fish meuniere.

Sun Wukong ate the gumbo. When they finished, she ordered bread pudding, of which she ate only half, and coffee. He had green tea and pecan pie. He delicately scraped the whipped cream off, and Hulda claimed it for her coffee. It was comfortable, and he realized he might have become a part of her ebb and flow, a part of her routines.

"Hulda," he said, when they finished dinner, "I've taken a place. It's a small place. A condo, they call it. Modest, but I think enough."

She looked at him with interest. "That's lovely. You really do mean to stay?"

"I thought we could share it," he rushed on, worrying his napkin between his hands.

She stared for a moment, and he thought he had been a fool, too rash after all. A tiny smile played at her lips, and uncertainty. "Share it?"

He cleared his throat and nodded. "Together. We could live together."

Her face brightened and she laughed, "Well," she said. "Look at us."

Relief flooded through him. He hadn't misread things after all. He smiled.

He reclaimed his hat and extended his staff again, and she turned to take up her distaff. When they reached the street, he offered his arm, and she took it. He swung his staff around, no longer leaning on it as a cane, his former spring returned to his step.

"I hope we can hear the boats on the river," she said, leaning into him, "From our condo."

"We can. I hear their call every night."

At the end of time, Sun Wukong found himself hopeful for the future.

DISTANCE

Nonfiction by *Mike Cooper*

The speed of light is 186,000 miles per second. It is theorized that this is the fundamental limit of speed: nothing can go faster. Meaning that if you were traveling in a car going the speed of light and you flipped the headlights on, it would still be dark in front of you.

Sound and light travel at different speeds. My father taught me to count the time between the flashes of lightning and the thunder. Five seconds equals one mile.

I remember one night when I was eleven and the lightning and the thunder came at the exact same time—almost as if the thunder came first. Everyone met downstairs immediately afterward, outside my youngest sister's room. My father went outside to check the house and the trees; my mother held us and told us that everything would be fine. It was only lightning.

The light we see on the moon is from 1.33 seconds ago. The rays from the sun take 8 minutes and 20 seconds to get here. When we see Jupiter in the night sky, depending on where we are in our respective orbits, the light has been traveling for 35 to 52 minutes. The light from Pluto, who was kicked out of the solar system for being too small, takes 5 ½ hours to reach us. If Alpha Centauri, our nearest star neighbor, decided to blink out of existence today, we wouldn't know for 4 years. The light from the binary stars Mizar and Alcor originated 83 years ago, which, at the time of this writing, would have been 1940, when my mother was two years old. The star Dubhe, at the upper right tip of the dipper in the Big Dipper, sends light from the year 1900, 123 years ago, the year my grandfather was born. The light from Betelgeuse, the star that makes Orion's right shoulder, is from 430 years ago, about the time that Catherine de' Medici was born. My grandfather and my mother were also Italian.

We see light from stars in the heavens that may no longer exist—haven't for a long time. Blown up. Gone nova. Cold and dead.

The first time someone you love dies is the hardest. The first relative of mine who died was my grandfather—my mother's father. As a child, he bounced me on his knee. I planted roses with him, picked dandelions for soup. Later, I went to his apartment in the middle of the night to pick him up when he fell. I sat with him on his deathbed. After he died, I looked into the night sky and focused on the second star in the handle of Ursa Major, The Big Dipper, which I now know is called Mizar. I'm not sure why, but I decided that he was there, that he was Mizar, and that was where I spoke to him in the years that followed.

Our galaxy, the Milky way, is 100,000 light years across. The nearest galaxy, Andromeda, is 2 ½ million light years away. A light year is 5.88 trillion miles. That's 588 followed by 10 zeros. They say that humans can't comprehend large numbers. We try to count the stars, the grains of sand in our hand.

We sent Voyager 1 into space in 1977. It is 14.6 billion miles away now, traveling at 38,000 miles per hour. It communicates with us through radio waves, which move at the speed of light. It takes about 19 hours to hear from Voyager 1.

My mother died when we were on vacation with our one-year-old daughter in 1997 when Voyager was about 4.6 billion miles away. My mother wasn't supposed to die. She was fifty-eight. She was healthy. She just forgot to wake up. We caught a redeye from Portland to Omaha. My daughter slept in my wife's lap. I watched the night sky out the window, and I saw the Big Dipper.

Alcor is a smaller star slightly to the left and above Mizar. I am older now than my mother was when she died—my vision has declined and I can no longer see Alcor with my naked eye, but at the time, on that black night in the thin upper atmosphere, it shone brightly. And I saw, without the obstacle of time or distance, my mother, a happy child, bouncing on her father's knee.

THE ULTIMATE REVENGE
Fiction by *Barbara Cole*

He drew back his foot and, like the baseball player he once wanted to be, raised his right leg high, and kicked in the window.

That was enough. He could not take the noise any longer. It had become too strong. Was he going crazy, he asked himself.

The bellowing kept coming. Its intensity had been increasing for the past two hours. Again and again and again. Little reprieve for his ears. Did not anyone else notice? Why didn't they do something? Where were they? Didn't they care? Who would do such a thing? He thought his eardrums would explode.

Now his foot hurt. And his hand was bleeding from the glass. The window was thinner than he thought and the glass had shattered glass bits over the animal and him.

The beast looked scared. It continued to bark. Would it never stop?

What did he do now? What should he do? Who should he call?

Gingerly he put his hand up toward the broken window. Easy, now, he told himself. He must be gentle. He was scared but so was the dog.

He had stepped around the corner, into the janitorial closet when the car arrived and parked. Only after he heard the door slam, the click, click, click of stilettoes and the elevator bell followed by the howls, did he know what was to happen.

They'd played a trick on him again. They'd got to him another time. One more time. When would they stop?

First, it was the drip of the air conditioner outside his room. No, he couldn't afford the luxuriant cool air, but they had installed one next door just to irritate and hurt him.

Then the photographs appeared. Shoved under the door of his cage at the garage, the envelope held scenes of men making love with one another. They had put them there just to remind him of his aloneness. He'd get back at them some day. He'd find a way to get revenge.

Now this.

He opened his hand a few inches from the jagged window. The dog sniffed at his outstretched fingers. The animal seemed to sense that it was all right. But what did he do now? Why was he doing any of this? Why didn't he just leave the dank, dreary parking garage and let someone else handle it?

He inched his hand closer to the dog's open mouth. Out came a pinkish tongue, licking a finger in front of its mouth. No sound came from either of them.

He stepped back. Looking at the blood on his hand, he knew he needed to have it cared for soon.

The dog stayed. It could have jumped through the window of the station wagon and made its way to freedom. Yet it stayed.

Another bark. And another but this time softer, more as if it called for attention.

Where were they hiding now? Could they see him? Did they want him to be placed in an uncompromising position with this animal? Did they want him to appear to be a fool to himself and to the dog and yes, to them? Their revenge.

But revenge for what? He didn't even know who they were. Or why they continued these attacks.

Now the dog crept closer. Just inches, but closer, nearer to him, putting its head through the open space. The dog sensed his fright and moved gently as if not to frighten him. The man knew his emotions were different from what he normally felt when near someone.

Silence.

The dog sniffed. And again. Then stretched its neck a few inches closer to him. What did it want?

He had no food to give the creature. Nor had he any bones or anything that seemed appropriate. Yet the dog remained with a soft, gentle stare at him. Again, the man reached forward with his bloody hand. He spoke a greeting.

Startled by his own voice, he realized he wanted to stay with the dog for a while. No drivers would want to leave the garage until the symphony was finished. What did it matter what they said to him? So what if they had sent this dog to bother him? He wanted to be near the animal.

Yes, it had been a long time since he had been near anything really alive. Who could you trust being near? You couldn't trust any of the fellows on other shifts in the garage. They'd trick you every time they could. Earlier he'd thought that they might be doing those things to him, but he had decided that they were too involved with their inside gambling and prostitution takes to want to bother with him.

And you couldn't trust any of those so-called women who pretended that he made a difference to them. The only way he'd make a difference to them was that he was one more notch on their missionary belt, someone they'd try to help but couldn't.

He knew about them. They were all alike. They told you at first how you reminded them of their fathers. When you tried to be the way you really were, they said they didn't like your drinking or your brown shoes or whatever. There was always something.

No. It was better to just leave everyone and everybody alone.

Keep to yourself. That's the best way to get through life. Pretend as they pretend. And then leave them alone.

Now he felt a little differently. The dog sniffed again, giving another timid bark. This time the man stretched his hand a few inches closer. The animal stood quietly. A huge sigh tumbled out of the animal. Almost a sigh of relief.

Another sigh, a slight sound and then the dog lay down in the dark back seat. It looked up at the hand the man had now placed in the opening. The dog stuck out his huge tongue, covered the hand and licked it again, blood and all. He edged a bit closer and nuzzled the hand against the furry neck.

Another sigh of relief.

This sigh was not from the dog. It was the man who sighed with relief. The dog seemed eager now to say something and yes, to touch. How long had it been since anything had touched him? He didn't even touch the people's hands as they gave him money when they left the parking garage. No, better not to touch. Someone may not understand and complain. You never knew what would happen these days.

But the dog wanted to touch him. And lick his hand. And nuzzle him. Maybe even love him.

Maybe even love him.

That, that would be his ultimate revenge.

RAISED BY BOOKS
Poetry by *Samantha J. Reynolds*

For my mom, who made sure I was raised by books.

I've always been wild, a dreamer, "off the hook."
But that's to be expected, since I was raised by books.

You aren't taught any rules when books are your guide,
so that dreams unbridled are left to grow inside.

Louisa May Alcott taught me most manners I know,
and I resolved to grow up and be exactly like Jo.

I came of age with Ramona thanks to Beverly Cleary
and Junie B. Jones, whom I do still love dearly.

Wardrobes and treehouses took me through time and spaces
to beautiful, terrible, wonderful places.

I saw Big Friendly Giants who liked humans and took one.
Trees that were giving, and trees that grew in Brooklyn.

There were scarlet letters, mockingbirds, mice, and men
whose lessons I didn't fully comprehend back then.

I fell in love with Tom Sawyer, Huck Finn, and other crooks.
No bad boy is off limits when you're raised by books.

I was inspired by stories like Nancy Drew,
and (if you couldn't tell) Where the Sidewalk Ends, too.

I discovered we each have a monster inside.
From Frankenstein, Dracula, Jekyll, and Hyde.

Many stories taught me that when love is true
it matters who you are, and not what you do.

I learned hearts can't break, even when they shatter.
For hearts, like humans, are made of stronger matter.

Have you ever wondered if a sad ending's not true?
Then maybe, perhaps, you were raised by books, too.

But it's not about endings at the end of the day.
It's about every happy moment we get along the way.

So how dare I have hope with how grim the world looks?
The answer is simple: I was raised by books.

HUNGER AND MOTHERHOOD

Nonfiction by *Dani Nichols*

As I type this, my baby is chortling happily at the toys on his bouncer, specifically a plastic, wildly pleased-with-itself sunshine that mostly eludes his grasp. When he catches it finally, he thrusts it into his mouth with the fervor of a starving man at a buffet. I joke with my friends that he's the kind of baby who makes you want to have ten more. He's chubby and happy and giggles easily. He curls his little fingers around your hand in a way that makes you feel like the most important person in the entire world.

He has the chocolate skin and black-coffee eyes of Africa, while I bear the green-apple eyes and undercooked-pancake complexion of my Irish ancestors. I refer to us as food because that's invariably what people say: "Oooooh, what a little chocolate chip!" an elderly Black woman in Target cooed at me with wonder.

"Oh, he's your brownie bite!" said another in Safeway. "I just want to eat him up!"

Babies and puppies are the universal delicious things in the universe, I've decided. But my nuzzles into his yummy hair and the sweet compliments from passersby come at a cost—he was not always mine to savor.

I'm reminded of this occasionally by the bluntness of strangers—for every hungry grandma there is a skeptical, pickier one.

"How'd this happen?" asked one such onlooker, gesturing with a bony finger at the coffee-colored face peeking out of the baby carrier on my chest. I stammered what I hoped was a kind explanation, but it was an ugly reminder—color-blindness does not exist, especially here in not-exactly-diverse Central Oregon. As much as he is one of the essential tastes on my palate, to others he's an anomaly, a new flavor they can't quite explain or pinpoint.

Not everyone understands; this I know. But those who do feed us. When I arrived at the rural, understaffed, and out-of-date Southern hospital to meet the child I hoped would become mine, he was lying alone in a plastic crib that reminded me of a Tupperware container for last-night's spaghetti. I'd driven several hours, flown all night, driven several more hours, and stumbled into the maternity ward with only the desperate love of a mother's heart propelling me. Only after I sat down with this miracle of a person in my arms did I realize I was starving. I dug in my purse for a granola bar. A kind nurse saw me furtively chewing, sitting as displaced and unmoored as the child I held, on a stool between the nursery and nurse's station.

"Honey, I can get you on the list for some food from the cafeteria," she said. "But you don't want it, our food is real bad. Why don't you leave the baby with us and go get you somethin'."

The maternity nurses were clearly stretched thin; the child I had come to rescue wasn't the only one who needed it, so I was shy to avail myself of her kindness. But finally, the rumble in my gut became impossible to ignore, so I waited for the baby to fall asleep and then ventured out to find food.

I found a Chick-fil-A, relieved to see a brand I recognized, and then realized it was Sunday afternoon, and it would not be open. I drove across the street to the next available option, a small-town milkshake and burger joint with teenagers in paper hats joking behind the counter and flirting with one another as they spilled Coca-Cola out of paper cups in puppy-dog clumsiness.

I got chili-cheese fries because I hadn't eaten anything more than a few pretzels and a granola bar in nearly 40 hours and felt daring. Belatedly, I added a milkshake too, which made the paper-hatted teenager grin at my hungry fervor.

By the time I made it back to the hospital with a greasy paper bag in my hand and a milkshake already half-finished, food was again forgotten, and all I could think about was the baby. What if he'd cried alone, with no one free to tend to him? What if someone from his biological family had arrived? What if he was never meant to be mine?

When I got back into the maternity ward, the charge nurse met me at the door and waved me past the imposing security guards. "I need to talk to you," she said.

My milkshake threatened to turn around in my gut and come right back up. I squeezed my hands around the crinkled paper bag of my dinner to keep from trembling. *Adoption is risky love. I always knew this might happen. He's a child who needs love. I don't have a right to keep him if there's someone in his biological family who will care for him.* These thoughts and more swirled around my mind as she pushed his crib into a small private room. I watched him glide in front of me, still asleep in his little Tupperware, like the most nourishing and soul-filling of meals, as I prepared my heart for hunger.

"Here," she said, thrusting several gift cards into my hands. "There was a failed adoption earlier, and these are from the family. The nursing team all agreed they should go to you. Take care of yourself, and him."

There is food that satisfies, like granola bars and chili-cheese fries, and then there is food that does more than ease temporary pain. It lingers on your palate and in your memory, like grandmother's blueberry muffins or a warming holiday feast, tastes that nourish long after the meal is over. When I think of that overworked and sorrowful nurse, the way she met my eyes and gave me hope when she could have kept it for herself, I think of the latter. I picked up the baby, who still wasn't mine, who'd been loved by another mother for months before I arrived, who was now supported by a maternity wing of kind professionals rooting for him. I held that precious, delicious life to my still-hungry-self, and I cried and cried.

Now that baby is cooing and cackling to himself, soon he will want another bottle because, as I joke, he eats like a linebacker. We're home; home in every sense as he is ours now, legally, and spiritually and completely. To celebrate, the day of his finalization hearing, my husband smoked a brisket, bursting with the legacy and flavor of a Texan upbringing, and I made roasted butternut squash topped with caramelized onions and bacon and goat cheese, sizzling in a cast-iron skillet. We popped locally grown sparkling wine and toasted to life and love and wholeness and satisfaction. We ate with the joyous gratitude of those who have known hunger.

"This is the body of Christ, broken for you," the priest says gravely. "This is the blood of Christ, spilled for you," we hear. In this faith, those who are hungry are fed, those who thirst drink from Living Water and thirst no more. This is sustenance that does not look away from pain and suffering. Indeed, it is the essential human experience of redemption and sorrow in one bite, the tension of sacrifice and love embodied.

It's essential to my understanding of God that my faith is represented in spilled blood and broken body, in rumbling stomachs and parched throats, in feasting and gratitude.

When my son and I are out together, folks often say, "Oh he's so yummy!" and I think about how we eat to celebrate, to survive, to grieve. My motherhood is a story of an empty belly, of yearning, of the deep ache that settles in our gut when hope is deferred. It is also the joy when it is finally, unctuously realized, the both/and of painful gratitude, of knowing that my fullness was paid for by the emptiness of another.

Sometimes at night, after a dinner of macaroni and cheese and "three more bites," I read *Where the Wild Things Are*. On the couch, with my three miraculous and delicious children snuggled around me, I say with fervor, with deep, lived-in understanding: "I'll eat you up, I love you so!"

BANNING BOOKS PLAYBOOK
Fiction by *Kristine Thomas*

Misty Lake Superintendent Charles Brown anxiously surveyed the crowd, counting 127 teachers each dressed head-to-toe in a red shroud.

And another 128 teachers wore T-shirts in the school colors of aqua and pink and were called Brown's "Mighty Grizzly" mascots who were instructed exactly what to say, do, and think.

Lambs of Christ Congregation Minister Drue had dictated to Brown the school board agenda, blessed by the seven male school board members to advance their propaganda.

Board chairman Owen and vice chair Dressler cautioned Brown everything had to go as planned, otherwise, his contract would not be renewed, and he would be canned.

Clearing his throat, tapping the microphone, and straightening his tie, Brown flashed his bogus smile as he told his first lie.

"To the prestigious and honorable faculty of the Misty Lake School District, let's celebrate the tremendous work you have all done, the varsity football, boys' basketball and baseball teams are all number one."

Barely five-feet tall, AP English teacher Ms. Bronte stood on her rickety, metal folding chair, angry after twenty-five years teaching that she was suffocating in a dystopian nightmare. Pointing at Brown, she yelled, "What are you going to do about the district's low-test scores? Teachers need the tools and freedom to do their jobs, or we might as well work for the same pay at grocery stores."

"Now, now dear Ms. Bronte, I don't want you to hurt yourself or get hurt," Brown said with a smile. "Everyone, everyone, please sit as this presentation is going to take a while.

"First let me begin by appointing Coaches Route, Lamar, and Wilkens each as sergeant in-arms who are instructed to expel anyone oblivious to my intellectual charms. And the person or persons behaving inappropriately will be escorted away and will be docked a week's pay."

Before another teacher could complain, Brown was quick to explain.

"Our quaint country town is being threatened by an ominous storm cloud, and now is the time to make the district's students and parents proud. Tonight, we stop the left's wokeness agenda by fighting their vitriol and it's time we listen to our true great, genius president and take control. In this very room, there are people brainwashing our children with the woke ideals. Today is the day we must stand up and repeal any and everything that prevents our good, faithful children from receiving the authentic education this community is perceiving. Beginning today, school board members have unanimously agreed, our precious children can no longer read: *To A Kill a Mockingbird* because killing birds is bad, or *The Catcher in the Rye*, a book that's incredibly bland.

"The mere idea of *One Flew Over the Cuckoo's Nest* leaves our board aghast, and why read *1984* because what's the point about learning about the past? Add to the burn pile *Harriet the Spy* and *Adventures of Huckleberry Finn* because we don't want our students to get any ideas from an irresponsible girl and boy. And let's burn *Gender Queer*, *All Boys Aren't Blue*, and *The Absolutely True Diary of a Part-Time Indian*—all tied to that woke ploy."

AP English teacher Mrs. Tyler quickly raised her hand to let the pompous superintendent know her stand. "Everything you said about those books is fiction and you are only spreading falsehoods to cause friction." Mrs. Tyler raised her fist triumphantly as she was escorted away. She had more to say, "Everything you are doing is preventing our students from learning and thinking in a critical way."\

Brown nodded once and his golden boys escorted Mrs. Tyler out of the room, only pausing a moment before continuing his tale of doom and gloom. "Next, we are talking about health and what our students need to know for them to develop healthily and grow. Let me make it perfectly clear, a cow's a cow and a steer's a steer. Boys are boys who play with balls and girls are girls who play with dolls."

Mr. Anderson tried to stifle a giggle, until he burst into an uncontrollable laugh, wondering if the superintendent was aware of his gaffe.

Cluelessly, Brown continued, "Teachers are prohibited from talking about periods until girls are in the sixth grade."

Health teacher Miss Parker and fifth grade teacher Miss Wilder jumped to their feet to voice their dismay, utterly tired of watching the game Brown was attempting to play. For years, they had kept their silence when listening to the good old boys like Brown ignore the community's and school bullies' violence.

"Are you talking about the period used at the end of a sentence?" Miss Wilder asked.

"Are you even aware the average age for a girl to start her period is in the fifth grade?" Miss Parker broadcast.

"Coaches, please show those women the door for they are exactly who we should all abhor." The superintendent still had more wisdom to depart about what the school board considered to be art. "Vulgar, immoral, and tacky adequately describes the work of the so-called sculptors and painters. I don't care about the backlash from elite, left-wing haters. Our children are hereby forbidden from studying Michelangelo and any artwork our esteemed board does not like."

Chemistry teacher and union representative Mrs. Curie said, "Congratulations Superintendent Brown, you have won because all 127 of us dressed in red are done. We will no longer teach in a district completely out of reach."

Librarian Ms. Atwood was the last teacher to leave the gym, but not before taking one last jab at him.

"Charlie, I have known you since you were in third grade and your behavior is nothing more than nonsensical hullabaloo. And by the way, I am here to remind you, the book you checked out—*The Handmaid's Tale*—is seven weeks overdue."

THE BEGINNING

Fiction by *Jennifer Forbess*

My life had to start somewhere. The story of an hour starts at the beginning of an hour. The story of a day starts at the beginning of the day. Where did the story of my life start? When I was born? Yes, and no. When my parents were born? Probably even before that.

I was not thinking about this for some great philosophical reason. I really just needed to know who to blame. I had new problems every day, and I was getting pretty sick of it. This morning, no lie, all the smoke alarms in my apartment went off at the same time. No good reason that I could see, no fire or anything. I couldn't reach them, couldn't even think with all that screeching and screaming, so I grabbed my backpack and my work uniform and fled. Got dressed in my car, scrunched down so no one would get a free peek.

Yesterday, the problem was that I had another argument with my boyfriend, Troy. Well, an argument I manufactured about him leaving his junk around my apartment. Even though he had his own place, we spent most of our time at my apartment, and it was cozy. I didn't really mind his junk. I just needed something to pick on.

As ready as I could get in my car, I texted Troy about my smoke alarms and headed to work. I have worked at Glory's Diner since high school, almost six years now. The owner's name is actually Gloria, not Glory, and she has become like a second mother to me. She's not anything like my mother, who was all about making the best of everything, never getting upset, never complaining, doing whatever anyone wanted her to do. Gloria doesn't take crap from anyone. She says exactly what she thinks, and she doesn't sugar-coat it. She's like a human lie detector. A long time ago, I gave up trying to tell her anything other than the truth.

So, wouldn't you know, on my way to work, another problem. I was on Gandy Boulevard, just over the bridge, morning sun in my eyes. I started to see little whips of white smoke from under the hood. Not good. I slowed and pulled over, put on the four-way blinkers, turned off the car. Now that I had stopped, smoke poured from under the hood. Definitely a problem.

The road was packed with morning traffic going into Tampa. I pulled the hood release and slid over to the passenger side to get out. The morning was already bad enough without being run over by some dick with his head in his fancy coffee.

I didn't know much about cars, but I've heard of cars overheating. Might be that. I squeezed my eyes shut. There had to be a good solution for this problem; single people had their cars overheat sometimes, and they solved the problem. What did they do?

Shit.

I pulled out my phone and called Troy.

The phone rang, and Troy answered. "Hey, Babe. Did you get to work already? That was fast."

"I'm on the side of the road. My car is smoking. Could you tell me …"

"No problem. Where are you?"

"Gandy, near West Shore. I just need …"

"I'll be right there." He hung up.

Dammit. Just like him.

I sat on the grass by my car and waited. The St. Augustine was poky and sharp on the skin of my legs, which were barely covered by the skirt of my diner uniform, but it was a beautiful morning. The air off the bay was light, warm, liquid, like water flowing around my limbs. The sun was warm on my back, but not scorching yet, like it would be later. It was a quarter-to-nine. I pulled out my phone and texted Gloria that my car was broken down, and I might be late to work. I tore blades of grass into tiny segments to mark the seconds.

Troy was basically a good guy, great even. We met a year ago at the hospital in St. Pete, when my mom had her second, and final, heart attack. He worked in the mortuary, and he came to her hospital room to collect her body. Definitely a morbid way to meet someone, but he was distracting when I really needed some distraction. He took me for some dinner, which turned into after-dinner drinks, which turned into making out in the car when he drove me home, which turned into some pretty great sex. I never slept with guys on the first date, and it wasn't even a date really, but he was so cute, dark curly hair, dreamy eyes, and he seemed to care about me. After sex, after Troy fell asleep, I was snuggled up against him, and I had a distinct feeling that my mom and I had been set free.

That was a year ago. About a month ago, I had another distinct feeling. The problem with Troy was that he cared about me too much. He would drop anything, in any moment, no matter what, to do something for me. At first, I loved this about him. Growing up, when I called my father for help, he would finish whatever he was doing, get a snack, call his brother, mow the lawn, and take out the trash before coming to help me. It felt good to be at the top of someone's priority list for a change. But, after a while, Troy's undivided attention turned out to be just as bad as my father's inattention had been. What started as, "He will always do anything for me," had turned into, "He will always do everything for me." It made me feel like a child who wasn't capable of doing anything for myself. It was smothering. It was like having another father, which was the last thing I needed.

My new distinct feeling was that I needed to know I could do things myself, so I didn't get myself into a situation like my mom's, where her only way out was to have two heart attacks and die. I needed to know I could take care of myself, and with Troy around, that was never going to happen. I had come to the unfortunate conclusion that I had to break up with him.

But he was such a good guy! He was caring, attentive, supportive, funny. He never ignored me, raised his voice, or disregarded my feelings. How could I dump someone who never screwed up? It was very confusing. The only answer I could come up with was to get him to dump me. Hence the manufactured arguments, whatever I could come up with, even if they were petty or stupid. The stupider, the better, actually. If he left me because he thought I was a bitch, he would be able to put me behind him, and we could both move on. But he was incorruptible, sinless, inhumanly perfect, and he forgave me no matter what kind of crap I pulled. He was like glue, or pitch, or snot maybe, sticky, like a second skin I couldn't get off. He was turning me into someone I didn't recognize.

It would have taken Troy ten minutes to get from his apartment to where I was broken down, but he pulled up behind my car nine minutes and thirty seconds after I called him. He jumped out, carrying a bottle of bright green liquid. I already had the hood up. At least I knew how to do that.

"I got here as quick as I could. Grabbed some antifreeze. Should fix you right up." He winked at me.

"You stopped for antifreeze and still got here in under ten minutes? Did you run over a small child or a dog while you were going a hundred miles an hour?"

He threw me a look. "Ok, let's see here."

He had a hand towel in his pocket, and he used it to open the radiator cap. He looked around the engine and under the car.

"Don't see anything leaking." He poured the antifreeze into the radiator, replaced the radiator cap, and looked under the car again. "No dripping. Start up the car."

The car started right up, acted like nothing had happened. Even my own car seemed to be against me.

Troy insisted on leaving his car on the street and riding to the diner with me in case anything else happened. He chattered about nothing. After a few minutes—we had turned onto West Shore—he finally noticed I wasn't saying anything.

"Hey." He put his hand on my leg. "I've been thinking we could take a vacation together. A little time away, no distractions, no stress. We could go someplace warm, Mexico or the Bahamas. Someplace we could lay in the sand, get a tan, relax."

I couldn't resist. "Why would we want to do that?"

"What—lay in the sand, or relax?"

"Either."

"Isn't that what you do on vacation?"

"Just lay there and think about all the ways your life sucks? Doesn't sound relaxing to me."

"Well, where do you want to go?"

"With you? Nowhere."

Troy took his hand off my leg.

"Okay," I conceded. "If we have to take a vacation, let's do something exciting. Climb Mt. Everest. Deep sea dive in the Mariana Trench. Go to space."

Troy sighed. "Maybe this isn't such a good idea."

"Finally, we agree on something."

There was silence in the car. I knew I was torturing him, felt bad because he'd come to help me. He had taken at least an hour out of his day to make sure I was okay. Granted, I hadn't asked him to do it. But he also hadn't done anything wrong to deserve this. Well, not directly.

The biggest of my current problems, the looming one, the monkey wrench in the whole deal, was that it was the sixth day since my period should have started. Almost a week of long, anxiety-ridden days. It was horrible timing. Just when I had decided I needed to be on my own, I might be pregnant. I hadn't told Troy, and I hadn't been able to bring myself to take a pregnancy test. Every day, I told myself I couldn't be pregnant, my period had to start. But, again and again, it hadn't. I felt trapped, desperate, alone.

We pulled into the parking lot at Glory's Diner. We both got out of the car, and I grabbed my backpack and started walking toward the colorful glass doors without a word.

Troy watched me walk away. "Have a good day. I love you," he called after me.

Halfway to the door, I turned back. "Why?"

"What?"

I strode back to the car and leaned across it towards him. "Why do you love me?"

"Umm … well …" Troy dropped his gaze, and then peeped through his lashes at me. "You're my girl."

Usually, that would have melted me, but I was frozen solid. "Why am I your girl?" I looked steadily at him.

"Cat, what's wrong? Are you worried about your car?"

I threw up my hands, muttered to myself, "Why do I even bother?" I turned toward the diner, took a couple steps, but then turned back to Troy. "I've been such a bitch to you." My voice was rising. "Why the fuck are you still with me?"

A woman, herding two young children into the diner, threw me a glance.

"Something's going on, Cat." Troy's voice was soft, and his arms hung at his sides. "You've been going through something. But we're good together. I'm just waiting for you to come back."

This was the moment. I felt the words in my mouth, "We're over," but I couldn't say them out loud. My belly ached, and my chest tightened with fear. Of what? The wrong decision? Hurting Troy? Thoughts and feelings rolled around together. I couldn't make sense of them. *Why can't I do this? Who am I?* I left him standing in the parking lot without a word, probably confusion on his face, though I didn't look back to see.

In the diner, the early breakfast rush was wrapping up. About half the tables were still occupied, dirty dishes on the other half, the familiar smell of strawberries and old bacon grease. I headed for the back room to drop my backpack. *Get a grip, be an adult, whatever that means.* I put on my apron over my uniform, jerking the strings tighter over my stomach than I usually did, and smacked the swinging door with a satisfying bang on my way out of the back room. Work would calm me down, burn some excess energy, and then maybe I could decide what to do.

Gloria eyed me as I collected dirty dishes. She followed me into the kitchen. "Car okay?"

"Yes, apparently it's fine. It overheated." I sprayed the dishes, chucked them into the dishwasher.

"You okay?"

I didn't answer, didn't know what the truth was.

"Troy helped you with the car?"

"Of course, he did. He always helps." I had finished the stack of dishes, but Gloria still stood there, looking at me. I shook my wet hands, and water droplets arced through the air. I leaned over the sink, my stomach a ball of fire.

"Cat." Gloria crossed her arms over her chest.

"I don't know, Gloria! I just don't know." I turned to face her. "He loves me so much. He won't leave me. How can I leave him? What if I regret it? What if I can't do it? What if …"

"Is there something else?"

Damn whole-truth Gloria. "Yeah." More quietly. "What if I'm pregnant?" I couldn't look at her face. I fiddled with my fingers.

"Are you?"

"I missed a period a week ago." I could feel the tears welling up.

"Well, that's not long. Might just be stress."

"I know." The tears rolled down my cheeks, and I sniffled.

"You haven't taken a test?"

I couldn't answer her. A sob escaped, and I put my hands over my wet face. Gloria enveloped me in a hug, and I leaned into her solid warmth.

She gave me a minute to cry, then said, "So you're afraid of leaving Troy." She stroked my hair. "You're right to be. It's scary to be on your own. But what if you never do it? You'd be scared of it your whole life."

The truth of this made my body straighten and my mind start to clear. My mother had never been on her own, had gone straight from her parents' house to her husband's house. Maybe she had been afraid, and look where it got her, stuck in a bad marriage. I had sworn I would never let a man control me, and Troy was nothing like my father, but I was still stuck because I was making myself stuck, controlled by my fear of being alone. *Who am I, if I'm not someone's girl?*

"What if I leave him and screw up my life? Troy's a good guy. Maybe it's wrong to leave him."

"Does it feel wrong?"

My body was humming. The fire in my stomach turned to fizzing. "It feels scary." I took a deep breath before continuing, looked into Gloria's eyes. "Staying with him feels wrong. Like fake or something."

The corner of Gloria's mouth tweaked.

I turned to the sink, grabbed a towel, and wiped my face. "But what if I'm pregnant?"

"Even if you are, would you want to live fake?"

I thought about my mother again. "Nope."

"Let's find out." Gloria swirled into the back room, emerged with her purse, and blew past me out of the kitchen.

She was gone for a long time, and the diner got busy. I worked the room, talking with customers, taking orders, and delivering food, clearing dishes, filling coffee and water. It was a simple job, but I got in the flow of it, swept along by the energy of the dining room, and hours passed before I realized.

The late-morning rush had eased when two police officers entered the diner.

"Sit anywhere," I called, carrying an armful of dishes to the kitchen. But they were still standing near the counter when I came out. "Two for breakfast?"

"Do you know someone named Gloria?" the taller officer asked.

"Yes, she's the owner of the diner." I glanced at the clock. Eleven forty-five. Two hours had passed since Gloria left. The drugstore was in the next block.

"Is there a quiet place we can talk?"

In the cold, windowless back room of the diner, the officers told me Gloria had collapsed in line at the drugstore. She had a pregnancy test in her hands. The ER doctor suspected she had a heart attack. She had died at the hospital.

After the initial shock eased, I called Troy. I didn't tell him about Gloria. I didn't want him to be with me or console me. I wanted to feel Gloria's death all by myself, start to finish, as I had not felt my mother's death.

"It's over," I said over the phone. "Get your stuff out of my apartment before I get home." Troy started to protest, but I hung up. Eventually, I might explain it to him, but not now.

When I got home, my apartment felt different, chaotic, dark. The smoke alarms were off. I silently thanked Troy for solving that problem before he left. The coffee table was littered with detritus: balled-up tissues, a half-burned candle, a painted rock Troy had found during a walk, an empty bottle of hand lotion, several dirty dishes. The sofa was hulking, dirty, monstrous. The kitchen table was equally cluttered, unusable, dirty clothes draped over the backs of chairs.

"I'm free," I said to the empty apartment. "I'm ready."

No one answered.

TWO SHEDS
Poetry by *Pam Tucker*

Two mossy, drooping sheds stand side by side
in Monty's field. Old timbered roofs once tight
now welcome birds that dip inside to hide,
and through the broken beams fall streams of light.
Those weathered walls give dubious shelter now,
admitting any through the sagging doors—
the nimble mouse, the fruit tree's reaching bough,
and butterflies that skim the dusty floors.
Inside, neglected tools begrudge their fate—
old rusted gears, bent wire, a harrow blade,
as prisoners condemned inertly wait
and serve their time by faithless time betrayed,
while on the roof, outspreads the velvet moss
to cover, bless, and thus assuage the loss.

A MOTHER'S HANDS
Nonfiction by *Maureen Heim*

It was a chilly November morning when my mother-in law passed away at the age of 87. It was only days later when my husband inherited boxes and bins full of her clothing from the assisted living facility where she spent her final days. As the oldest and nearest son, it fell on him to do something with her earthly possessions. Not surprisingly, none of his six sisters wanted the dated fashions.

Her boxed belongings were stacked around our foyer like Jenga blocks. For days we navigated between the containers that held the essence of who she was. What was I going to do with all these clothes? We needed to reclaim the space they were taking up. How could I reduce this mountain of garments? When my husband walked by, I tilted my head to the side fanned my right arm out to indicate the boxes and casually said, "How would you feel if I cut these up?" He gave me a quizzical look like he thought I was joking and walked away.

Earlier that day as I was pondering the situation, it occurred to me that maybe I could craft something out of these garments that might be meaningful to her nine children. I pulled up a chair, sat down in front of a stack of boxes, and started opening them one by one looking for inspiration.

The first box contained numerous pantsuits, sweatshirts, shawls, and sweaters. My mind was blank. The simple solution was to haul everything to Goodwill. I didn't want simple. I wanted meaningful. I needed a different tack. I tried not to think of them as the items they represented and instead looked at them as fabric that could be fashioned into something else. Still silence. After going through a few more boxes, I ran my fingers across several recognizable sweaters and the creative right side of my brain came up with an idea that grabbed me, and it yelled "Mittens!"

I started digging through the boxes looking for as many wool sweaters as I could find. My next stop was the internet. My search was on for instructions on how to work with wool and how to find a simple yet attractive pattern. After I engaged the left side of my brain, I downloaded a pattern and created a template. The design I chose for the mitten was constructed with one piece for the back of the hand and two pieces for the front of the hand, separating the thumb and palm from the fingers. Inside one of the boxes was a velvet robe that was perfect for a mitten liner.

To avoid shrinkage, I washed the wool sweaters in hot water and dried them in high heat before cutting the wool into pattern pieces. I wanted them to be beautiful as well as useful so went to a thrift store to find more wool sweaters to complement the colors and designs of the sweaters she used to wear. I reasoned that if the mitten was made from 70-80% of her sweaters it still embodied her.

When I was satisfied with the test mitten, I set up a workstation. Hours passed as I started cutting wool into pieces and started coordinating colors. As I envisioned the final product, I discovered I enjoyed the creativity so much I wondered if I would have enough material to make mittens for the granddaughters as well. Before I knew it, I had committed myself to making 35 pairs of wool mittens.

Each mitten set was lined up with liners, fronts, backs, and cuffs. As I was sewing it gave me time to think about the meaning of this gift. I consulted the right side of my brain again and created a poem about the significance of a mother's hands to the rearing of a child. I hoped each time my sisters-in-law wore their mittens they would think of their mother holding their hands.

Sitting at my sewing machine amid piles of wool my brain would not be quiet so off it went and came up with names for each of the mittens that signified her favorite vacations, hobbies, and places she lived.

When the completed and named mittens were lined up on the table one of my sons walked by and said, "Hey those are really cool, do I get one?"

"Of course," I replied as I smiled and walked back to the box of supplies grateful that my mother-in-law wore a lot of sweaters.

I lost my mother as a child so had some idea how her loss would affect my husband's family. How could I surprise them with this heart-felt gift? His sisters were planning a girl's weekend getaway in another state in a few weeks. Now I had a deadline. I consulted ahead of time with one of the sisters in person. She was stunned and touched when I showed her what I created for her. She was completely on board with presenting my gift to the rest of her sisters. We wrapped each named pair of mittens with the poem I wrote and tied them with ribbon. She flew out with the mittens the next day.

A couple of days later I got a FaceTime message late at night from a brother-in-law who crashed the girls' weekend. He said he had something to show me. When he held up the phone, my sisters-in-law were standing in a row each holding up their hands showing off their coveted custom mittens. Each one in turn personally thanked me for the thoughtful gift and shared with me what it meant to them.

When it was time to hang up, my brother-in-law said he would have contacted me earlier in the evening, but the girls were all crying so hard they couldn't talk. Before he hung up, he tearfully said, "Boy did you hit a home run with this one!"

PASSING OVER
Fiction by *Cameron Prow*

In the early dawn I usually sleep through, I find myself walking down a long hall like those at the nursing home where Dad lived the last month of his life. Door after door, room after room—no end in sight.

"Come here!" A voice I never expected to hear again hails me. A shadowy figure ahead beckons. I take a step, pause.

"Hurry! Not much time," his voice rasps.

I follow, hesitantly. *Is it really? No, it can't be.* And yet … that voice.

The disjointed apparition moves in a jerky fashion down the corridor. I increase my pace, trying to catch up. The ghostly form disappears around a corner. About halfway down a second endless hall, a white wisp of smoke curls up from a gap under a gray roll-down door.

Fire! I look for an alarm, some way to warn other occupants of the building.

From behind the door, I hear: "You can make it. Hurry!"

If the voice were anyone else's, I'd ignore it. But I haven't heard my father speak since my last visit the day before he died. The need in his voice is an appeal I cannot refuse.

Gingerly, I lay my hand on the metal door. Instead of too hot to touch, the surface is icy. I grab the handle at the bottom, pull the door up a couple feet, then drop to the ground and scoot under it.

As I stand up, the door lands with a dull thud on the floor in front of me. *Am I trapped?* A handle on this side suggests I can get out the way I came in. Somewhat reassured, I turn around to survey this new space. Tables and chairs suggest a recreation area, but the room is empty of life. Everything is gray except the white mist snaking across the floor toward my feet.

The furniture appears to shift around unless I look straight at it and concentrate. Maybe things here are real only if I believe they are.

"Dad?" I whisper.

"Yes, yes," his voice interrupts, in the impatient tone I know so well.

"But you're supposed to be …"

"Dead? I am."

"Then what …"

"… am I doing here? Need you." His smoker's voice is scratchy.

"What for?"

"Energy."

The stale air is hard to breathe. Nothing feels real. Perhaps I'm dreaming—dreaming my father is still alive.

"Wake up!"

"I don't understand. What can I do? You're dead."

"Tired. Need to … get to … next stop."

Again my attention wanders. I remember viewing his shrunken body in a coffin at the memorial service. *How can he talk to me now?*

"Pay attention!"

I look up. While I have been following the memory trail to assure myself Dad is indeed dead, the shadow figure across the room has faded to an indistinct amoeba-like shape.

His husky voice, though fainter, is oddly compelling. I want him to keep talking to me, dream or not.

"What do you want me to do?"

"Get ... knew me ... best."

"Who?"

"Your mom ... strong thoughts. Your energy ... hers ..."

"She won't listen to me."

"Without her ... you ... I'm stuck!"

His insistence I do what he demands convinces me, as always. I turn to go. Then swing back.

"How can I contact you if she agrees to help?"

"I'll watch. Go to ... where ... you are."

I pull the gray metal door back up again and roll under it. The walls in front of me are now the light green I remember, an efficient color that fades little with multiple cleanings. Voices and the screech of a chair being dragged over a vinyl floor in a nearby room surround me: sounds of life.

I turn back to the doorway I just passed through. Nothing there now but a solid wall.

What my father needs from me is as impossible as spinning straw into gold. Mother and I have never been close. Her bitterness over my choosing to live with Dad after their divorce has lasted longer than their marriage did. We barely acknowledge each other's existence.

Can I get to her in time?

She's driving to Southern Oregon tomorrow to visit her favorite daughter, the one who stayed with her, and two little girls who adore their grandmother.

I cancel my plans for lunch with a friend and throw basic necessities into a small overnight bag. Driving over the Cascade Mountains to Mother's apartment in Salem, I wonder what kind of energy one can give a person who is dead. It doesn't seem feasible anything physical can pass between us.

Now that I have time to think instead of react, I realize Dad shouldn't have appeared as a figure at all. By his own wish, his body was cremated. Last week, I finally scattered his ashes along the river running past my childhood home.

So how can he appear to me in physical form? My mind picture of him looming over me is a child's memory. Does the essence of what he was depend more on what I remember than the reality of "ashes to ashes, dust to dust"?

Perhaps the energy Dad needs is from those with the longest sense of him. On the one-year anniversary of his death, Mother sold the land where they built a house together, raised a family. The struggles they went through to make a new life in Oregon two thousand miles from their hometown now appear to her as an extended honeymoon time of working toward shared goals.

My younger sister never forgave Dad and me for abandoning our family. She hadn't seen or spoken to him in the last ten years before he died.

As I review my life with Dad, I realize I have more to offer than my sister. My memories are full of the chores I shared with Dad: fetching tools and holding the flashlight when he was repairing the tractor or family car, stacking firewood for the ever-hungry furnace, feeding the cows, sheep, and goats that kept the forest from reclaiming land converted to pasture.

Which of Mother's memories would contribute the most energy? All I heard for years before she and I stopped visiting was how Dad's mother sabotaged her marriage. Is her constant grieving keeping my father from passing over?

What happens to Dad if I can't convince Mother to help?

DAD, BATMAN, AND CORNBREAD

Nonfiction by *Dan Murnan*

"Come on, Son. The new Batman TV show is going to start soon," my dad shouted from the kitchen. I was so excited. My dad had been telling me about this new superhero show for weeks. I loved superhero shows. Superman and The Flash were my two favorites. Superman could fly faster than a speeding bullet and leap tall buildings. I didn't understand how someone could be a superhero without any superpowers. My dad explained that Batman was super smart, clever and had neat inventions like the Batmobile. I ran from my room leaving G.I. Joe to fight his own battles as I slid into my favorite place in front of the TV.

My dad was a carpet guy, coming from a long line of carpet peddlers. His dad, Grampa Charlie, owned the largest carpet and rug business in Omaha, Nebraska called "Murnan Rug." This meant that we always had the most luxurious wall-to-wall carpet in our house. This latest carpet edition was a beautiful slate colored plush pile fabric that could support a bear. Add this plush pile to a full inch of padding and the carpet would envelop your feet as you walked, leaving footprints like walking on a sandy beach. My dad would always say that padding was the most important part of carpeting, and he lived what he preached! I settled into my favorite spot in the living room like a robin in a newly made nest.

I yelled to my dad, "What channel is the new show on?"

"Son, I think it's channel 4, but look it up in the TV Guide to make sure. The guide is on my chair, unless Mom threw it away with the morning paper today," my dad responded. Luckily, I found the TV Guide under the chair and looked up Wednesday.

"Yep, It's channel 4 Dad," I replied.

"Okay, Son, remember that you have to point the TV rabbit ears up and to the left, towards downtown Seattle for the best reception."

Springing up from my carpeted nest, I quickly changed the channel dial to 4. Another perk from my dad being in the home furnishing business is that we were always getting cool appliances. Our latest new gadget was a "huge" 21-inch color TV, a first on the block and a rarity for 1966. It also was so strange that the TV dial had 13 channels. We only had 3 channels to watch, why would the dial have 13? Who could imagine having 13 channels to watch?

***

The channel selector was on 4 and the TV rabbit ears were pointing towards Seattle, we were ready to go! I snuggled into my favorite spot.

"Dad, how much time before Batman starts?"

"Son, it's 7:25 p.m. so 5 minutes before the show starts." I got to thinking that I ought to phone my best friend Mike and remind him to watch Batman. I would normally invite Mike over to watch the program, but it was a school night and Sister Mead gave us a lot of homework that was due the next day. I wanted to avoid the fury of Sister Mead and the possibility of the ruler on the back of my hand at all costs!

I found the phone on the table and unwound the long extension cord to reach the couch. Our new phone had nice large finger holes that made rotary dialing so much easier. Unbelievable as it sounds, my dad said that in the next couple of years, we would have push button phones instead of rotary dials. But for now, I "dialed" LA3-7789. After a few rings the phone was answered.

"Hey Mike, the new Batman show is starting in 5 minutes, are you going to watch it?"

"Hi Dan! I sure am, with my brother Chip. It sounds like a really neat show!" Mike replied.

"Okay great, we can talk about it tomorrow at recess." I hung up the phone and raveled the long extension cord back into the next room. Then I smelled it, the unmistakable aroma of cornbread muffins in the oven! My dad was the ultimate king of after dinner baking. His favorite was making Jiffy cornbread muffins. Singing to the tune of Frank Sinatra's "My Way" he would work his cornbread magic conjuring up 12 perfect muffins.

I was a little surprised that he was in the kitchen this early as we had finished dinner only an hour and a half ago. Tonight, Mom made my favorite home cooked meal; meatloaf, mashed potatoes and corn. We were a good Nebraska family, anything with a green shade rarely made an appearance at our dinner table. Out of the oven the muffins would come with just the right combination of crusty top and a moist middle. Muffins cut in half with lots of butter and honey was my favorite way to eat cornbread. But dad's favorite style was warm crumbled muffins in a bowl with milk and sugar. I gotta say, as the years went by, I became a convert to this way of eating my cornbread.

My dad was a contrast of personalities with a huge loving heart buried beneath layers of pressurized granite in the form of 1960's stoic masculinity. An Irishman at heart, he seemed much larger than his 5'9 and 190lb frame. His bald head and firm jaw highlighted his tough brown eyes giving away a hint of his Golden Glove boxing championships of the past. And the man could YELL like nobody's business! The type of yelling that in mere seconds would wake you from a deep sleep to fearfully clinging to the ceiling. As the years went by, as weird as it may sound, I came to understand that the "YELL" was the love for his family escaping his heart and making its way through the cracks of his granite barriers.

With the muffins out of the oven the entire house smelled delicious and comfy.

Dad yelled, "Son, get the TV trays setup so we can watch the show while we eat our cornbread." Wow, I thought, this must be a special night to get the TV trays out. Usually, the TV trays were limited to TV dinner night. My favorite TV dinner was Swanson's Hungry Man Salisbury Steak with tater tots and peas. The kicker to this meal was that it came with a big square of apple cobbler that tasted amazing right out of the foil tray. The peas and carrots went under the TV tray to Rusty, our 110lb yellow lab who was a canine garbage disposal. He came in very handy at dinner time.

I grabbed two TV trays from behind the bookcase and set one up in front of my dad's chair and one up in front of the couch. Dad and I filled the TV trays with cornbread just as the theme song to the new Batman program began. The catchy theme song caught our attention as we saw the Bat Signal for the first time. Batman and Robin slid down the Bat Pole down into the Batcave and raced to the Batmobile. Off rocketed the dynamic duo through the Bat Tunnel to save Gotham City against dastardly arch criminals to the likes of the Joker, Penguin, and the Riddler. Dad and I were hooked! A short 30 minutes later the show was coming to an exciting end and we heard those famous Bat words, "SEE YOU NEXT WEEK—SAME BAT TIME—SAME BAT CHANNEL!"

For the next three years on Wednesday evenings at 7:30pm, Dad in his comfy leather chair and I tucked away in the warm weave of polyester, enjoyed our cornbread muffins while watching Batman and his sidekick Robin save the world. Little did I know that almost 60 years later, I would still remember those enduring Wednesday nights with my dad, Batman, and cornbread.

VERDE (EXCERPT)
Fiction by *Jeffrey W. Kramer*

Chapter One

Francisco Soto sat on his deck overlooking the ocean, listening to the waves thumping along the shore, warmed by the golden afternoon sun. His house stood on a thin strand below high sandstone cliffs facing the sea. His eyes traced the long outward curve of the Malibu coastline, southward toward the beaches of Santa Monica, around the bay's broad expanse of blue, to the distant peninsula shimmering in the hazy summer light. But he saw none of this.

His mind was on death. Sudden death, unexpected and inexplicable death. One moment a man might be walking along enjoying the sun on his face, the wind in his hair, birds singing on a spring morning. The next moment, blackness. He was … then he was not. Just like Rob Larsen, one moment a man full of life, the next a crumpled body lying on the bottom of a picturesque canyon, dusty and lifeless flesh.

The newspaper report had few details of Larsen's untimely demise. The headline read "Local Malibu Geologist Found Dead in Verde Canyon." The article was brief. Larsen was survived by his wife, Emma, and an adult son. He was discovered by a young couple hiking with their dog along a nearby trail. The county authorities believed it was an unfortunate accident, a slip on unstable earth and a fall hundreds of feet down the rocky hillside.

"Damn it," Soto muttered, running his fingers across the newsprint as if to erase the painful news. He knew Larsen. The man was a Malibu old-timer. Larsen had always been fit, experienced in the mountains. And at one time, to a lonely kid, Rob Larsen had meant everything. Soto tossed the newspaper onto the deck, then watched as the stiff onshore breeze scattered the sheets and plastered them against the glass door behind him.

He also knew Verde Canyon. It lay hidden in the western reaches of the Santa Monica Mountains, a spine of rugged upheaval stretching along the twenty-seven miles of Malibu coastline. It was still undeveloped, the way it was when Rob Larsen had first taken him there so many years ago. Soto had loved those adventures, trailing after him and Larsen's own boy as they climbed the narrow trail from the beach, thrashing through the tangled underbrush along the narrow path, finally reaching the deepest recesses of the remote canyon. There Sycamore trees huddled around a small pool fed by the winter rains. In the shadows of the towering canyon walls, wrapped in the stillness and quiet, he had felt its power. Rob Larsen had loved this place and taught Soto to love it.

He rose and stretched, then gazed out at the endlessly rolling sea. Wind chop had spoiled the glassy morning water when his surfboard had slid gracefully along arcing waves in the early light. He let his mind wander. It took him back to when he had left home for college and law school, to when he came back and chose to live in the city. His law practice had kept him busy. He had married, made a name for himself in the rough and tumble world of high-stakes litigation, and divorced. He should have come back to Malibu sooner, he now knew. And he should have reconnected with the man who had given him so much. Now it was too late.

When his cell phone rang, muffled under a towel and faint against the crashing surf, Soto nearly missed it. He grabbed the phone with irritation, pulled off his sunglasses, and read the number. The call was forwarded on his office line. Sighing, he accepted the call. This was the price of working from home.

"Francisco Soto?" It was a woman's voice, nasal and with an accent he recognized as New York. "We need a good lawyer. When can we meet?"

"Who's we?" he said. "And who are you?"

The woman identified herself as Rachel Goldstein, the President of the Malibu Nature Foundation. Surely he had heard of their organization? He had not and said so.

"We're a group of local citizens opposed to the Bouchard Company's proposed development," she went on. "We would like to hire you to stop it. When can we meet?"

"Wait a minute," Soto said. "Slow down. How did you get my name?"

"Lynn Bailey," the woman said. "I take it you know her?"

"Ah yes, Lynn." She was the publisher of the town's longtime local newspaper. If Lynn had given her his name, she must have had a good reason.

"You're familiar with the Bouchard Company's plans?" the woman asked.

"No, not exactly," he said.

"The 200 home luxury subdivision and golf course? Bouchard's been doing a good job of flying under the radar. But the word's gotten out."

"Go on. I know something of Richard Bouchard. Where does he want to build now?"

"Verde Canyon."

"Shit—"

"Do you know it?"

"Yes," he said. "Sorry, I'm usually not so crude."

"Shit is right, no need to apologize. So, when can we meet?" she said. "How about Wednesday evening?"

"Sure," he replied, recovering some of his professional demeanor. "That should work."

"Good," the woman said, her tones clipped. "The meeting will be with our board. In my home." She gave him the address.

"Do you know where that is?" she said.

He did. The home was on Sweetwater Mesa Road, high on a bluff overlooking the Malibu Pier, with an unobstructed view of the coastline and the ocean beyond. The high rent district if ever there was one. These people would have some serious money.

"Be there at seven," she said. "And don't be late." She hung up without waiting for a response.

Soto stared at the phone for a moment before putting it down. He didn't care much for being told what to do. He also wasn't looking for more work. Especially now, with a strong swell from the coast of Mexico lighting up the surf along Malibu's south-facing beaches. But if a big-time developer was trying to put a golf course in Verde Canyon, the threat would be serious. The thought of it was deeply offensive.

And then there was Lynn. She would be furious if he refused even to meet with these folks. He pictured the look on her face if he blew them off. At this, his mouth curled into a slight smile.

His thoughts were interrupted by a pair of seagulls quarreling overhead. Gathering the scattered newspapers from the deck, he turned to go inside. Reflected in the door's broad glass panes he caught a glimpse of himself, faded green board shorts, shirtless, lean and muscled, the light brown hue of his skin deepened by the sun. This was who he really was, he thought, how he wanted to be. He had never been eager to put on a suit and tie, to spend those long hours in office buildings and courtrooms, sedentary and shut away from the natural world.

Before moving inside he paused, his eyes drawn again toward the sea. Light sparkled from the ocean's surface, a humid breeze ruffled through his hair, yet his mood was dark. He couldn't stop thinking about Rob Larsen. A good man had been taken from this world. Maybe it was just an accident. Somehow he didn't think so.

Chapter Two

Soto sped west along Pacific Coast Highway, enjoying the well-tuned hum of his four-door German sedan. The car was more than twenty years old. With its blunt Bavarian styling it didn't look like much. But if you were a car geek you knew better. The car was one of the fasted production cars of its day. Even now it could hold its own with all but the fastest vehicles on the road. He glanced at the speedometer and reluctantly eased up on the gas pedal, letting the car slow to ten miles per hour over the limit.

On his right, the rolling manicured lawns of Pepperdine University stretched up a large slope toward the hilltop campus; on his left the ball fields and scrub lands of Bluffs Park reached toward the ocean. As a kid, he had played soccer and baseball on these fields. Passing them now, he found himself thinking about those long ago days and his fingers tightened on the wheel. Rob Larsen was part of those memories.

The highway began a slow descent to Corral Canyon Beach, where lines of roiling white water cascaded onto the sand in hazy morning light. He was on his way to see Lynn Bailey, the owner, publisher, one-woman editorial board, and chief reporter for the *Malibu Seaside Herald*. He was sure he would find her at her usual morning spot. Before meeting with the Malibu Nature Foundation, he wanted to find out what she knew about them.

He turned left from the coast highway into a long driveway that wound up a slope to The Westwind Cafe. The restaurant sat on a scruffy hillside overlooking Zuma Beach, a broad expanse of sand stretching more than a mile northward toward distant beach-front homes. As Soto entered the small cafe, he saw Bailey sitting at her favorite table in the corner, letting her morning coffee grow cold. Her gaze was fixed on the ocean below, where just beyond the breaking waves a family of dolphins bobbed lazily along through the glassy water, slowly down and then to the surface again, rounded backs glistening in the early sun. She turned and looked up as Soto pulled a chair out to join her.

"Francisco Soto," she said, "How nice to see you this morning."

"Beautiful day, isn't it?" he replied, taking a moment to study the curling shore break visible through the restaurant windows. Then he got to the point, because Lynn wasn't one for small talk. "I got a call yesterday from a woman calling on behalf of something called the Malibu Nature Foundation. Should I thank you?"

"You're welcome. I recommended you, you know." She glanced up from stirring her coffee and raised her eyebrows. The corners of her mouth twitched almost imperceptibly, as though she were suppressing a grin.

"Well," he said, "thank you, I suppose. What can you tell me about them?"

"They want to stop the Bouchard Company from developing Verde Canyon. Rachel Goldstein heads up the group. She's very sharp, very rich, and has plenty of time on her hands. Her husband Simon heads up a large investment banking firm. He spends most of his time on the road."

"I'm surprised I haven't heard anything about them, the Foundation I mean."

"They're new. And not very experienced as activists. They could use someone like you."

"I'm meeting them tonight, but I have some concerns. You know I'm not taking many cases these days."

"So I've heard you say."

"I've been busting my ass for too many years. I'm tired of it, tired of all the conflict."

"Of course."

"And I've got better things to do."

"Like surfing, I suppose you mean?" She shrugged her shoulders. "That of course is a noble pursuit."

He started to protest, thought better of it. She knew him too well.

"Getting back to this foundation," he said, "I'm not optimistic about their chances. Stopping Bouchard won't be easy."

"I'm sure you'll explain that to them. But I hope you take the case."

"Why?"

"There's the canyon of course. I would hate to see it spoiled."

"But why me? There are plenty of lawyers in this town."

"Not like you. Not as good as you." She tucked a few strands of graying blonde hair behind an ear, looked down sadly at her cold cup of coffee, then back again at him with a mock look of innocence. "Just my opinion."

He caught the eye of a passing waitress and pointed at Bailey's cup. The young woman hurried over with a new cup and a pot of hot coffee.

Bailey ignored the new cup and filled her old cup to the brim with the steaming liquid.

"And then there's Rob Larsen," she said.

"You think there's a connection." He did not say it as a question. "I figured you might know something more. You usually do."

"Thank you, I'll take that as a compliment." She paused.

"You know about that canyon, don't you?" He waited for her to continue. She could be frustrating and he was in no mood for her riddles. He tried to wait her out, but she simply sat there, meeting his gaze, bifocals resting on the end of her narrow nose, her plump round face impassive.

"Yes, I certainly know the canyon," he said. When it became apparent she wasn't going to say anything more, he continued. "Rob Larsen took me there when I was a kid. I've loved it ever since."

"I didn't realize you knew Rob."

"I hadn't seen him for years. But there was a time when he was very important to me."

"How so?"

"It wasn't easy growing up here, not for a poor Latino kid like me. He took me under his wing, treated me almost like a son. It meant a lot to me."

"Rob was a good man. He touched a lot of people in this town."

"So he did. I can't stop thinking about his death."

"What else do you know about Verde Canyon?" she said. "Remember, I'm a reporter. I gather information. I don't give it away. At least not until I publish it."

"Thanks to the call I received yesterday, I know The Bouchard Company wants to put a major development out there. I know Larsen was a geologist. He probably wasn't out hiking in that canyon just for the fun of it."

"The County Coroner doesn't seem to think there's anything to investigate," she said. "To them he was just a guy hiking along a rocky trail who slipped, fell down a hillside and died from a blow to the head. They're treating it as an obvious accident, file closed. Imagination is not their strength." She caught his eye and smiled. "I don't buy it."

"Too bad we don't have any good investigative journalists in this town," he said. "Someone to get to the bottom of what really happened."

"You might be surprised," she said, dumping a spoonful of sugar into her cup. "I have my ways." She stirred the coffee with slow, deliberate strokes, then carefully settled the spoon on the edge of her saucer. "Will you take the Malibu Nature Foundation case?"

"Maybe. You've made it plain you think I should."

Lynn Bailey gathered her purse from where it hung on her chair and pushed away from the table. She stood up slowly and with some effort, willing her considerable girth into motion. Her skirt stretched taut across broad hips. She pushed it down a few modest inches and brushed some crumbs from the front of a cashmere sweater that had seen better days. Then she patted him softly on the cheek, like a mother encouraging her young child.

"Yes, I do think you should," she said.

"Why?"

"Rob's death is too convenient. Maybe you can get to the bottom of it. And save the canyon. I would like it if you would try."

Bailey gathered up her purse, then waited a moment before turning away. "And if you won't do it," she said, "who will?"

He watched her work her way across the small cafe, then out into the glare of another bright and promising Malibu day. He noticed she had left him her bill. Shaking his head, he motioned for the waitress. But he couldn't help admiring this woman. She knew how to get what she wanted. She knew he wouldn't want to disappoint her.

MESQUITE MELODY
Poetry by *Ted Virts*

      Forty-feet across, ragged arms drifting green
           scratch a half-circle in sky.

From within the Mesquite
      a hundred-mouthed, multi-toned song
         moves above the small brick porch,
            cacophony of call and caw.

Mesquite and me in mirrored stare
      our years—similar
         our limbs—soft-leafed invitation,
           sharp-thorned protection.

Thrasher and Warbler
      huit and chirp.
Sparrow and Dove
      sing and hoot.
      The wind, a whispered roar.
      Tree song.
      Setting sun.

1969 PEACE MARCH

Nonfiction by *Janet Best Dart*

My knuckles turned white as I approached U.C. Berkeley, my inner voice screaming to turn back. Telegraph Avenue was lined with men clad in black pants and long-sleeved black shirts. Their navy-blue ballistic vests bore bright yellow chest-width labels branding each as SHERIFF. Alameda County Sheriffs in riot gear. Just as I had seen on television.

It will be okay. They're just here to protect us, right?

Taking a deep breath, I rode by on my ten-speed, looking past the sheriffs to the sidewalks teeming with musicians, street vendors, and teens and twenty-somethings sporting long hair held with woven headbands across their foreheads. Girls in peasant blouses and shorts sat sipping tea at outside tables. Shirtless men wandered by in bellbottom pants. Riding past small cafes and bookstores, I breathed in a mixture of cigarette smoke, marijuana, car exhaust and incense.

After spending my Freshman year at U.C. Davis, sixty miles and a world away, I was home.

I rode past the sheriffs and locked my ten-speed to a bike rack, then joined some thousand other students walking through Sather Gate, the south entrance to U.C. Berkeley. The bronzed arch, green with oxidation, isn't a gate that closes, but more of an entry gateway, taking me from Telegraph Avenue into Sproul Plaza, the major site of student protests, hallowed ground to me. The stone-faced sheriffs lined Sproul Plaza, and several gazed down from the rooftops, making me jumpy.

The usual Berkeley fog hadn't shown up that day. The trees were bright green, the sky brilliant blue, allowing the sun to warm our skin as we traded our sweaters for braless tank tops. The Campanile glowed, calming me, beckoning me to climb its thirty-eight steps from the elevator to the top deck. *Maybe after the march*, I thought, anticipating the view of San Francisco on such a dazzling day.

Sproul Plaza was filled with the vivid hues of flowered skirts and tie-dyed t-shirts, jeans and bell bottoms, long hair, Afros, hoop earrings, and dangling necklaces. The scent of marijuana drifted through the air as doobies were passed from hand to hand. *So different than U.C. Davis,* I thought, remembering the nearly silent peace march last spring. Now, reveling in the medley of colors, I joined the booming chants of "No More War" and "Hell No, We Won't Go." The Berkeley students radiated passion, a contagious belief that we could stop the war.

Wearing a long skirt and tank top, I walked in my handmade leather sandals, happy that I had splurged on them. A long-haired hippie who had set up shop in a VW van near the campus had outlined my feet then cut the leather to fit, instructing me to immerse my sandal-clad feet in water, the same way an outfielder soaks his glove wrapped around a baseball. I had never owned shoes that molded my feet so perfectly. I had never owned more than two pairs of shoes at a time.

Helicopters hovered overhead, obscuring the sun but not eclipsing our chants and our singing of "We Shall Overcome." *Ahh, the newscasters are here*, I thought. *Maybe we'll be on TV.*

We marched past the sheriffs standing shoulder-to-shoulder, their stern faces visible through the clear visors of their helmets. Their left hands clutched twenty-four-inch batons; their right hands hovered over holstered guns.

We gathered in front of the Student Union to listen to speeches against the war. Brushing against fellow students, I threaded my way toward the front to hear.

"Get out of here, Pigs!" Four shirtless men with scraggly, mousy-blonde, shoulder-length hair tucked behind their ears appeared from nowhere. They ran between the speakers and the throng of protesters, toward the sheriffs.

What the hell? I thought. *Why are you doing this? It's a peace march.* "Stop!" I shouted, along with others, hoping I could prevent these guys from taunting the police.

The grim-faced sheriffs raised their batons, taking a few steps closer to the crowd.

The taunters threw rocks at the sheriffs.

The sheriffs returned fire with canisters that emitted a foggy substance upon hitting the ground.

The helicopters circled lower, their whirling and chopping overpowering the sound of the crowd. They spewed white gas over us.

These aren't newscasters, I realized. *They must be police helicopters.*

The sheriffs closed in behind us, waving batons, herding us out of the plaza back toward Sather Gate.

My eyes stung and watered. *So, this is tear gas*, I thought, lifting my long gauze skirt to my eyes. I could barely see through my tears. Wiping my eyes only made it worse.

Four guys ruined the whole march! And because of only four disruptive guys we all got sprayed with tear gas.

Students started running. I feared a stampede.

"Slow down!" I shouted, purposefully walking, trying to quell the panic of the crowd as they ran.

A young woman fell as the throng scattered. Fellow students carried her up the steps of the Administration Building. A sheriff stood atop the building with a bullhorn, his words echoing across the plaza: "Everyone disperse."

I made my way out to Telegraph Avenue, eyes still stinging. The thunder of the helicopters blotted out the sounds of the crowd and the traffic. The sheriffs pushed a long-haired student onto the hood of their patrol car, handcuffing him and holding him down with a forearm pressed on his neck. A woman was sprawled face-down on the sidewalk, a sheriff kneeling by her side, handcuffing her hands behind her.

Protesters shouted, "Let them go! Let them go!"

My body trembled as I watched the sheriffs threaten them with their Billy clubs. Wanting to run, I instead walked stiffly, looking over my shoulder.

My stomach churned watching my peers being handcuffed, knowing they would be transported to Santa Rita prison. Joan Baez had served a forty-five-day sentence there after a 1968 sit-in at the Oakland Draft Board. It was a badge of honor to serve time at Santa Rita.

I don't want to go to jail, I thought, terrified at the prospect, realizing I wasn't willing to go to jail for my principles.

I slowly walked up Bancroft Way to another campus entrance and found my bicycle. Tears welled, but not from teargas. As my morning optimism had turned to defeat, my energy was spent. Tucking my skirt under my bottom, I rode forty-five minutes across Telegraph Avenue, from Berkeley to Oakland, barely registering the cars that sped close by me.

I carried my bike up the stairs to my apartment, leaned it against the wall.

I leaned next to it and closed my eyes.

I let the silence enfold me.

THE CRITICS
Fiction by *Evelyn Moser*

Three women—what we used to call "of a certain age"—met once a month at Upper Crust for coffee and to critique each other's writing. Georgia was a world traveler and artist whose travelogues, mainly about museums, appeared in the local newspaper from time to time. For this meeting, she presented a draft of her trip to Madrid, concentrating on the Prado Museum.

Unlike Georgia, Marilyn and Eloise were unpublished, but were struggling to find their way into print. Marilyn had spent part of her childhood living in a lighthouse and was presenting a piece about lighthouses on the Northern California Coast.

Eloise was not writing from her own experiences but trying to bring her research of early California to life, particularly from the late eighteenth and early nineteenth centuries, concentrating on the life of Junipero Serra, the Franciscan father who was the spearhead in building the California missions.

Marilyn read first. Her essay described three lighthouses in the San Francisco area: One at Point Sur, another at Alcatraz Island, and a third at Battery Point, which, she said, is not a tower but a house with a light attached. In order to see the lighthouse at Alcatraz, one has to reach the island by boat, which Marilyn did, making the trip a part of her story. Eloise said that she liked Marilyn's description of her boat trip across part of the bay and that Marilyn made it fit well with her descriptions of the island's isolation and its direful purpose.

Georgia's article for the newspaper covered her preparations, including a description of all the articles of clothing she packed for the trip and the rationale for taking each item. It then covered the Prado museum itself, which she explained was designed by Juan de Villanueva. She then moved to a discussion of the painting, *Third of May 1808* by Goya. She followed by giving some history of the Napoleonic War in Spain.

Marilyn commented favorably on Georgia's use of language and her topic. Eloise agreed although she thought Georgia could have said less about her packing since the space in the article for her wardrobe rivaled that for Goya.

Eloise's work was a fictionalized story of the death of a priest, Father Serra. She selected this portion of her research to present because it was singularly odd. Father Serra took a long time to die. Although those in the house with him and the many in the village all knew his death was near, he refused to lie down. Eloise read:

"'Come lie down on your cot,' urged Father Francisco Palau.

'I will get plenty of rest soon enough,' Serra said as he limped to the door to answer the knock. The woman who entered was yet another parishioner wanting a memento from her dying priest. He told her, 'I have given everything away except my blanket. I won't need it any longer, so take it with my blessing.' He folded the rough blanket and placed it in her arms. She bowed slightly in thanks, smiled, and went out the door.

'If anyone else comes, I would have to give up my robe, which is all I have to cover my dignity.'

Fray Francisco did his best to administer Extreme Unction as the dying man paced the floor. Stepping quickly, Francisco followed him about and crouched to apply the oil to Junipero's feet. In addition to the strangeness of the scene, it also became clear that Junipero, like many mortals, was afraid to die."

Eloise tried to make the scene real. Depicting this historic time had become important to her. During her research of journals and a biography, she also visited some of the missions and discovered that the fathers had found new ways to build and to farm. They also rediscovered places that were not on their maps. She wanted these people to live for her readers too. When Eloise finished speaking, Georgia sat quietly at first, then gave no comment except, "I thought you were writing children's literature." Eloise didn't know how to respond. She stammered as she tried to explain that she was interested in different kinds of writing.

Marilyn sighed, placed her elbows on the table and said, "Can't you spice it up with some sex?" and made a cute face.

"He's dying."

"I know, but it needs something spicy … like sex."

"He's a priest."

"Well, priests have sex. Maybe he had an Indian mistress on the side."

Eloise said, "Well … this one was uncomfortable with women." She had read that Serra was shocked when he saw naked native men and deeply relieved to hear the women wore clothes.

Marilyn added helpfully, "If you have to tell history, you should make it fun for the reader—not boring." She folded her hands under her chin coquettishly.

As the meeting dwindled down, Georgia mentioned there was a writing workshop coming up. Eloise decided to go. She needed more help and hoped a workshop led by professionals would be her answer.

***

The lecture and reading session Eloise attended at the workshop was for fiction writers and was led by someone named Lee Hammersmith who wrote romance novels with his wife under his name. The first student writer to volunteer read a passage of a man's first romantic encounter with a certain woman. Eloise thought it sounded pretty good and was probably from the writer's own experience, but Lee Hammersmith yelled the most cutting remark she had ever heard from an instructor to a student.

"So, all you're telling me is that this guy had some kind of foot fetish! So what?! It's a piece of crap."

The writer yelled an obscenity back, called Hammersmith a "son of a bitch" and stormed out of the room.

This did not look promising.

Eloise elected to ask Hammersmith to read her scene privately and comment only to her. She had done a little editing of the death scene of Father Serra and hoped she had improved it. After reading her piece, he handed the paper back to her and said, "Why not just say, 'He lay down and died.'"

"But that isn't what happened."

"It would be so much better. He just lay down quietly and died." He looked serene. *But that isn't what happened*, she thought

***

Eloise gave up on the project. She had wanted the story of the Franciscan fathers to be told as interestingly and as truthfully as possible and at one time thought she could do it, but it was painfully clear she wasn't up to it. She stopped trying to be a writer. It was apparent to her that she couldn't reach a standard that teachers or editors or even writing groups would deign to work with.

Decades went by and when she moved out of her house to something smaller, she had to decide what to keep and what to discard. The extensive notes she had taken from volumes of journals kept by the Franciscan Father Juan Crespi and a biography written by Junipero Serra's friend, Father Francisco Palau, were now faded and moldy from water damage. A flood in the garage years ago had destroyed many boxes of belongings, but it was painful to think of parting with these items. Her notes were difficult to read and because of their condition, couldn't go into her new home. Yet she could not get the idea of relating a fictionalized story based on facts out of her mind.

The thought returned from time to time as it did this particular day as she walked aimlessly toward her new home when she heard someone speaking.

"So, I see you threw away all your notes. How long did it take you to accumulate them?"

"Hmm? Who said that? Is it you? It's you, isn't it? In my head." It took her a moment to recover. "Well, yes, I did need to throw them away. I'm not up to doing what I want to do anyway. And there's another problem. If I tell the story as fact, that is, non-fiction, it could lack humanity that fiction can bring to a story. If it is fiction, it isn't exactly fact. I want to tell the truth about who the people—well who *you* were." She ventured to ask him directly, "So what happened to you after—you know?"

"It was very interesting. I was carried on the back of a messenger, an angel. As he left Earth and flew over a most depressing place, he seemed to dip his wings slightly over a dreadful cavern seven circles down where I saw people with prideful looks beaten down by demons. I was afraid I was going to be dropped and left there. It is the place I feared most when I was a physical being."

Eloise knew from his description that Father Serra had seen the circles of hell described by Dante in the *Inferno,* and the worst of them was the seventh circle reserved for the cardinal sin, pride. She had spent so many hours studying the life of this man, and now listening to him speak she felt as though she had been transported to another world. She also felt human compassion mixed with elation at what was happening within her own mind. In her studies, she had tried to decide whether Serra was a saint or a sinner. She had concluded that he, like most humans, was both.

"I know that was what you fought against in your lifetime, and I felt sorry."

"Don't pity me on that account."

"So, you went to Heaven then."

"Not right away," he answered, "The angel set me down in Purgatory. I had some things to work out. I think you have an idea what they were."

Eloise had concluded after volumes of reading that Father Serra had been suffering throughout his lifetime and that many of the unexpected things he did, such as refusing to allow a doctor to cure his leg wound and wearing a hair shirt, were done to humble himself. More to the point, he beat himself raw. While self-flagellation was not uncommon in his time, his beatings were so severe that his friends worried about him.

"Eventually, I was received in Heaven. The problem now is you and your writing, which you have given up."

"Everyone's a critic," she said defensively.

"Actually, I am of two minds about your wanting to make my life public. On one hand, I think you should leave it alone; on the other, you're suffering because you can't. You say you want to tell the truth. You should know this: The kind of truth you are looking for is over-rated and is relative. I can read your thoughts; you think it is odd for a priest to say truth is relative. Pay attention. The *kind* of truth you are looking for is relative, not absolute Truth which is constant.

"I met someone in Heaven that you would be interested to know. In fact, she was a compatriot of yours. Her name is Emily. She says that in writing one should tell the truth, but tell it slant."

"If I remember right," Eloise said more haughtily than she intended, "Emily Dickenson said truth should be told gradually, not all at once, so that the hearer can bear it. Are you saying I should fudge the facts to suit some end?"

"You're not listening, or else I'm not explaining well." Father Serra tried not to show his annoyance. "Let's try it from this angle: Things occurred in my life. On occasion something happened to me, or I did something. Then a good friend of mine, either Fray Francisco or Fray Juan, wrote about it. So, the event or statement, whichever it was, filtered through that writer, and each of them had an agenda. Fray Francisco made it clear he wanted me to be canonized and I believe Fray Juan for the most part wanted the mission to look as noble as we believed it was." He went on, "Here's another problem. Did you read the volumes in Spanish?"

"I looked at the Spanish pages in Juan Crespi's journals, but my Spanish is very weak. I read them in English."

"There you go." Serra had made his point, "The story is filtered through a translator next, who selects nuanced terms according to the translator's best effort, but that person also has an agenda, whether realized or not."

"I suppose that means I have an agenda too."

"Of course. That fact doesn't mean you shouldn't tell the story. It means you will put your own 'slant' on it. Now, which particular part of my life interests you right now? How can I help?"

Eloise was excited that the one person who could help her was not only willing but appeared eager to do so. "When you are dying, you refuse to give into that fact. You are pacing around. At one time you cry out that you are afraid."

"Yes, I was."

"Something happened to change that. What was it?" she asked.

"Suddenly my fear was gone. If you are writing a fictionalized factual story, you will have to figure it out for yourself." With that, the father left.

Eloise sat at her computer pulling in what she knew for certain about Junipero Serra. He had hardly known his family, but he had two close friendships in his life from boyhood through university and throughout his time in the Americas. One of them was with him at the time of his death. Francisco Palau had traveled from Mission San Francisco to be with him. The other friend, Juan Crespi, had died and was buried in the church in Mission Carmel where he and Junipero Serra had served. Why wouldn't both these friends, she thought, be with him at this important transition?

She also realized from his journals that at the end of his own life, Crespi knew Serra very well his virtues and his faults. In order to tell the truth, however, she needed to tell it slant as Father Serra told her to do. Why not, she decided, bring Juan back as a spirit to comfort Junipero? He would be a second priest to present the Eucharist at the same time Francisco is administering the Holy Oils. If this occurred, it would make sense for Junipero to say, suddenly his fear was gone.

She would have to find a priest's breviary. She wondered, should it be in Latin? She continued to make notes. This just might work, she thought, as she began to write.

DOORS
Poetry by *Joan Gordon*

After walking through griefs door, I'm happily weaving again once more. And finally see with better clarity, my new reality without my identical twin, as I step in, into a passageway showing a beginning and new day or another way.

Doors can be closed or open, leaving the possibilities wide-open. It can be an exit or entrance, allowing us a quick glance or a chance to advance. Or is it an outlet or vent, a descent or assent? An escape or way out, no doubt. A place to walkout, turnabout or bring all about. Something to withdraw into or emerge from, depending on the direction you came from.

A threshold on which to grab onto and hold. A stronghold or place to remold being genuinely bold. It can be looking from the past steadfast, seeing the contrast or peeking into the future at last. Or a place to stand, taking time to let thoughts expand from life's changes unplanned. Is it a downfall, a place to stall or an approach with access to all? Whichever way we choose, it can be an excuse or possibly light our fuse. Whether on your way out or in, it is a portal from which to begin. Yet another door to pass through, a see-through to a different avenue.

A closed door is protection or rejection and exclusion, leading possibly to confusion. A closed door does however abandon the old, allowing an embracing of the new to behold.

An open door empowers us to explore. An open door is welcoming, greeting and acknowledging a new beginning. It is a challenge or opportunity to grasp and seize onto, to make-do or actually breakthrough. To turn a liability into a viability. Unlock its magic and feel delight, as moving from the dark, into the light.

A doorstep is a temporary domain, not a spot on which to remain. A doorway is meant as a transition, a bringing of ambition to a new mission. Whether from childhood—to adulthood or leaving a piece of us behind, a door is there to remind that no matter which way we go, we are being led to internally grow. Doors provide the point of change, a pass-way, pathway, or interchange.

The door to my 'Loom Room' is open wide, to bring creative ideas inside, where they are applied. Allowing me to get past griefs door, looking for more, as I again restore and move on as best I can, with my newfound plan. After my twin was risen, taking advantage of what I was given, being again driven. To live life to the fullest and really enjoy, like a child with a new toy. Seeing all there is to see with increasing glee, helping myself to the world around me. I'll enjoy each day as it comes, looking for more positive outcomes. Like me again weaving away or back on my bike today, having a really good day, as I take on new challenges/goals and find the true key to open the next door waiting there for me. I'll keep moving forward to strengthen and advance, taking that chance to enhance, from life's circumstance. All because in the meantime, that door in time, gave me downtime to find a new outlook for a lifetime. And before we know it we've stepped right on through, holding onto our memories along with something new to look forward to. Thank you.

SEE NO EVIL
Nonfiction by *Ted Haynes*

Uganda 1971

The police station was a three-room concrete building in the small Uganda town where we gave up hitchhiking for the day. There was no hotel and they wouldn't let us sleep in the jail. We decided to spread our sleeping bags behind the station. It seemed the safest place. There was a woman sitting on a bench and five more people standing on the porch at the front of the building. A policeman in a green uniform told us the people had ridden a bus from a remote village to bring the woman to the hospital and now they were waiting for the ambulance. The woman's husband had shot her with an arrow.

"Why did her husband shoot her?" I asked.

"He was Kakwa," said the police chief reluctantly. The Kakwa were a tribe from further north in Uganda.

"Why would that make him shoot her?" I asked. The policeman wouldn't answer.

We looked at the woman—small, quiet, and uncomplaining—and wondered whether the story could possibly be true. The woman, perhaps in her thirties, lifted aside the wrap she was wearing to show us a six-inch shaft stuck in a clean round hole in her flat brown abdomen. Nothing leaked or oozed. A half-hour later the group gave up on the ambulance and began to walk the woman slowly to the hospital.

I'd gone to Kenya on a hiking tour. We saw the game parks, camped in the bush, and two of us climbed to the top of Mount

Kenya, up ice and vertical rock for the last two thousand feet. An adventure. A risk. I was 26.

I stayed after the Kenya tour and persuaded a girl I'd met in Nairobi to hitchhike through Uganda with me. I will say "girl" rather than "woman" because, in our twenties, we were both blissfully naive. Children. Some advised against our adventure because Uganda's new president, Idi Amin, had taken power in a coup d'état two weeks earlier and was an unknown quantity. But we had read so often of Third World countries changing leaders that we thought it wouldn't affect us.

My experience in Kenya was that white people were still a privileged race in Africa. Kenya and Uganda had gained their independence from Britain less than nine years earlier. Africans' habits of colonialism sustained a respect for the wisdom and power of white people despite whatever foolishness they might exhibit. In Uganda the locals asked me again and again what I thought of the new regime and what they should do about it. I hadn't even read the newspapers. I advised them badly, though unintentionally, and I disappointed them all.

After easy rides across Kenya, we entered Uganda with an Israeli man of about 40 who told us he was going there on business. He took us on a short side trip to see the enormous rapids below the dam that marked the beginning of the Nile. I had kayaked rapids in New England and I was awed by these mountains of water. I was further astounded to see an African not just kayaking the waters but swimming them. What an athlete! What a skilled and courageous man!

The Israeli urged us to sing as we drove over the dam. And keep looking straight ahead. We sang "Jamaica Farewell," the Harry Belafonte song, and I was proud to know a verse the others didn't know. I rolled my eyes left toward a small bay above the dam. There were floats like long brown balloons lying in the bay and I thought they must have something to do with fishing. When I asked the Israeli about them he reminded me sharply to keep looking forward.

He dropped us off at an inexpensive hotel in Kampala while he went to stay at the Sheraton. He invited us to have dinner with him and my companion quickly accepted for both of us. I was not so intrigued by the Israeli and would have preferred to eat African food in a local restaurant.

Before dinner I went out to find a safari driver named Emmanuel. He had driven my girlfriend with her family on a tour the previous summer. My girlfriend was enchanted with him and wanted us to meet. The shopkeeper in a local duka knew where to find Emmanuel and he appeared 10 minutes later. After a smiling but guarded greeting Emmanuel asked me what I thought was going to happen in his country and what he should do.

"There are no more safaris," he said.

I told him I didn't know what would happen but I thought the uncertainty would pass and he should wait it out. He wanted me to come back in the evening to have a talk with his friends. I apologized that I had dinner to go to at the Sheraton.

Why did the Israeli want to have dinner with us? He seemed to be a spy with a very thin cover and we were his fortuitous additions to that cover. Maybe he just wanted company. Maybe he had designs on my companion. He didn't tell us the country was descending into chaos. He didn't tell us to get the hell out of Uganda as fast as we possibly could.

I did not have designs on my companion. Our purpose was to see Uganda, not to kindle a romance. We made a good team. She was visiting her sister in Nairobi when we met. The sister had married a Kenyan she had met in Boston and the sister's house was a gathering place for aspiring Kenyans who had gone to college in America. It's possible that one of them was Barack Obama's father. The one time I visited their house, a group was eagerly awaiting a visit from "Daniel" who may have been Daniel Arap Moi, future president of Kenya.

The girl and I awoke the morning after our Sheraton dinner to the vigorous and continuous hammering of metal. It sounded like the largest autobody shop in the world. At 11 o'clock it stopped abruptly, followed by a scream. Then silence.

We took ourselves on a walking tour of Kampala and found our way to the university. On a grassy lawn between two buildings two women, one black and one white, were learning a dance and laughing about it. They were happy to see us.

"It is a dance of the Kakwa people," they told us. "Isn't it silly?" I didn't know that Idi Amin was a Kakwa and the tribe had leapt into power when Amin led his military coup. In my naïve disposition to all things indigenous, whoever the Kakwa were, I announced that I didn't think the dance was silly at all. Fear clouded the faces of the two women.

"Are you a friend of the Kakwa?" one asked.

"I don't even know any Kakwas."

The women looked relieved. I changed the subject by lifting my chin toward a city-block-sized field below us about 200 yards away. I asked about the man wearing a dark suit and a white shirt sitting on the ground in the middle of the weeds. It was a hot day and he was waving his arms as if he needed help getting up. I asked what he was doing there.

"The president says to kill anyone who goes into the field," answered one of the women.

That seemed preposterous. Why would the president of an entire country concern himself with one man in a field? And in the middle of a city surrounded by buildings, buses, and traffic lights, who would tell the police to kill people for helping a man in difficulty? The police should take the man to a hospital if he were injured, and then, if he were a criminal, to jail. There were men in uniform dawdling on the sidewalk, not standing guard or threatening anyone, and civilians, including a woman in a very nice dress wringing her hands, walking back and forth and looking anxiously toward the man in the field. We almost went down to help him ourselves.

The following day we hitch-hiked 300 miles across Uganda to Fort Portal. Our first ride was with an African woman in a Mercedes who spoke excellent English but would not engage us in conversation. She said she had to stop at her house. It would have been a well-kept middle class house in America and nicer than any other house we'd seen on our trip. We waited in the car for at least half an hour before I knocked on the door to ask if we should wait longer or catch another ride. She told me snappily to wait. She was rich and sophisticated by Ugandan standards and was too habituated to white people to defer to them. We were the means to an end—to make her safer, her presence a little more formidable, as she drove us to a town outside Kampala where she dropped us off.

We rode most of the way in a truck—my companion in the cab with two Africans and I in the truck bed. I found it more comfortable to stand up and lean on the cab than sit and feel the bruises from every bump in the road. We arrived after dark at a compound and met the owner, a British ex-pat who ran an agricultural business. He gave us a concrete floor to sleep on and we requested, courteously at first and then with arguments, that he or his men take us into Fort Portal as we had originally understood. He didn't want to send the men out again but he reluctantly agreed. We stayed in a small roadside motel, far from elegant but very clean.

At breakfast the next day we were approached by a group of Indian men. A doctor among them asked us what we knew about the Amin government and what we would recommend the Indians do. We had nothing to offer and they left us in disgust.

From Fort Portal we hitchhiked to Murchison Falls, a famous site farther north on the Nile. We were picked up, grudgingly, by the man with the agricultural compound that we'd met the previous evening. He happened to be going to Murchison as well. He said his men had run into trouble returning to his compound from taking us to our motel. He didn't like us—we had complicated his life and we offered him nothing in return. It was a sense of solidarity that compelled him to stop. We were fellow white people. "Europeans" was the term though we weren't Europeans. Whites were in the minority and we were vulnerable. We had to stick together even if we didn't particularly like each other, even if we didn't trust each other.

The man was going to bring more of his workers back to Fort Portal and he had us wait at the lodge near the falls while he gathered the men. There was a metal rack on the lawn where the management left meat to attract animals and birds. Guides had pointed out marabou storks to me in Kenya as one more animal to photograph and claim to have seen. But marabou storks, I'd decided, were the ugliest creatures God had ever created. They stood up to five feet tall on thin bony legs. Long dusty black wings hung from their shoulders like an undertaker's coat. Their very large bills were the color of weathered bone and their big heads were bald like a vulture's. A wobbly, fleshy pouch dangled from their jaws. Five of them were picking at the broken remains of a bloody red skeleton.

Going back, our unfriendly businessman assigned me a bench seat, along with nine of his workers, in the bed of his canvas-covered truck. I was by the tailgate in the bumpiest and dustiest seat. Hardly anyone spoke the entire trip.

I wanted to see one of the lakes in the rift valley and we hitch-hiked from Fort Portal to a lodge overlooking Lake Edward. As we left the asphalt and walked up a dirt road to the lodge we saw an open truck driving rapidly toward us and raising a cloud of dust. There were men standing in the back gesticulating wildly. I thought we should hide from them. We slid down a bank and lay flat in the weeds. The men came by laughing, banging on the side of the truck, and waving machetes in the air. They may have been drunk.

The lodge was luxurious compared to the places we'd been staying. We skipped the expensive dinner and ate bread and cheese we'd brought with us. I was reading *Keep the Aspidistra Flying* by George Orwell. A man who rails against the pursuit of money is finally persuaded by his girlfriend and his miserable life to accept the middle-class life he despised. I realized the adult within me would soon nudge my venturous youth aside.

There were few people at breakfast the next morning and the mood was somber. The staff wistfully regarded us from the back of the room as though viewing a familiar and orderly scene for the last time. They knew far better than we that the tourist business was over for Uganda. There would be no job tomorrow. They and their families might be in danger. My companion, as oblivious as I, told the waiter the toast was burned. The man laughed, not at her, but at surprise that anyone would worry about burnt toast at a time like this. But he went to the kitchen and brought us new toast, a perfect light brown.

We were lucky getting rides all the way back to Kenya. A Brit took us from the lodge to Fort Portal. Another took us in a nice, air-conditioned car most of the way to Kampala and stopped at a private coffee depot where he worked with other ex-pats.

The men sat around a table quietly drinking beer. Ignoring us, their conversation started with, "What should we do now?" Their talk proceeded slowly, broken by long silences, and came to the conclusion, repeated in turn by some of the men, "It's over." Back on the road with the same driver we passed Africans standing by sacks of coffee they'd grown on their own little farms.

"No one is coming to buy their coffee," said the driver. "But they don't know what else to do."

We were picked up by another British ex-pat who took us to his sugar plantation. Workers were lifting sugar cane out of big trucks and running it into a rusty machine that squeezed out sugar-filled juice.

"We can't sell this sugar anymore," the man said sorrowfully.

"Then why are they doing this?" I asked. His face contorted and his eyes pinched.

"They're used to it. They feel good doing it." He stepped forward as if to tell them to stop. What they were doing was pointless. But he held himself back. He was used to the work too. He liked to see the men working, the mill turning, and the juice flowing out.

Our next-to-last ride was with an American in a sedan. A man about our age. He first said he worked for an American company that imported auto parts. Later he admitted he worked for the CIA. He had an Indian couple with him that seemed nervous. He was driving them to Kenya but he didn't want to take us with him. He took us to a lodge near the border and treated us to lunch. He asked an American family with two small children at another table to take us across the border and they did. They were nervous and it took a while for the parents to relax after we were through. The CIA man had said to tell people we met in Nairobi to stay out of Uganda.

Idi Amin ruled Uganda as a military dictator for eight years, slaughtering at least a 100,000 of his fellow citizens, terrifying the rest, strangling democracy in its crib, and laying waste the entire economy. He expelled and seized the property of sixty thousand Indians who made up the business and professional classes and accounted for most of the government's tax revenue. He abandoned the substantial support Uganda had received from Israel.

I read a biography of Idi Amin years later, sitting safely beside a river in Oregon, and I surveyed my memories in the light of fresh knowledge. The brown floats I had glimpsed in the water were the bloated bodies of Amin's political opponents. The man I saw swimming was already dead. The banging of metal we heard in Kampala hid the sound of men being tortured and killed. The marabou storks were picking over a human body. The men waving machetes in the back of the truck were probably Kakwa who had just terrorized and robbed the lodge we stayed at. The fear, confusion, and sinking hearts I saw throughout Uganda were real.

Emmanuel and his fellow safari drivers left Uganda to look for work in Kenya. The ambulance may not have come for the woman with the arrow in her stomach because she was not Kakwa. Did her husband shoot her to prove his loyalty to the Kakwa? Had he wanted to kill her for a long time and, now in a lawless country, he did it freely?

I saw my traveling companion in Nairobi a few times before I left.

"We were lucky," she said.

We were.

THE PRICE OF INEQUALITY FOR WOMEN & GIRLS AFFECTS GLOBAL INNOVATION

Nonfiction by *Diane L. McClelland*

To increase the leadership opportunities for women to make needed changes in society, we must put a stake in the ground now to change the conscious and unconscious bias by men and women, towards women and their ability to contribute meaningful success to ideation and innovation. This is critical to increase the gender equity for women that translates into greater innovation, collaboration, and societal global wealth. This bias even comes unwittingly from women themselves, who don't realize the power they have to use *global collaborative innovation*™ with other women as a growth strategy to achieve internal satisfaction and external success.

  Change is needed to develop training for women and girls that helps them recognize they have everything they need to be successful to break down barriers. It comes from their inner perception and the lens they use when they look in the mirror at themselves. What do they see? Who are they? Is there an inner incongruency of the inner self and how they show up in society similar to *Imposter Syndrome?* Do their behaviors mirror how they feel deep down within themselves? Do women and girls take time to be quiet, without distractions, to sit with themselves alone and openly think: *"What is important to me? How can I change the vibration level of my energy to attract more abundance and the life I love? My happiness is my responsibility and choice. It is an inside job."*

The bottom line is to take responsibility every day to make choices for our lives that are consistent with our inner core values.

What if women made a concerted effort to think of "we" rather than "I" to create a global tidal wave of a sea change in the "field of possibilities" for all women, no matter their zip codes? How would our world change? What new ideas could be co-created? What new innovative products or services would be offered that could bring our global citizens together who are honest brokers of ideas and could make a societal impact?

It really is simple! Women have the numbers! There are 385 billion women in the world and 285 million global women business owners. Women live longer, are major purchasers of products and services, excellent communicators, and lead many campaigns for human rights that change perceptions and create new laws protecting citizens whose freedoms are at risk.

Women are the center of the circle of change. They are the key to our society's future for innovation, gender equity, and wealth. It is a simple continuum: Begin with girls 9-12. Introduce them to using curiosity to be aware of their environment and possible gaps of missing solutions. Ages 13-18, encourage them to join the Girls STEAM Institute® Global Team Challenges, develop a business idea, and pitch their business ideas to a panel of judges for feedback about the commercial viability of their ideas. Women business owners' mentor young future entrepreneurs and fund the needed startup capital to bring these ideas to market. These young female entrepreneurs are trained by the seasoned women entrepreneurs and become vendors in the supply chains of the seasoned women's businesses. When the seasoned women entrepreneurs decide to sell their companies, the younger women entrepreneurs with supply-chain experience become the new owners of the seasoned businesses and maintain the corporate goals for diversity in their supply chains.

Major factors for this continuum model to be realized, that increase net worth and wealth for women, require personal development and leadership programs to prepare young girls to develop self-awareness and self-sufficiency, resulting in self-confidence, using curiosity and empathy to make a difference in society that encourages *global collaborative innovation*™.

NEIGHBORLY CONVERSATIONS
Fiction by *Anna Marie Garcia*

February 2, 2000

Shifting in my chair, trying to get comfortable with my book, the mid-morning silence was interrupted by a familiar knock. "Coming," I called, moving slightly slower than usual. I opened to my neighbor Celine's relieved smile.

"Okay, I'll admit it, I was a little worried when I hadn't seen you in a few days," she said.

"I pulled a muscle in my back doing yard work. Probably hauling the branches I pruned. It's much better though."

She had me sit while she made us tea and pulled shortbread from my cookie shelf. "Have you met the new neighbors?" she asked as she filled my cup.

"Well, that's almost funny. I saw them going into their house last week, so I tried to see if I could pay the boy to do some yard work."

"How'd that go over?"

"Strange. The mother acted like I was a criminal. Sent the boy in the house, said he wasn't available to work for me, and abruptly followed him inside. I didn't even get her name. Have you met them?"

Celine said her encounter had been similarly odd. She took a cake over Saturday to welcome them and explain the neighborhood watch program. The woman closed the door and stood outside. Gave her first name, Rachael, but no last name. She hesitantly relinquished her home phone number, but made it clear it was only for emergencies, not to be added to any lists or given to anyone else. "Skittish and distrusting, I'd say."

"Maybe she'll warm up after she's been here for a while," I said. "What do you want to do about giving me her phone number for the child watch roster?"

Not wanting to breech trust, Celine said she'd have to think about it, then asked when I was last watching the street. I easily remembered it was Friday morning, because I hurt myself that afternoon.

"Lacy called me Monday evening. Her daughters ran home out of breath after some man yelled, 'Hey girls,' out his car window and motioned them over. They didn't get a car description, but Lacy alerted the school and drove them both ways Tuesday. She was concerned when she hadn't seen you. Unfortunately, she works today, and Shelby has a late class so she can't help either."

I assured her I was good enough to sit outside after school. Said I'd call Lacy to tell the girls to come to my house if they were scared and would let the school know if I saw anything suspicious. Celine shared the neighborhood's appreciation, then handed over the new neighbor's number.

"Promise," I said, "I won't call them to chat."

"Make a list of the yardwork you still need finished, and we can talk about it on the weekend," she said as she put her cup in the sink before letting herself out.

That afternoon, Gabi and Vanessa waved at me from across the street as they walked past. I watched them open their front door and go inside. A few minutes later they called to let me know everything inside was fine and they weren't scared. My back was starting to throb, so I went inside to continue my watch from a more comfortable chair.

Before I even sat down, I saw a man I didn't recognize driving slowly down our normally tranquil street. His head smoothly swept side to side as he surveyed the scene. I reached for my pad and pen but couldn't see his rear license plate and didn't readily recognize the generic looking make of the car. I watched him until he turned the corner, noting the car was dark green and he was wearing glasses.

To my right, I saw the boy next door approaching from about five houses away. He glanced towards my porch, quickly looked right and left, then focused on his front door. Despite his bulging backpack, he was maintaining a quick pace. As he neared his front door, I noticed the green car had circled the block. He slowed and watched the boy enter his house from about seventy yards away.

He parked in front of Celine's house and sat there for a moment, focused on his steering wheel. My trembling hands reached for the phone list, as my stomach started to knot. I knew the girls were alone in one house, the boy alone next door, and no other adults home nearby. I wasn't sure if I should call 911 or wait to see what he was going to do. He looked out the driver side window straight at the boy's house. I didn't hesitate. I called 911, gave a brief synopsis and dialed again.

"Answer, come on answer." The machine beeped on and the best I could do was speak to the recorder, "Hello, this is your next-door neighbor, this is an emergency, please answer. You are in danger. Pleeease Pick UP! A suspicious man in a green car has been driving through the neighborhood. Come on, answer. He followed you home, I saw him. I'm trying to protect you."

The answering machine clicked off without an answer. I redialed.

"He's coming up your walk. Don't open the door. DO NOT OPEN THE DOOR!"

"Hello. Who is this?" a youth answered reluctantly.

"I live next door in the blue house. I try to watch out for the kids in the neighborhood."

"I'm not allowed to talk to the neighbors."

"Don't open, he's at your front door."

"Why are you calling me? How did you get my number? My mom thinks you're weird and nosy. She told me to stay away from you and not talk to the old lady next door."

"I understand, but this is an emergency. I already called 911 and the police are on their way, but I want to keep you safe," I said as calmly as I could muster.

"Why? How do I know you're telling me the truth?"

"Because you're a kid and I'm a retired teacher, and I watch out for children. I really am trying to help you. Believe me."

"I'm not a child. I'm twelve. Who's the guy?"

"I've seen him drive through the neighborhood. I think he's a predator … Good job not answering the door. He's walking around the side of your house now. Get to a place he can't see you. Closet, counter, anywhere, quick," I directed, inching towards the rear of my house. "He's looking in the side window."

"I'm down behind the kitchen counter," the boy said, his anger waning and his voice fearful.

"Good. Stay there until I tell you, then get as close to the front door as you can. Stay low and away from the windows."

"Did you really call the police? Is this some crazy old lady game?" he questioned. His rapid breathing audible.

"I'm trying to help you. Now. Go to the front. He's not looking inside. He's scoping out the back of your house and your backyard. Get to the front of the house. Stay low. Don't try to look out the window."

"Should I lock myself in the bathroom?" he asked.

"No bathroom. If he gets into the back of your house I'll tell you, and then I want you to run out the front door. If he doesn't get in, I'll give you other directions. The police should be here any minute."

"How long? Why aren't they here? Did you really call them? Is this a trick?" he hissed.

"I told them to get here fast. The man just tried the back door and then he reached up and cut your window screen with a knife. I think he's looking for something to climb on because he couldn't get up to the window. Do you know if the window's locked?"

"I don't know. I'm scared. Are you sure I shouldn't lock myself in the bathroom?"

"Since he's trying to get into your house, I think we should get you out of it. Do you understand?"

"My mom told me not to talk to you. She thinks you're really strange, and, and … you sit outside when kids are walking home from school. AND crazy."

"LOOK," I said, "I'm 68-years-old and four feet eleven. Who's scarier, me or the man trying to get into your house?"

He took several panting stutters, "I, I thought I saw a man watching me yesterday. He creeped me out."

"He's standing on your garbage can and trying the window … It just opened. Are you near the front door?"

"Yes."

"When I say now, you open your front door and run to my house. My door isn't locked. I'll meet you there as soon as I can walk from the back of my house."

"I'm shaking."

"You can do this. I'll beat that man myself if I have to. I will NOT let him hurt you. He's half-way in the window. NOW. GO. RUN TO MY HOUSE!"

RIDGELINE

Poetry by *Corbett Gottfried*

Whatever it takes
to get to the top.
Struggling up the side of the ridge,
gasping for breath.
My heart pounding,
my head dizzy.
New boots,
blisters on my heels.
Leg muscles screaming,
cannot take another step.
Sweating beneath layers of clothing
and heavy backpack.
Keep tripping over rocks
and snagging myself on sagebrush.
Freezing wind picks up;
my face is numb.
No trail to follow,
just creating own switchbacks.
Progress up is slow,
impeded by rock outcroppings.
Cannot remember
why I am even here.
This is insane,
but I need to finish it.
Finally make my way to the top;
feels like I will pass out.

The view is more spectacular
than I had imagined;
I can see for miles,
I can touch the sky.
The effort was worth it,
I feel closer somehow to God.

PASTA CORTONA

Nonfiction by *Karista Bennett*

The deadline for the winemaker's contest is looming, and of course, I haven't even begun to write the essay, which is due by midnight. My desk is overflowing with client menus that need to be completed and emails that demand my response. As I sit at my desk berating myself for having procrastinated, my scruffy little terrier stares at me with a puzzled expression from under my desk. I'm sure he's wondering who I'm talking to.

I am a chef. Can I write a 500-word essay that isn't solely focused on food and still have a shot at winning? A trip to Italy to discover the secrets of Italian winemaking seems like a dream. I can do this; I'm going to enter. It takes me all day to weave my story into the essay, and when I'm finished, I feel a sense of satisfaction, a smidgen of pride, and a little surprise. The essay is good: I might have a chance. It's 9pm, and I have three hours to spare. I hit the send button and breathe a sigh of relief.

In the next several months, I spend much of my time lobbying for votes, and now the contest is nearing the end. Making it to the final three is an exhilarating experience, and I feel grateful to be acknowledged for my work and to be among such great company. The final decision will be announced in a few months, but daily life, a move to a new state and work, are keep me busy, and the thought of winning slips from my mind.

Moving day has arrived, and my youngest daughter and I load our luggage into the car, place our little terrier and his crate carefully between our seats, and head out of our beloved town for the last time. After a few hours on the road, we stop in a small rural town just outside Portland. My 15-year-old daughter has been begging me for the last hour to let her get some highway driving practice with her permit, and I finally relent. I climb into the passenger seat, buckle up, say a silent prayer to the universe, and give our little dog a biscuit for being so good.

As my daughter drives the car back onto the highway, the clock reads mid-afternoon, and the sun is high and bright. It's one of those magnificent Pacific Northwest summer days when the sky is cloudless and the color of a cornflower blue crayon. The car windows are down, letting in the warm summer breeze that gently brushes our faces. My daughter looks at me for a quick moment and smiles, and I know she's proud of her good driving skills. For a few moments, we ride in silence, relishing the beauty of the day.

As we approach the city, I shift into driving instructor mode to help my daughter navigate the complex highway system. My cell phone rings, but I don't recognize the number. A woman on the other end of the line identifies herself and begins to talk about the winemaker's contest. As she continues to speak, the wind and traffic noise suddenly go silent. I glance at my daughter and see her mouth moving, but I don't hear a word she's saying. All I hear are the words, "you won a trip to Tuscany." Just as I look up, I notice we're driving across a bridge, and the sign on the bridge reads, "Welcome to Oregon." It is a surreal moment. We had just driven into our new home state, and now the woman on the other end of the phone tells me I am going to Tuscany. Life is about to get interesting.

The plane ride to Italy isn't quite the delightful experience I had imagined. I envisioned cozy scenes from movies, where passengers look comfortably seated with soft blankets, and gracious flight attendants that serve delicious-looking food and cocktails. Instead, I find myself in a stiff and cramped middle seat, sandwiched between my husband on the right and a very tall, unpleasant-smelling man on the left. As much as I sympathize with the man's discomfort, I silently hope that he will stop moving so his odor won't reach my nose. I keep reminding myself that I will be in Tuscany soon and this entire plane trip will be worth it. And so, I order another gin and tonic.

During the long flight, I contemplate admitting to my husband that while we're in Italy, I want to visit the little village of Cortona. We have already planned our itinerary for the week, and Cortona isn't on the list. The second week, I'll be busy with the winemaker's tour, which is exciting, but I know there won't be time to see Cortona.

I have read the book *Under the Tuscan Sun* so many times I could recite it from memory. The adventure, the food, the culture—everything about the book speaks to me. And of course, who hasn't seen the movie adaptation? I have a yearning to visit Cortona, but I hesitate to admit this. I am not a giddy, dreamy-eyed tourist, or at least I don't want to be one. But I crave to experience the village through the eyes of the locals, to feel the unique culture deep in my bones, while drinking in the landscape and sampling the local cuisine.

Our last day in Tuscany together is quickly approaching, and I'll soon be on my way to meet colleagues for the Winemaker's tour. My husband asks me, "What do you really want to see on our last day here?" I take a deep breath and reply, "I really want to visit Cortona." He smiles and says, "Then that's what we're doing tomorrow."

The train ride took longer than I expected, or maybe it was my excitement making me impatient. As we emerge from the train station, I feel a sting of disappointment. The little town is cute but not the magical village I envisioned. My heart begins to drop and as we get into a taxi, I ask the driver about the village. "Oh, do not worry Miss!" he says. "We have to drive to the top of the mountain to get to the village." I had barely shut the car door when the taxi driver speeds off in the direction of the large mountain that sits above the train station. He expertly navigates a long, narrow switchback road up the hillside which leads to the entrance, and I feel my heart begin to pound.

Walking through this iconic, medieval village feels like a dream. Steep, narrow cobblestone streets are lined with enchanting stone buildings, each with doors painted in bright colors. Church bells ring in the distance, and a warm breeze carries intoxicating scents of nearby trattorias. Local residents walk among us, speaking heartily in their romantic language. As two older women pass by me, one of them, an angelic-faced Noni, gives me a nod and a smile, as if she knows I am now under the magical spell of Cortona.

Our day in Cortona is idyllic, and we exhaust ourselves meandering every corner of the village. I can't leave the village without tasting a traditional Tuscan meal, so we find an outdoor Trattoria that overlooks the *Piazza della Repubblica*. Directly across the *Piazza* from our table is the large Town Hall Building, complete with a majestic-looking clock tower that looks as if it stands guard over the village.

As we wait for our food, a young couple in wedding attire emerge from the town hall building and walk onto the balcony. They wave to wedding guests below and to everyone in the *Piazza*, and then to everyone sitting at the Trattoria. We all wave back and I feel lucky to have witnessed this couple's special day. The stunning raven-haired bride, wearing a ruffled white gown, begins tossing red roses off the balcony, creating a breathtakingly romantic moment.

Just as the bride tossed the last rose, my plate of food arrives as if on cue. It is a silky linguine bathed in a white wine cream sauce infused with garlic, and mixed with cabbage, mushrooms, and shaved Pecorino Romano. The dish is aromatic and intoxicating, garnished with paper-thin slices of black truffle and fresh parsley.

Swirling my fork into the pasta, I ensure that I gather a little of each ingredient. The flavors dance on my tongue, and I know this will be one of the most exquisite meals I had ever tasted. I savor each bite, relishing the perfect combination of flavors and textures.

The days race by and my tour of Italy has ended. As I fly home in a more comfortable aisle seat, the memories of mouthwatering food remain fresh in my mind. Still bemused from my adventure, I grab my journal out of my bag and jot down my experiences from the trip, including that most magnificent day in Cortona. I want to remember every delicious moment and the glorious linguine that I had so immensely enjoyed. I decide the first thing I'm going to do when I get home is recreate that luscious pasta dish.

A decade has passed since that trip to Cortona, yet it remains vivid in my mind, as if it was yesterday. I have since tried to recreate that mouthwatering pasta dish with some success, and now I call it Pasta Cortona. While it is heavenly, it's not quite the same as the linguine I had that one special day. Perhaps the magic lay in the chefs' hands, in the locally grown ingredients made with love, or the moment I savored it.

Pasta Cortona serves as a delightful reminder of that perfect Autumn day I spent in Cortona, Italy. It reminds me to relish the simplest pleasures in life, like a warm breeze infused with the scent of luscious food or a friendly smile from a stranger. It's a reminder to find the magic in every moment, whether at home or in an enchanting village like Cortona, Italy.

Pasta Cortona

I believe recipes are guidelines so feel free to adjust ingredients to your tastes. This pasta dish is not heavily sauced so be sure to use high quality ingredients for the best results. Have fun, experiment, and create your own taste of Cortona.

Serves 2 (or 4 as a starter)

Ingredients

10 ounces linguine, cooked to package directions
2 tablespoons butter (salted or unsalted)
4 tablespoons good quality extra virgin olive oil (start with 2 tablespoons and add as needed)
2 cups sliced mixed seasonal mushrooms (like chanterelle, cremini, and shitake)
2 large cloves garlic, finely minced
1 teaspoon minced fresh thyme
1 tablespoon chopped fresh Italian parsley
¼ cup white wine
1 small to medium head Napa cabbage, halved lengthwise and thinly sliced into ribbons or shredded
3 tablespoons grated fresh Parmigiano Reggiano or pecorino Romano (good quality cheese is key here)
Pinch crushed red pepper flakes
Salt and pepper to taste
Drizzle of black truffle oil (or thinly shaved black truffle)
Serve with fresh grated Parmigiano Reggiano or pecorino Romano

Directions

Prepare the pasta according to package directions.

While the pasta is cooking, heat butter and olive oil in a large skillet over medium heat. When the butter/oil is hot, add the mushrooms and sauté to your preference. Mushrooms quickly absorb liquid but will eventually release the liquid when they've finished cooking.

Just before the mushrooms are done, add garlic, thyme and parsley to the mushrooms and season with salt, pepper, and a pinch of crushed red pepper.

Stir in the wine letting it simmer for a few seconds. Next toss in the thinly sliced Napa cabbage, and continue to toss with the mushroom garlic mixture, adding additional olive oil if needed, until the cabbage is wilted, or crisp tender.

Take the skillet off the heat, sprinkle in grated parmesan or pecorino, and season to taste with salt and pepper if needed.

Drain the linguine and toss with the mushroom cabbage mixture and plate immediately.

Drizzle each plate of pasta with black truffle oil (or thinly shaved black truffle) and shaved pecorino or grated parmesan.

OUR HOUSE
Fiction by *Eric Moser*

Spiritual relations hanging around the old house were actually the least of Larry Howell's troubles. It was the upkeep. It had broken his father and it was doing the same to Larry. When the roof began to leak, he slept on the parlor sofa downstairs. When the basement furnace broke, he used the fireplace exclusively. He kept his clothes in a bureau in the foyer, his business records in a laundry basket under the dining table. He ate out most of the time.

Three generations of Howells had lived, and more than a few of them had died, in the house. Haunting would have been normal. Still, it was large enough for everybody/everything: two stories, a tower, a garret tucked under a steep pitched roof overweighed with dormers.

Larry was the last Howell in residence. His older sisters had fled. Each hardly a day out of high school, in a quick succession of years.

The house had been built by Larry's grandfather, who willed it, along with a highway convenience store to Larry's mother. Neither of which, obviously, his father wanted. The old man had tramped sullenly through the greater part of his life, shackled to another man's things.

His parents died at home, one following the other, neatly bracketing Larry's senior year in high school. It was left to him to keep the store, mind the house, send the profits to his college student sisters. That was fifteen years past.

The real haunting began shortly after.

It was little things. Brief, faint unpleasant smells that set him searching the house for a dead mouse the cat brought in. The laughably hackneyed draughts, the creaking floorboards he could ignore. There had always been raccoons in the attic in the spring, and the wind had moaned through the warped door frames for years. But the nighttime presences, or sense of them, that awoke him suddenly in the dark. Those made his very soul shirk into a little space, deep in his chest.

He therefore began to edge out of the house, willing it to die, leaving it behind in sections as in strategic retreat, until he was perched full time in the front parlor, its bay windows open in all but the worst weather. He stayed up each night watching television until he passed out, a sleeping bag twisted around him.

Larry hadn't slept well in a year. Not since Emily left. Well, he never slept well, excepting the six months she had spent under the sagging roof, the wonder being he supposed, that she had stayed for even the first night. He recalled the morning after, she grinning back at him over a bare shoulder, standing at the bottom of the stairs about to take his dare to go up. Of course, the house had a reputation.

They had spent the night on the floor, in front of the fire, which was practical, even if romantic. Emily now wore that ridiculous sleeping bag like a cloak, somehow looking provocative in the way it smoothed over her ample hips and one round shoulder. Larry had a sudden intimation of a resilient and practical Emily, and he was less afraid then of the effect the house might have on her. He was seized then with an exquisite agony so unique in his experience he did not recognize it for love.

Emily worked in a bakery making pretzels. Larry went there for coffee, he didn't much care for pretzels. She worked at a little window, rather like pizza parlors, so customers could watch the dough thrown into the air. The motions in pretzel making were less lyrical and more like whipping a snake to death. Larry was drawn to her immediately. He didn't know why exactly. Who knows about attractions that way? When he first saw her, flour caked up to her elbows, and a smidge of it on the tip of her nose, he was sold.

One day he pointed through the window and grinned at her. "I want that one," just as she was tying the knot. She fought to control a look, won, and smiled sweetly. Emily tried some sleight of hand when it came time to take his pretzel out of the oven, but he caught her at it and they had a small laugh together.

"Careful, it's hot," she said, while she handed it over the counter in a tissue. Her long fingers, cupping the warm pretzel, she placed directly into his waiting hands. "I'm not supposed to give them until they cool down." He sat down and smirked back at her, his mouth full of steaming pretzel. The next day she came around the counter to sit with him. When he asked her out, she said yes.

Now she was running up and down the upstairs hallway yelling, "Come out, come out, wherever you are!"

Later that morning, the house thoroughly exorcised, they lounged on the front porch. Larry was having definite thoughts of another night with Emily when she conceived the notion of fixing the place up.

Her ideas were rather naïve and decorative rather than restorative. Still Larry allowed himself to be drawn into the plan, being as agreeable as she was excited, but captivated by the daring intimacy of planning anything with a woman. They went from room to room, her hair still smelling vaguely of apples after her shower, her face shiny like a freshly scrubbed one.

After ignoring the house for so long, he feared it would prove more a resurrection than repair. He was sure there was dry rot in the joists, termites in the beams. Water had run down inside the walls; the wiring was the providence of the 19th century. Still there was much to recommend it. The birch floor, cherry cabinets, red oak wainscoting. The claw-footed bathtubs were original, as were the terra cotta ceiling in the dining room.

With a premonition of disaster that made him physically shiver, he set to work. He opened up holes, in exploratory fashion, to find rot so thorough that it dashed any hope he might have had.

Emily showed up after work often and helped out a little, fetching tools, holding the end of a measuring tape. Mostly she cooked for them, set the table, cleaned up afterward. It was companionable, though Larry felt balanced on the most precarious of reasons. Which was, that for the time being, Emily's imagination seemed seized by the house. She talked every day about its possibilities for a bed and breakfast. He saw it as a 5,000 square foot chimera waiting to swallow them both.

But then one evening she showed up at the house with a carload of belongings. She suggested she rent an upstairs bedroom that Larry had first tackled in his renovation. He thought such an arrangement a curious fabrication but said nothing to upset the calm and agreed. They slept in her room most nights, though occasionally down in the parlor after a poor night's sleep upstairs. Emily never said anything, but those next days they both moved around each other as though there was something left unsaid and best left that way.

Emily's friends dropped by. Mostly curious, some apparently concerned.

Larry's sisters visited, one after the other, like cautious cats poking their heads around the corners and sniffing into rooms that previously hadn't seen a coat of paint in thirty years. Emily was proud of the changes. He hung back and let her do the talking, following her gesturing to the rehabilitated molding and terra cotta as if seeing it for the first time himself. The better to ignore his sisters hooded looks. Each of them suffered being pulled through the place like tourists with more graciousness than he would have thought, until he finally understood the hope they must harbor with this girl. A man with three older sisters was used to being told how to behave.

And each managed a moment alone with him to ask about, well, you know … it. No, he told them in turn, he hadn't really noticed anything, at all. Lately. All lies of course. But he was beginning to worry for Emily's sake. He could see something in her expression lately. And there was the quick dart of the eyes suddenly down a darkened corridor, he knew he wasn't meant to notice.

Unsurprisingly, she was soon on her way out the door for the last time, her face framed that very instant by the wilting begonias she carried in her arms. While Larry stood by, he reflected on how their relationship had come apart as easily as it had come together. The problem he decided was a breezy sort of irreverence for facts, like inhabiting a truly condemnable house and deciding it could be anything different. It was a kind of playacting what they had had been doing. "I just don't know how anyone can know anyone well enough," she had said about it.

"Enough for what?" he asked, confused.

"To love them, we all seem strangers."

"I love you," he said for the first time as he held the door for her, for apparently the last time.

She had the two pots of begonias, one pressed against each breast. "I feel sick right now. Love isn't a stomachache."

He followed her to the curb where she got in and started her car. It caught finally even as the battery began to fade. She sat with both hands on the wheel, arms stiff as if already bracing for an impact. At an idle, the car's engine thumped in a slow bass beat. He knew she was holding the accelerator down to the floor, waiting for the engine to rev up. Standing on the curb, he was enveloped in puffs of blue exhaust, syncopated to the dead stroke of a non-firing cylinder. His lungs labored.

"I know how you must feel." She had to yell over the detonation pings. "I wish I could say something to you."

"Now?"

"Not now."

"Then I really don't think you know how it feels."

"I'll call. I promise."

Promise? He mouthed the word carefully. She nodded grimly, ground the car into gear and was gone.

He stood on the curb a while hating to go inside and remembering exactly what it had felt like when she was going the other way, bringing her belongings into the house in jaunty little back-seat loads each evening after work.

Emily didn't go far. A few blocks to an upstairs apartment in another old place; three stories, clapboard siding, gables at all angles, it had been long portioned into a dozen tiny apartments. He drove right past it on his way to and from work and felt self-conscious doing so, except it was the same route he had taken every day for fifteen years. No fault surely could be found with him for maintaining such a habit. He knew which apartment was hers because of the red curtains with a white sailboat print that were in a second story window that use to hang in his kitchen. He thought they might hang in her kitchen too, right above the sink. The red-draped window was a siren call to him. In summer the window was open morning and evening, and sometimes the curtains wafted outside the frame.

One early evening, watching the red curtains flagging, as if waving to him, he ran into a parked car on the street. If he had thoughts of driving off it was no use because he couldn't restart his car. He was bringing groceries home and the bags had split open casting a milk carton up against the windshield. He staggered out of the car, leaving milky footprints on the road, and stared at the bent-back hood and rising steam from the ruptured radiator. The door and front quarter panel of the car he had hit were caved in half-a-foot. Larry couldn't help glancing up at the window with the cheerful curtain.

A red-faced man had come out of the house of the parked car, cursing loudly. Larry thought to apologize but was becoming nauseous. He had to sit on the curb and lower his head to his knees. Still, the man kept it up, squatting in front of him and yelling. Larry was dimly aware of another car pulling up.

"The guys wasted," the red-faced man said. A cop replaced him in Larry's field of view.

"Are you all right sir?" the cop asked. Larry shook his head, afraid to open his mouth, to let anything pass his throat, even the air to speak. He lay down to put his head on the cool grass, the soft earth, next to the curb. He heard radio chatter, soon he heard sirens, different types mixed together. An ambulance, a fire engine. Someone, a paramedic perhaps, forced his eyelids open and shined a light into his eyes. Larry saw the dark form of a man within a blood red corona.

"You awake?" the man asked.

"I am now." Larry already felt better but thought it wouldn't do simply to get up and be better. It had always troubled him to think he was an inconvenience to others. Now that there were so many responsible, concerned people, fireman and paramedics and the police. It seemed best to assure them their time was not wasted. The man let go of his eyelids and Larry kept them closed.

"Do you know what happened?" the man asked.

"No," Larry said, unsure of the meaning of the question.

"You don't remember crashing your car?"

Now Larry understood. In an inspired instant he answered, "No."

He was whisked off to the hospital. It was a short trip, only a few blocks from his house. There an ER doctor peeled his eyelids back.

"What's seems to be the problem, partner," said a confident, over-loud voice.

Larry winced. "I don't know."

"You don't know? You can't remember?"

The light went away. Larry squeezed his eyes shut. "I guess I don't remember."

"You ran into a parked car. You don't remember that?"

"Maybe."

"Could you try opening your eyes again for me?"

"Sure." Larry opened his eyes to little slits in case the doctor was going to shine a light into them again. He focused carefully on a tan, chubby and good-natured appearing face.

"Any dizziness?" the doctor asked.

"Not now."

"How did you feel before the crash?"

"I don't remember." He had anticipated telling the lie while in transport, and now he savored it. Surprisingly there was no feeling of guilt, only of being unburdened. Larry closed his eyes again while study fingers probed his scalp for injury. It felt soothing.

He spent a good portion of the night going to and from radiology. Mostly waiting in the hallway outside, on a gurney. It was peaceful and he slept. He appreciated the bright lights and the clean walls and floors. The gurney's thin mattress was much more comfortable than the broken-down sofa.

Though the x-rays showed nothing out of the ordinary, "in that noggin of yours," said the cheerful doctor, he reluctantly admitted Larry for the night. In a room of his own, Larry was hooked up to a heart monitor. The room had a large window and a TV on the wall. He slept for ten hours, awoken only when the nurse opened the blinds to a brilliant, summer day.

After a brunch in bed, it was time for morning visitation. First were the store employees looking appropriately glum, but supportive. He was a good and fair boss. Then there was Emily. He didn't know how she would have heard about the accident; the pieces were probably swept up before she came home. Of course, it might not have been Emily's kitchen window after all. He was laughing quietly to himself over the thought when there she was in the doorway, wearing a familiar if complicated expression, and in her hand a small bouquet of daisies.

He felt strangely uplifted. Not just because he was glad to see her—he was delirious with the sight of her. But he had the thought that the next moment would provide the context for everything that had happened and everything that would happen for them both. And that, he understood in the same instant, was what was on Emily's mind as well. She hadn't just gone on without him when she left.

He sat up. Slowly she crossed the threshold of the room with the daisies held out, and before he could think to utter a word, he saw the smoke from out the window behind Emily. It was already a thick gray-yellow column rising up from some point very close by. Then he knew it was his house for no other reason than a sense of fit. His life had sharpened overnight into a series of portentous events that already had carried him far away from the ordinary. His distraction caused Emily to turn and look out the window.

"Oh, my God!" A hand clasped over her mouth. "It's your house Larry."

He lifted himself further. Yes. It was definitely his house on fire.

"Do you suppose anyone has called?" she said. "I don't hear sirens."

As if to answer her own concerns directly, a siren wailed from very close. He sank back onto the bed in relief. Emily's face appeared above him.

"I am so sorry, Larry." She was crying openly; tears sopped her cheeks. "All that work." She had laid her hands on him to comfort, placing the daisies on his chest.

He hadn't lifted a hand to the house since she'd left. He never would have again. It would be a mercy killing except he had a sudden fear the fire would be incomplete. He sat up again. No, it was all right. Bright orange flames darted from a dormer window. The roof was already a goner.

CHEATGRASS
Poetry by *David Cook*

It's late summer on the desert high
Hiking dusty trails with smoky sky,
Their nodded heads flowing as I pass
A raft of ever-present cheatgrass.
Will they shed their many seed
And the native grass impede?
Or will they nourish a wildfire?
Either way, the weed earns our ire.

AMIDST A PANDEMIC
Nonfiction by *Kathryn Mattingly*

My mom and I were very different people, and we certainly weren't as close as I think both of us would have liked, yet in some ways we were very bonded. I believe she knew that. It took her death, however, for me to fully understand that bond and everything that prevented it from being stronger. Fortunately, we had wonderful closure in a Starbucks parking lot over specialty lattes in paper cups. We'd sat there sipping our hot drinks just as COVID hit the states and social distancing was gearing up. It was the precipice of a new normal. Small businesses were rapidly closing and restaurants were widening spaces between tables. Carryout and drive-through windows were soon to be the saving grace of those who frequented chain food establishments. In my heart I knew the trip to Starbucks might be the last time I ever saw my mom, so I kept my promise to visit that day despite going against public opinion.

  She died of sudden heart valve failure on March 30. That was one week after our lattes in the parking lot. I knew she only had six to twelve months to live unless she could get the surgery she needed for a valve replacement, but unfortunately the hospital canceled her surgery date to accommodate the onslaught of pandemic patients. We hoped she could hang on until they resumed regular surgeries again, but that didn't happen.

  Something about those two hours sipping lattes had been magical. We didn't say anything profound, heart wrenching, or pivotal. It was bigger than words. It was a feeling. It was like she knew. And like I knew. Love and understanding was in the air. It settled peacefully between us in the front seat. When I dropped her back off at assisted living I gave Mom a big hug, despite employees monitoring the lobby to prevent hugs at a time when we needed them the most.

My mother's sudden loss was a game-changer in many ways, causing me to reflect upon my lifelong relationship with her, how it formed and shaped me in so many admirable ways, yet was a conundrum in other ways. I miss talking to her on the phone and I miss her unconditional love, which I somehow knew I had, even though words were not her strength. I think my biggest takeaway is to be sure and use my words to encourage and inspire my own children, to make it clear how proud I am of them. To let them know that they are loved.

I'd like to say I grieved her loss, but honestly, I didn't have time. The week she died I was quarantined with my 90-year-old father who was in the latter stages of Alzheimer's. It would take up to three days for his COVID test results to be returned. If the results were negative, I could place him in memory care. During those three days of quarantine in the assisted living apartment my dad was completely disoriented and confused, because the love of his life whom he'd spent 72 years with was suddenly gone. He asked me about Mom multiple times each day but never understood when I told her she had passed. At one point on the third day something in his eyes registered reality and he cried. Then almost as if it were a blessing, he forgot again.

This man had been my superhero.

He influenced my life more than any other person on earth.

His sweet, gentle spirit was always alive and well within him, despite not knowing who he was, where he was, or why he was there. When I checked him into memory care I knew he wasn't long for this world, especially considering he could have no visitors. Although he was in an excellent care facility, what did the man have to live for if not visits from his children and grandchildren? Of course, the Catch 22 is that, amidst a pandemic, such visits could also have caused his demise. If there had been any way possible to bring him home and care for him myself, I would have, but his needs were overwhelming at this point in his disease. I will say that in hindsight I wish I had brought him home anyway and hired people to care for him. It's a decision I can never change and will always regret. The one silver lining, in not being present when he passed, is that he passed on Easter Sunday. No one loved Jesus more than my dad, and so it seemed fitting.

Watching my father slowly decline in mind and body over a decade was agonizing. No one ever believed in me as much as he did, not even me. While sorting through wills, estates, and powers of attorney, I reflected upon the true meaning of life, which I have decided is love in the form of faith, family, and forgiveness—especially for ourselves.

I would like to say that losing my parents at the start and closure of COVID is the end of my story, but sandwiched in-between their deaths, my avid mountain-biking husband had a heart attack while on a remote trail.

And just like that, our lives were forever changed.

The paramedics took him out on a stretcher behind a quad. Four stents later we learned that he'd had a 90 percent blockage. The man was lucky to be alive. He called me after dialing 911. Couldn't breathe. Me or him! I called his cell phone every two minutes until the emergency crew arrived. When he was finally in the ambulance, I drove to our local hospital. They took my temperature before I could enter the building, and then asked me questions regarding possible virus symptoms. It was there I found out they had bypassed our small, local hospital for a larger, more efficient hospital in the next town over. When I arrived at the larger facility, they wouldn't let me out of the car at the emergency entrance. Someone wearing what looked like a spacesuit said I could wait in the parking lot and they would call me about my husband's condition. My view from the car was of temporary tents set up for COVID patients. Time went by very slowly waiting for that phone call.

I know I have had moments of taking him for granted, moments of frustration for having met and married so young, moments of angst from us being very different people, yet in all honesty, he completes me. Somebody once said you should find someone you love and then hold on tight because it's going to be a bumpy ride. I believe there is a lot of truth in that. I am grateful that our 50+ year ride has been smoother than not. We are no longer taking each day for granted.

On a happier note, the same day as my husband's heart attack, I found out that I would soon be a great grandmother. The call came through as I was racing to the hospital. I couldn't help but think about the circle of life and how my mother passed just as a new generation was forming. At this same time, I realized my own generation was suddenly vulnerable in so many new ways.

My husband and I can no longer think of ourselves as invincible or that we will live forever. Instead, we have updated our will. I can no longer pick up the phone and talk to my mom about everything and nothing, or just sit with my father and listen to Willie Nelson (his favorite artist). I have now held my first great grandchild in my arms. I have somehow transitioned from a carefree, slightly rebellious daughter to the matriarch of my family. In. One. Week. And during a global pandemic.

In truth, everything that happened within my family during COVID consumed me more than worrying about the virus itself. There are many blessings in all of this besides a new great grandson. The most immediate blessing that comes to mind is how our children had been there for us. Our oldest son gave wise and much needed counsel for decision-making regarding legalities of my parents' estate. Our oldest daughter stayed with me while being quarantined with my father (our children's grandfather) while our youngest son ran frequent errands for us. Our youngest daughter (laid off from her job because of COVID) chose to quarantine with her father and me at our home during this time of both the pandemic and personal crises.

All of these events brought our family closer together. There is nothing like a pandemic, losing loved ones, and a near escape from death to make you appreciate how precious and fleeting life is. What is clear to me now, if it hadn't been before, is that life is short and tomorrow is not guaranteed. The most practical advice I could share with others, after living through the most difficult time in my life, would be this: *Cling to your loved ones, because they will be your shelter in the storms of life.*

CARS: A LOVE STORY
Nonfiction by *Niki Rainwater*

Do you remember that song "Cars" by new wave rocker Gary Numan? It's stuck in my head as I sit in my father's Toyota Avalon, making short work of a bag of contraband cheese puffs, savoring each crunch.

When I was a kid, we lived next door to a big Irish Catholic family whose home was the hub of all the fun that transpired in our 1960's cul-de-sac. The Murphys had an equally big, red Chevy station wagon that held their whole crew, sans seatbelts, which were not mandatory at the time. The red wagon was, let's just say, "well-loved." The door handles were always sticky in a way I found oddly comforting, and one of the rear seats had a loose spring that sounded like farts when you sat on it.

The red wagon served the Murphys well and was miraculously litter-free, aside from the random parochial school sweater or swimming pool towel. Unlike my car, where just today I excavated a slice of mummified salami, six gum wrappers, a perpetually out-of-reach half full half crushed tissue box, and three mostly empty Hydro Flasks . Oh, and at least 17 cheese puffs lodged between the seats, and what may be a piece of Amelia Earhart's landing gear. My SUV serves as transportation, sure, but its chief function is year-round office on wheels, and it looks every bit the part.

What enchanted me most about the Murphy's red station wagon was that the Murphy children, all six of them and the dog, were allowed to *eat* in it. Like, actual food. My parents had one child and no pets, yet I was *never* allowed to eat in my father's 1963 rose beige Thunderbird. My mother did not drive and thus, I imagine, did not have much to say on the topic. The thumb-sized pill box of valium she kept in her purse gave her the acumen to pick and choose her battles. This was before "Women's Lib" empowered us to demand our say, burn our bras, and pull up a chair in the boardroom.

My father was no tyrant, but had grown up in a poor family where what few possessions you had you treasured like the crown jewels; a new car maybe even more so. When we would carefully climb in (notice, I did not say "pile in") to the T-bird and drive to Foster's Freeze for a frosty on warm summer nights, we stood on the sidewalk until we'd whittled our sugar cones down to the last lick. My mother always kept Wash'n Dri towelettes in her purse; no chance for sticky door handles here.

By the time I learned to drive during the tail end of the Ford administration, I was terrified by the size of my father's newest land yacht, a 1971 copper mist Buick Riviera that my friends and I dubbed "The Batmobile." My father washed this new car weekly, including the white wall tires, which he meticulously scrubbed with an SOS pad. He was, afterall, a career civil engineer, devout in all such endeavors.

I spent a good amount of my junior year in high school grounded for this or that minor infraction, the biggest of which was slipping in the front door after my 10:00 p.m. weekend curfew. Or maybe it was the fender bender I got into while my parents were at a Neil Diamond concert. It was during one such period of house arrest when, on my way home from church (one of three places I was allowed to drive; school and piano lessons being the other two), I made a brief stop at my boyfriend's house which was conveniently located on my dad-sanctioned route to and from home.

I bumped the curb while parking the Batmobile and immediately burst into tears when I saw the skinned, blackened white walls. The scrape would definitely be noticed by my father. Poor Tom ran into the house for an SOS pad. He knew my father as well as a boyfriend could and immediately went to work on the two smudged tires. His brother also came out to help, and then his sister. I applied the finishing touches and we all cheered at the brilliance of our work. When I drove into our garage not ten minutes later, my father was there to greet me, arms crossed, glaring alternately at me and his wrist watch, making note of the time.

Not only could he *smell* the fresh SOS fumes, he *saw* that the white walls were actually *cleaner* than when I'd left the house an hour earlier. That's where I'd gone wrong. Two more weeks were promptly added to my sentence. It wasn't about the tires so much as the fact that I didn't drive straight home after church. At least that's the story he stuck to through the years wherever he regaled, in jest, the errors of my youth, most often at the Christmas dinner table before an audience of extended family. By the time I was 20, I stopped going to church.

It's 2023 and I'm 64. My own children grew up on healthy, organic food. Of course there were also frosties, now called softserve, our shared biography of summer. We've enjoyed thousands of meals together, many of which were eaten in our Toyota Sienna van, just to spite my own childhood deprivation. My son and daughter ate in the van whenever it pleased them, without a word from me, until the day they each moved away to college where they no doubt ate in their own cars. I eat in my car too, mostly when it's stopped, sometimes when it's not. My father is now 90 and his driving is limited to a four-wheel rollator, where he shuffles around the house, transporting things from this room to that. There is a ring of melted plastic where he recently set a pot of mac and cheese, hot from the stove. He doesn't seem the least bit bothered by this. But then it's not an actual car.

My father loaned me his Avalon this week while my SUV is in the shop. In the twelve years he's had it I've never sat behind the wheel. "Be sure to keep it in the garage," he said, "and wipe it down with a soft towel if it gets wet." His cars have always lived in the garage.

Old age has softened him in certain areas of his life, to be sure. He bought me my dream car for my 60th birthday, on his actual birthday, when I had been thoroughly content with my 12 year old van. It was the sweetest of gestures and one I appreciate with every tree-ring layer of my life.

I'm sitting in front of my house in the Avalon now, amid the most glorious Central Oregon rainstorm. My garage is too loaded with box after box of memories for this beast to fit inside. It makes perfect sense that "Cars" is playing in my head just now. It's a catchy song, only slightly danceable, but very drummable on the steering wheel. Signature 80's all the way-heavy on the synths, paired with an intriguing use of the tambourine on percussion. It's the perfect soundtrack for a memoir of car adventures. A clap of thunder booms overhead. I remember that my mother's last purse in this life still housed Wash'n Dri packets, and that the Valium had long since been replaced by Rescue Remedy. She would laugh if she could see my fingers now, caked with sticky crumbs. I can feel the memory of her hands as we high-five on either side of the veil. My lap is covered in a dusting of powdered yellow fluff, and I've just dropped a cheese puff between the seats. I swear it was an accident.

I'm not picking it up.

WHAT I HUNGER FOR
Poetry by *Nadra Mlynarczyk*

What I hunger for is a renewed happiness, independence, strength and freedom.

To be who I want to be, when I want to, and how I want to live.

What I hunger for is to maintain the ability to be actively physical, with well-being in both mind and heart.

What I hunger for is to keep close a cherished group of "old" friends, while making new ones in time.

What I hunger for is to eventually be just as "beautiful" on the outside as I am on the inside.

What I hunger for is to learn how to become the best writer I can be using my past life experience and future endeavors with idolized mentors who have taken me under wing to reach my fullest literary potential, someday making it a new career.

What I hunger for is more "humor" and less sadness in the world.

What I hunger for is safer environments for current and future generations to thrive in this country, as well as around the world.

What I hunger for is that our young people (infant to high school) are safe in our schools, without endless fear to attend.

What I hunger for is climate change to stop 'disturbing' our worldly ecological environments so current and future generations may enjoy and experience the vast array of unique forests, rivers, oceans and grasslands.

What I hunger for is no more wildfires that diminish to ashes the normal everyday livelihoods of many.

What I hunger for is that life "opens up" post pandemic.

What I hunger for is that the front-line workers of the pandemic are receiving help now just as much as the rest of us were to keep us safe.

What I hunger for is medical cutting-edge technology continues to discover and locate ALL the "biomarkers" for rare and uncommon diseases that affect mass populations today.

MY SUMMER AT CAMP RILEY HORSE CAMP

Nonfiction by *Patti Lopez*

I had just separated from my husband and was walking down the aisle at my horse boarding stables. As I walked up to my purebred Arabian horse's stall, I noticed Muferrin was not there, and several flakes of uneaten hay lay on the floor. I searched the entire stable area. Muferrin was gone. My gelding was like my child. I broke, trained, and showed him. He meant everything to me. We even had the same birthday!

    I had a sickening thought: What if my husband had taken and hidden him? Worse, I confirmed that my husband had the horse but would not give him back to me unless I agreed to almost nothing in the property settlement. My lawyer wrote my husband a letter saying if anything happened to Muferrin, my husband would have to repay the cost of the show horse. My husband did state that Muferrin had gotten a little injured and also that he did not always remember to supply my horse with food and water. I was frantic and hardly slept.

    I put an ad in the local newspaper about my missing horse. A couple of weeks later, I got a call from a girl who said, "I board at Lakeview Stables, and I think your horse is here!" I called my sister, Kathleen, and together we traveled to my husband's storage area where the horse trailer was located, but the gate was locked. We lucked out and followed a vehicle into the storage lot. Then, we couldn't raise the trailer up high enough to attach it to the hitch on my vehicle. Kathleen used vice grips and WD40 to solve the problem and said, "Every woman needs a pair of vice grips and WD40."

We headed out to the stables, and boy was Muferrin glad to see me. He had some mild injuries on one leg. Apparently, my husband had put him in a barbed wire fenced pasture, and Muferrin had gotten caught in the wire. My horse had also lost some weight.

I loaded him in the trailer and drove several miles to a horse boarding facility that was extremely private and well protected. I thanked God for rescuing and keeping Muferrin safe. My husband removed all money from our bank accounts and did not feel I needed a dime to live on, even though we had both worked our landscaping business.

"Your mother can support you," he said. My mother was barely surviving on social security. I took my husband to court and won a judgment against him, but of course, he decided not to pay.

Fortunately, after how my husband dealt with me, I did not miss him or feel sad about the end of our eight-year marriage. But I needed someplace cheap for Muferrin and me to live. I had heard about horse camps in the national and state forests where they had corrals for horses within a camp spot for people, so I called the Mt. Hood National Forest Department. I was told that a horse camp called Camp Riley had no fees that summer because the water system was not working, but the area had two creeks for watering horses and a small town 15 minutes away for obtaining water for people. I visited the camp and thought it would be a wonderful way to spend the summer before getting a job and an apartment. From the camp, I could also see beautiful Mt. Hood and the Cascades. These mountains would become my true inspiration for the rest of my life.

I began getting ready for my summer in the forest while staying at Kathleen's apartment and bought a tent. I practiced setting up a tent in her living room. Next, I went to her ex-husband, Bill's house to learn how to use a fishing pole. I practiced casting the line in his front yard. Bill asked me what I was going to do about cooking food and light at night. I said, well, I'll just build a fire. Bill knew I'd had NO camping experience, so he told me to get a gasoline cook stove and a lantern. Thank God for his advice.

When I was ready to pack up Muferrin and move to the mountains, I found a good camping spot near the bathroom. There were no showers, however. Then I set up my tent. I had a bad neck from a fall off Muferrin, and the process put me in pain. That day the weather was good … until it started raining … and did so for practically the next six weeks!

At first, the camp was completely empty. I would get awfully scared late at night, alone in my tent, when a car would drive through camp. Muferrin and I rode along close trails and dirt roads, but I didn't go up in the mountains due to the snow still on the trails in early June. Also, I was a little nervous to be up in the high mountains by myself.

A couple weeks later, one person showed up at the campground, a single man in his fifties named John. I was in my late twenties. He had a camper but no horses. Because of the incredibly rainy late spring that year, that camper became very important to me. Also, it didn't help that I had bought a very small tent and could barely change my clothes in it. Big Mistake.

In mid-June, seven men with horses trailered into Camp Riley. I immediately ran over to them. They told me they were going to ride in the mountains, up Horseshoe Ridge, and I asked if I could join them. They said I could come along, so I quickly saddled up Muferrin. We had no sooner gotten on the trail than it started raining … hard. The guys wanted to continue, and I wanted to stay with them. It was also a cold day, especially as we travelled further up the mountain.

When we finally got on top of Horseshoe Ridge and tied up the horses, we couldn't see the amazing view through the clouds. The guys tried to pathetically start a fire in the rain to warm up. We were all freezing, and it was an hour-and-a-half ride back to Camp Riley. We mounted up. The plan was to ride a different trail back to camp called Cast Creek Trail. Well, we couldn't find the trail. We rode in circles in miserable weather. Eventually, someone broke out a flask of whiskey. The guys passed it around, and I helped myself to it as well.

One of the guys recognized the turnoff for Cast Creek Trail. This trail was named right because we rode in an old creek bed, almost straight down. Streams of rainwater made the route dangerous for both horse and rider. We found we could not ride our horses as our saddles were slipping onto the horses' necks because the trail was so steep. We got off and led them. At one point, a branch got caught in Muferrin's bridle, and one of the guys quickly removed it for me.

We got back to camp thoroughly soaked, but I'd gotten up into the mountains! Years later, I would tell people that I left part of my spirit in those mountains. I don't think I'll have it fully back until I return on a good Arabian horse.

John, the guy who let me share his camper, who had become my boyfriend, was in the process of getting divorced. He didn't have the income to rent an apartment while things got straightened out. He would tell me of his history over the past several years at Camp Riley when he owned horses. I heard about many of the great rides. We even discussed the idea of going to the largest cattle ranch in Oregon, located in Paisley, and applying for jobs herding cattle from summer to winter pastures and doing other work on the big ranch.

I was open to just about anything at this point in my life … having had my whole world turned upside down from losing a business, a home, and a marriage. We even fantasized about riding the whole Pacific Crest from Mexico to Canada, though a trip like that would cost thousands of dollars, require major prep, and two very "together" people, none of which we had or were.

It was kind of a magical summer once it stopped raining. Near the stream, there was a homeless lady living in a grove of trees with her two children. She even had living room furniture under some trees. I met new people all the time who were passing through, and I got to do more riding.

Sharon arrived on July 1 to be the camp host for the month. She was an old friend of John's, and she became my friend as well. She turned out to be a lot of fun. Sharon had both a husband and a boyfriend named Richard. She didn't ride much because her plate was full. Sharon's husband would come up on weekends because he worked during the week. On Sunday nights, he would pull out of the campground, and within minutes, Richard was there. Practically every night, we would all meet at Sharon's campsite and sit around the fire. I enjoyed hearing more exciting tales about rides out of Camp Riley.

After Sharon left at the end of July, John managed to re-injure his back by taking a fall. He stayed at his brother's home in Milwaukee, and I stayed with Sharon at her home. John and I had taken in a kitten, and the kitten stayed with me.

When John was on the mend, we decided to go over the mountain to Central Oregon where it almost never rains. Muferrin was stabled at Sharon's place, but the kitten stayed with us. We travelled over to a camping spot on the Deschutes River, near an Indian reservation. John suggested I use my fishing pole and try to catch a fish from the Deschutes River. Although I did not have a fishing license, nor experience fishing, I decided to try.

I almost immediately caught a rainbow trout. Almost as quickly, a Fish & Game officer, who had been watching me through binoculars from the hill above, presented me with a fishing violation ticket. The fine seemed high to me since I had almost no money. This was just the start of a bad camping experience.

The next night I told John, "Don't let the kitten out in the middle of the night when you get up for a smoke." The following morning our precious, vulnerable kitten was gone! As a devoted animal lover, I was very upset.

I questioned everyone at the campground, though it was 6:00 a.m. I then walked across to the store and was told that an Indian had taken the kitten and gotten on a bus to Madras. Though John was still recovering from his back injury, I told him we had to pack up the camper and head to Madras. "I just got out of a hospital," he yelled. "You are more concerned about that kitten than me!"

Despite John's frustration, we packed up and left the campsite to find our kitten. First, we hit a bar where, unfortunately, we found a lot of Indians at 7:00 a.m. One of them said, "Oh, I saw a guy in here with the kitten. I tried to buy him a martini." Then others chimed in. Everyone was having fun with me.

Then I got the bright idea to go to the local police station. I reported the theft to the sheriff who asked me for basic details like how much the cat was worth. Then he asked me who I was travelling with. When I didn't know John's last name, he seemed disturbed and said, "You don't know the last name of the person you are travelling with?"

I had nothing to say …

We drove to Warm Springs, to the reservation police station. I had a name for the man we believed took the kitten, and I also got John's last name! The reservation police were nice, but they informed me that unless I was reporting a serious crime, I had no right to file a complaint against the Indian since the reservation was a separate entity from the United States. I was assured that Indians truly valued life, and the kitten would probably be well taken care of.

John and I decided to be hosts at Camp Riley for the month of August. I did some riding but not as much as in July. I was starting to think about what I would do next. I had no interest in living with a much older and disabled man in his camper for the rest of my life. I knew it was time for me to find a place to live, get a job, and start supporting Muferrin and myself. I wanted to build a new life as a smart, resourceful, independent single woman.

Muferrin and I moved on, but I will never forget the challenging, exciting and humorous adventures that summer at Camp Riley. Muferrin lived 32 years and was buried on my ranch in Central Oregon. Now I ride Muferrin's grandnephew, Domino. Over the decades, I have been blessed to own several of my beloved Muferrin's close relatives. Part of my spirit remains in those mountains. Someday I'll unite my spirit riding up in those mountains again, on a good Arabian horse.

SHIRLEY

Nonfiction by *Bob Sizoo*

I slid my auto shop textbook and slim notebook higher up under my arm, you know, like some prep school rich kid holds his books.

Shirley stood in the outdoor corridor leaning against the steel post, arms crossed beneath her breasts, her left foot bobbing slowly, pivoting on her right ankle. As I neared her, she uncrossed her ankles.

The roar of her panty hose-clad legs sliding against one another startled me. "Hi again, Shirley."

"Oh, hi Bob. How was your day?"

"As usual, my daily journey through the hallowed halls of learning rewarded me with vast knowledge." I wished I had a borrowed a physics book or copy of Jane Austin on top of my dramatic saga of the internal combustion engine. But I'd have to settle for being a wiseacre, as Mr. Stanford, my wood shop teacher, used to call everyone, knowing the "nickname" he was really thinking would get him fired in 1966. I intuitively knew that one could be smart and not have a sense of humor, but one could not be both dim-witted and clever. And it was better to present oneself as an intelligent slacker than as a dullard working up to his potential. "How about you, how was your day?"

"Oh, about the same. If I were any more illuminated, you'd have to wear shades." Shirley looked down at the gigantic stack of textbooks at her feet. "And I look forward to my exciting date this evening in the company of these handsome textbooks."

Until March of my junior year in high school, I suspected that I probably wouldn't ever go out with girls. Not that I didn't want to—girls appeared fun and soft, and, of course, mysterious, but they all seemed to prefer guys with fast cars, athletic prowess, and good grades. My dad's family station wagon, my basketball team dropout status, and my apathy and alienation-induced 2.3 GPA rendered me ineligible on all counts. It seemed the only thing that could make these requirements unnecessary was a pocket full of folding money, and the dollar-a-week allowance I received failed to impress even the most desperate gold digger.

Then I met Shirley. She was blonde, attractive, smart, lived on the beach in a big house with a pool—everything a teen in a surfing and money-obsessed subculture would value, a girl for whom an unmotivated son of a cop would be patently ineligible. We began talking almost daily in the breezeway outside my auto-shop class; she waited there for her friend Judy to come from the other side of campus, and I pretended to need to be at that spot as well.

Glancing down at her books, I said, "You're here every day at this time. I know you're a college prep major; don't you have a sixth period class?"

"I took a year of algebra in junior high, so this year I have a free sixth. How about you?"

"The industrial arts major isn't quite as demanding as the college prep ones. They like to get us off campus as soon as possible." Judy walked up and greeted us. I picked up Shirley's books. "Here, I'll give you a hand with those books. I'm going out to parking lot, too."

After a couple of weeks, I found the courage to ask Shirley to the Teenage Fair at the Hollywood Palladium. Bill Peterson had just got his license, and we doubled. I don't remember anything about the no-doubt excessively commercial exhibits and displays, but I do remember her soft, cool hand in my hot clammy grasp. We kissed in the back seat on the way home, and she did some things with her tongue and my ear that I hadn't anticipated but found surprisingly pleasant.

By late April, we were "going together." I had given her my St. Christopher, a totem I had worn more in the rebellious spirit of a tattoo than one of religious faith. I had my own driver's license, and soon had a car—the era of double dates was all but over. She lived with her wealthy divorced mom who drank vodka straight in 12-ounce tumblers, and called it quits by nine o'clock, leaving us to our adolescent explorations on the deep pile carpet of the living room. I was set for a summer of ecstasy, knowing my parents weren't serious about taking me on the family summer vacation.

They were.

This was not just a weekend in Yosemite. My parents had planned a seven-week driving trip around the US. This was the year it had to happen, because my sisters were "old enough to remember it," and I was, at sixteen, for reasons I still don't understand, still an appropriate travel companion.

I begged to stay home, promising to keep the lawn mowed, the dog fed, and the house clean. Hell, I'd *paint* the house if they'd go without me. One gloomy July morning, we piled into the powder blue '59 Plymouth wagon, Dad's homemade plywood cartop carrier bolted to the roof, and headed across country to collect new decals for the rear side windows.

I had purchased a pile of new books for the trip. My plan was to refuse to look out the window of the car for seven weeks. I read three books in the first 2 days. Somewhere around the New Mexico/Texas border, I had a short conversation with my mom. "We didn't bring you all this way to keep your nose in a book all day," she complained.

"I told you I wanted to stay home," I cleverly retorted. Rolling my eyes, I went back to my reading.

Shirley had given me a ten-inch, pink, stuffed troll to remind me of her, as if I needed something to bring her to mind. For the first five weeks, I slept with it every night, hoping to embarrass my macho dad by walking into his FBI-Inspector brother's house in Arlington, clutching a fuzzy-haired toy, or at least raising the eyebrows of motel managers across the country. I always cradled a pink troll in one arm and carried my suitcase with the other.

When we arrived at the Washington Monument on a muggy day in August, my family got in the line snaking around the base, waiting to ride the elevator to the top. "I'm walking up," I told them, and challenged myself to take the stairs two at a time without stopping. I broke a sweat on about step number ten and arrived at the top just ahead of my family. I stood in front of the elevator door in saturated clothing, a small puddle forming at my feet. "I made it," I told them as they exited the elevator, greeting me with slight smiles.

In Savannah, Georgia, my parents and sisters toured the Juliet Lowe house, one of the few activities I wasn't forced to endure. Even my parents could fathom that a sixteen-year-old boy wouldn't benefit by a trip inside the house once populated by the founder of the Girl Scouts. I sat in the car and read. I cracked the window to provide enough oxygen to keep me alive and conscious, preparing a stale sauna for the rest of the family upon their return. Without air conditioning, the car interior never really cooled off until that evening.

At the 5-week mark of this miserable journey, I left "Shirley," as my family had come to call the troll, in a motel in Florida. I didn't realize she was gone until we were nearly to the Alabama state line. My guilt from not missing her was doubled by my realization that we were not about to backtrack three hours to pick up a stuffed troll.

As a testament to her sensitivity and unconditional love, my mom felt sorry for me in a situation where most people would be filled with smug satisfaction that fate had finally intervened and delivered to me the vengeful blow I deserved. She retrieved from the glove compartment a stamp and postcard from the Juliet Lowe house (her one little jab) and looked in the AAA Florida guide for the mailing address of the motel that now housed Shirley. Holding a pencil like an icepick, I wrote to the motel in large printing including malformed and backward letters addressed to "Motel Man" asking him to return my stuffed animal. For legibility's sake and to fit the postcard, I had my mom write our home address on the card. I signed it Bobdy. I believe the manager probably saw me walk in with that troll, and, after receiving my card, said a little prayer for my parents each evening for weeks thereafter, regretting his initial judgment of me.

The early evening, we arrived home, Shirley, the troll, waited on our dining room table along with seven weeks of mail gathered by the next-door neighbor. To my relief, Shirley, the girl, also waited for me outside our house in her car and met our family as we wheeled that big-finned Plymouth into the driveway after the Bataan Death Drive. I hopped out of the mobile family prison, ran my suitcase to my room, and flew back outside. Shirley and I drove straight to her house.

"Hi Mom," Shirley sang as we walked in the front door.

"Hello, Mrs. B," I called. We received no answer. Shirley's mom was already asleep and the empty vodka bottle on the kitchen counter assured us her sleep would be a sound one. We headed for the living room.

SILENT MOVIE
Poetry by *Pamela Mitchell*

I watch his screen in row ahead
Passenger absorbed in the drama

Movie begins: 2 kids on a playground
One falls   wounded leg

Mother rushes   band aids minor cut

     Something within me says there will be violence
     There will be a gun

Next scene: family at dinner table
Father argues with child

Next scene: father   pulls out   assault   rifle
Rushes out   to his car   there are police   flashing   lights

Next scene: Cuba   mother   flown to airport   injured
Mother   taken away   children crying   yelling   at father

Next scene: child has a gun   pointing at father

     November 19, 2021   a child carries assault weapon   illegally
     A child   kills 2 men   a child is acquitted of murder

Next scene: Morocco   sexy woman   beating another woman
Knives   guns   punching   choking

    Women embrace seductive system   system assaults women
    Deceit of the blind

    Friend shares photo in local paper:
    Women with guns   all walks of life   here   our community

    My daughter gifts me perfume   she sprays me: *Lovely!*
    I glance at bottle   its name: "Juliet Carries a Gun"

A PLACE CALLED NORMAL
Fiction by *Neal Lulofs*

Marcia almost collided with the girl. It was the first week of her freshman year of high school and she had pulled a thick book from her locker. When she turned, she was inches from Donna, her new neighbor. The one whose mother had a habit of tying her young son to a tree every time he wet his bed, which was often. In 1965 in Normal, Illinois, people like Donna's mother tended to think of abuse as a synonym for parenting.

Donna hugged a bright-orange school folder to her chest. She had on a plain sleeveless cotton dress with a skinny vinyl belt tied around the waist in a droopy bow. "Hey, neighbor," she said.

There was something about her that Marcia connected with—the defiant look behind her droopy eyes, being part of a peculiar family. They were going to be friends, she concluded. "Did you borrow that rope from your mother?" She motioned to her belt.

At first Donna wasn't sure how to take the comment. She decided it was funny. "Right out of the fucking gate with that? Okay then." She lifted one of the belt's ends that hung in front. "This is from her indoor rope collection. Soon to be a Normal fashion trend."

"Nice."

The bell began to ring. "Shitballs, do you know where you're going?"

"Biology." Marcia pointed to her book cover. "The study of living organisms."

"That excludes half the people here." Donna turned and disappeared into a sea of bodies crisscrossing the hall.

***

Lunch tray in hand, Marcia scanned the cafeteria for a place to sit, finding a spot on the end of a table where Donna was sitting with a group of freshmen girls who were gathered together for protection like a herd of exposed deer in a barren Illinois corn field.

"What's with the boys and all the long hair?" one asked.

"Yum. Fine with me," said another.

"Not the football jocks," Donna said. "Did you notice? Look at them." She nodded her head to the side in the direction of a table filled with players. "Hair shorter than a priest's favorite altar boy."

"I can't believe we're not allowed to wear pants," another said. "We're not at Epiphany anymore. What bullshit."

"My epiphany is I won't ever use algebra in real life," said another.

"They make them have short hair above the ears. And wear ties to games or something."

"It's so the old male teachers can stare at our legs. Pervs."

Could these girls be the same age as Marcia? Some, with their braces showing, rail-thin arms and underdeveloped breasts, looked like children. She felt older than all of them. She'd felt that way a long time, really. It's not that she didn't like to talk about boys or music or hair or clothes. She just felt different from most girls, like she was in between two things—one in the past, the other yet to happen. Maybe it was simply because she wasn't from this place. Maybe she'd be a different person if she still lived in the Netherlands, living a different life, moving toward a different future, as if there could be two versions of Marcia, the same person but not the same life.

She looked at her plate: fish fingers, baked beans, instant potatoes, a roll, a patty of butter covered by a tiny square of waxed paper.

"Fresh caught from the Illinois River," Donna said to her.

"It's like they're all trying to look like The Beach Boys or something. Not the football team, the normal boys."

"Is that the one with Herman Hermits? Yum."

"That's a band—the wrong band—not a person. And please stop saying yum."

"It's actually not bad," Marcia said. "The fish, I mean."

"Oh, you thought that was fish?" Donna said. "Where are you from again?"

A short-haired football player suddenly stopped in front of them carrying his lunch tray, the team at the table beside him watching and snickering. "Would any of you attractive freshmen ladies care for a finger?" He waited a beat, then angled his plate to reveal a lone remaining stick of breaded fish, remnants of baked beans and instant potatoes anchoring it in place.

"No," Donna said, "but you can have *my* finger." She raised her forearm, elbow on the table, and flipped him off.

"Touché," the boy said, half-smiling at her. He tilted his plate perpendicular. The fish finger slid down in slow motion, landing with a splat on the table between Marcia and Donna.

"Oh, my god," Marcia said after he left.

"That's Brian Aronson," Donna told her. "Junior. My brother is on the team. His dad's the coach. You just met the douchebag quarterback."

***

A few weeks later Donna talked Marcia into attending a Friday night varsity football game in Peoria. The school would be bussing students to the game. "We can watch my brother sit on the bench," she had told her.

On game day, to pass time before the busses left, they walked into town, cutting across the Illinois State University campus, which had dropped "Normal" from its name the previous year—*no longer normal* the joke went. Music blared from a dorm room window, the girls singing along, *We've got to get out of this place if it's the last thing we ever do.* They pretended to blend in with the college students, cutting back and forth across the quad as if late for class, trees ablaze with yellow and orange leaves of fall, Donna ogling a group of boys—men?—flinging a frisbee around, Marcia imagining she was on her way to attend a lecture on something like abnormal psychology or ancient history. She wanted to be the first in her family to attend college, but she doubted her father would see any point to it. Though she only lived a few miles from campus, it felt as far away as the moon—something she could see every day but couldn't possibly reach.

Downtown, they approached the local Walgreen drugstore, the city's self-aware motto painted on the building's exterior brick wall: *Normal, Illinois, Where Everything is Just as It Seems.* Inside, the store had an airless smell, with narrow, packed aisles, and a flickering fluorescent ceiling light above the checkout. There was a small section in back where a lone male pharmacist worked. Dressed in a dark tie and white coat, he glanced at Marcia and Donna without expression. The other side of the store featured a large counter area with wall-mounted mirrors spanning its length, backless swivel stools bolted to the floor, frayed strips of duct tape splayed across cracked vinyl seat covers, a still-in-use soda fountain front and center. The girls sat down and ordered cherry colas from a gray-haired woman who wore glasses attached to a chain around her neck. They watched her pump syrup into two Coca-Cola-branded glasses, add carbonated water from the fountain, scoops of chipped ice, straws.

Next, they browsed magazines. Mick Jagger was on the cover of *Tiger Beat*, which exclaimed "OH BABY!" and "SO GROOVY!" on either side of his boyish face, the lower corner declaring that The Byrds were America's answer to The Beatles and The Rolling Stones and Herman's Hermits and The Hollies and The Kinks and The Animals.

"I'll take The Beatles over everyone," Marcia said.

Donna looked at the article Marcia held up for her to see. "George has a crooked smile."

"Don't laugh. My dad doesn't want me listening to their music. Or any rock and roll, for that matter. Says it's all screaming. *When you have your own car, then you can choose the radio station,*" she said, exaggerating her father's deep voice and Dutch accent. "Makes for some boring car rides."

"Your dad's a little weird."

"Your mom's not exactly June Cleaver."

"No," Donna agreed. "We're more like the fucking Addams Family." She found a magazine with a male bodybuilder flexing on the cover, muscles oiled to a shine, his tiny, dark bikini trunks bulging. She pointed to his groin, touching it with her finger. "Have you ever seen one?"

Marcia's face went red.

"I've seen pictures," Donna said. "This one time I answered the phone in my parent's bedroom and had to take a message, so I opened the nightstand drawer and there was this magazine with a naked couple on it and the guy had this huge, you know, and the woman had her hand around it and the guy was like oh yeah. It was hilarious."

Marcia took a breath. "Okay, promise you won't tell anyone? This is so creepy. A couple of months ago I was walking out of the bathroom and my dad was just standing in his bedroom with his pants open, like he was waiting for me to walk by or something. He said now that I was starting high school, he wanted me to see one so I'd know what to expect."

"Jesus Christ. That's the grossest thing I've ever heard. I thought *my* family was nuts. Let's get out of here before I puke."

They put the magazines back and began walking toward the door. Donna stopped suddenly and snatched two pieces of Bazooka bubble gum from a shelf loaded with assorted candy, gum, and chocolates, wrapping her fist around the plunder. "Take some," she whispered.

Marcia's eyes widened. "I thought thou shalt not steal."

"I'm not in Catholic school anymore."

Marcia snatched a single piece and quickly followed Donna to the door.

"We're all going to hell," Donna yelled loudly, the bell above the door announcing their escape.

***

Arriving in Peoria, the Normal students departed the busses and walked en masse to the stadium. Donna pulled on Marcia's coat sleeve and asked her to come with her to the bathroom first. She led her behind the concession stand and toward a remote, dark area of the Peoria campus where there was a clump of tall trees.

"Are we peeing in the woods or something?" Marcia said.

"Better." Ducking behind a tree, Donna pulled out a crudely rolled joint, curved slightly from being in her coat pocket all day. "Have you ever tried it?" she asked, holding it inches from Marcia's face, slowly waving it back and forth.

"Is that pot? No. Where did you get it? What if someone catches us?"

"Stole this from my brother's stash."

"Football players don't smoke dope."

Donna shrugged. "I guess they do if they don't start. Or maybe they don't start because they do. Either way, are you up for it?"

"What will happen to me?"

"Your boobs will double in size and your poop will smell like flowers. What do you mean? You'll get high, laugh, want to eat an entire pizza." Donna lit the joint, inhaled, then held it out for Marcia. "Just inhale a little and hold it in. You might not even feel anything after smoking your first time."

"First petty larceny. Now illegal drug use. I'm beginning to think you're a bad influence." Marcia inhaled and immediately spun around, her lungs erupting, smoke stinging her eyes. After finding her breath, she said, "God, that's awful." She dabbed at her watery eyes with her coat sleeve, then took another hit, a seed popping with a crack as she handed it back to Donna.

"Didn't your parents teach you about *reefer madness*? We're going to turn into zombies before the night is over."

They made their way to the stands. Marcia couldn't really tell if she felt different, but she did feel buoyant sitting amidst a crowd of her classmates who were yelling and cheering, lights illuminating the stands and field, the edges of her ears growing cold in the fall air. Thanks to a second-half injury and contrary to what Donna had predicted, her brother not only played but intercepted a pass and was involved in several tackles, each time after which she would stand and scream her brother's name loudly—too loudly, considering Normal was on its way to a 21-point loss—swollen eyes, stoner grin. It was Marcia's first American football game and she made the most of it, participating in cheers, eating a hot dog and Cracker Jack, drinking watery hot chocolate. She was glad she and Donna were becoming friends—stuffing notes into each other's lockers, gossiping about peers and teachers, arguing about who had worse parents.

After the game, they stopped at the bathroom inside the school, a group of boys pushing one of their friends into the girls' bathroom, apparently hoping to see … nudity? Girls making out? What he got was Marcia washing her hands, Donna telling him to fuck off. They made their way to the parking lot where four busses were waiting side by side, three for the students who had made the trip and one to transport the football team, coaches, and cheerleaders, all with lights on, engines running. Donna and Marcia took a seat halfway back on their assigned bus, their chaperone, math teacher Mr. Alm, counting the passengers twice, then announcing to the driver "All present and accounted for," the convoy beginning the near hour return ride to Normal a few minutes later.

Less than halfway home, the busses pulled to side of the road. Mr. Alm conferred with the driver and stepped outside, making his way to the front bus carrying the team, returning several minutes later. "Listen up," he announced. "The team bus has broken down—"

"Just like the game!" a boy in the back yelled.

"—so each bus will have some new company. Make room, people."

A few coaches, including the head coach, some cheerleaders in short skirts and bulky jackets, and a couple dozen players lugging equipment bags piled onto the dark bus, headlights from the bus behind Marcia casting a spotlight on each new passenger, the jokey boy in the back introducing each like a stadium announcer.

"Well, if it isn't the pretty freshman girls I shared my lunch with," Brian Aronson said. "Slide over, will you?"

Marcia, seated on the aisle, hesitated, then nudged Donna to move closer to the window.

"How's that finger doing?" he said to Donna.

"Fine. See?" She flipped him off—again.

"You're a spunky one, aren't you?" Coat in his hands, he slid his bag under the seat in front. "Aren't you Schneider's little sister? He actually played tonight."

"I was there," Donna said. The bus heaved forward as the convoy got underway again.

He sat back. "Played better than me tonight," he admitted.

His body pressed against Marcia, their thighs, arms, shoulders synchronized with the movements of the bus. She could have slid closer to Donna, who was soon asleep, crashing from her high, head leaning against the window, but decided not to. She watched the bus driver wrestle with the oversize wheel, shift gears with a lurch and grind, the head coach and Mr. Alm chatting in the seat behind him, red taillights of traffic dispersed on the highway in front of them. The bus yawed back and forth, its seats rattling and squeaking above the engine's drone and occupant's muffled conversations. Occasional bumps in the road would lift everyone in unison, dangling them an inch or two above their padded seats, briefly suspended in time, before the laws of gravity and motion took hold and returned the world to its previous order.

Brian pulled his coat over his lap and arms like a blanket, closing his eyes as if intending to sleep. But Marcia felt his hand drop to his side and rest against her thigh. Then his fingers found her hand, placing it on top of hers. Her heart quickened. He curled his fingers over the backs of hers and gradually moved their joined hands to the top of his thigh, his other hand now also clasping hers. Then, shifting in his seat, he pulled her hand toward him, the side of her hand against his groin before she realized it. She tried pulling it away, but he held on, his grip firmer, his coat falling off his arms and below his lap. She was still for a moment, feeling like she was suspended over the seat again, momentarily between two worlds, observing this other Marcia. There was also this: She thought he had unzipped his pants and was now exposing himself, in the dark mistaking their clump of hands for his penis. With a surge of adrenalin, she wrenched her hand free, momentum carrying it across her body, whacking sleeping Donna on the forehead, then, boomerang-like, she swung her arm and smashed her fist into his crotch with all her will.

Donna and Brian let out terse groans in near unison.

"What was that for?" Donna said, bolting awake. "Are we in Normal?"

Brian slumped forward and pressed his forehead against the metal seat in front of him. "God damn." His voice was muffled by the seat back, his coat now balled up and pressed into the wounded region.

Marcia hooked her arm inside of Donna's, inching closer to her. "Not yet. Go back to sleep."

Despite the dark sky, she began to recognize some landmarks that signaled they were approaching Normal—the farm with its silo painted to look like an ear of corn, the under-construction interstate highway that would connect the city to Champaign, Indianapolis, Cincinnati, and a world beyond, the cluster of ISU dorms on the edge of campus, her world coming into focus. It was the first time she had the sense that she would leave one day, and that Donna wouldn't.

She shook Donna, whose arm she still grasped. "Almost home," she told her as the caravan carved its way through town, passing the city's motto painted on the side of the Walgreen's proclaiming that everything was just as it seemed.

MY MOTHER'S HANDS
Nonfiction by *Kore Koubourlis*

Clutch

I remember watching my mother's hands grip the wheel of our '73 Thunderbird. From my perch in the backseat, her hands were a focal point. I witnessed hundreds, probably thousands, of times as she methodically lifted each finger and then placed it back down on the wheel, firmly thrumming: *one, two, three, four*. A near-soundless dirge, drive after drive, as she ferried us to community art classes, the corner grocer, the County for free vaccinations.

For me, this pulsing practice of hers was connected to other phenomena I observed while watching my mother. Like, for instance, how her eyes rolled all the way back in her head when she yelled at us. Or like how she was in the backyard carrying the galvanized steel watering can and she fainted, and the ambulance came, and I was alone with her when it happened, and I was alone without her when they took her away.

I catalogue the birds of my childhood on the Palouse: sparrows, magpies, pheasant, and quail. I catalogue the birds of my adult life in the forests of the Pacific Northwest: owl, eagle, crow, and Steller's jay. I collect bird facts as if I were preparing to make a study: a group of eggs in a nest is called a clutch; migratory birds often lay just one clutch per season; human contact with a nestling need not necessarily cause the mother to abandon it. Not as a matter of biological fact.

My mother's hands are well-formed. A smooth, prettily shaped nail caps each finger. A parking lot fall one snowy January left her pinky finger crooked, bent upward at the knuckle.

To this day, I have never held my mother's hands.

Transmission

Researchers from the University of Cambridge recently discovered pre-natal communication in birds. They learned the mother bird communicates with her unborn chicks, transmitting important messages about life and the world they are about to meet, about availability of food, about survivability, about what are the chances.

Beacon-like, these maternal messages signal scarcity, or plenty, to the eggs waiting snugly in the nest. Birds' nests are made of foil, human hair, fur, twigs, lichens, feathers, string, discarded paper, a soiled gum wrapper.

Do we ever truly leave the nest?

Durability

Earlier this year, my mother introduced touch into our relationship. When she did, it threw me. I didn't know what to do with my arms.

Birds and mammals collect information from the surrounding world. They do this using the senses. This is how we live, and this is how we survive. Touch is a sense. Time has been called a sense.

My mother's sorrows marked my life with the heaviness of rock tied around belly. I learned from my mother how to wait and how to bear disappointment. I learned from my mother how enemies are made, and how they are kept. What I want to learn from my mother is, what nurtures rage that is passed with such awful durability outside of time from mother to daughter the same way birds regurgitate food for their offspring.

What I want to learn is how much time will it take?

Wings

One year, I quit my job and spent a great deal of time at my desk in a basement room looking out on the downward-sloping wooded ravine outside my window. This brought me to ground level and it brought me to my knees. I think maybe it'll be okay. I think maybe I'll be okay.

Did you know that birds spend more time plucking around in the dead leaves and the dust than they do in flight?

I remind myself: even poultry had wings at one time. And flew.

Taking Flight

At the end of a visit the year my mother turned 75, we shared our morning coffee on the deck that looked out over the woods behind the house. I noticed my mother's fragility then—and more and more with each visit—though her hands were the same. Through the dense forest foliage, the large wing of an adult barred owl flashed into sight. The owl, keeper of secrets, lit on a scrag about forty feet from us. Smaller birds circled, dove, and poked at the owl, protecting a nearby nest filled with the seeds of the new generation waiting to be born. The owl winged away, disappearing into the dense green.

We think of birds. We take flight. We travel far from here.

HOW TO HAVE EVERYTHING
Fiction by *Anastasia Lugo Mendez*

Jenna's iPod was prophetic. Set to shuffle, it started to play Beyonce's "Single Ladies" as soon as she plugged in her headphones. She wouldn't have thought much of the song, but a picture of her and Spencer smiled at her from the console in the foyer as she left the house. Next to the picture was a silver tureen that held only dust, and bookends pressed tightly together as if to forget the absence of their books. She turned the picture frame so that the happy couple faced the ugly mustard wall she'd asked Spencer to paint over several times in the past. He said it was Spanish Olive, not mustard, and that the color had won an award from the American Society of Interior Designers.

At the end of her driveway, Jenna bent down to re-tie her laces, tightening them down on her broken-in shoes. She glanced up and down the quiet street, lit by early summer sun, her neighbors still asleep, their coffee makers beginning to kick on. Some days Jenna turned left; others she turned right. Whichever she picked she would find her way to the main avenue leading through town. Today felt like a *left* day. She took a few minutes to warm up, jogging slowly to the avenue, passing a multitude of similar, but not identical, million-dollar suburban homes. Most of the yards were well-manicured, with box-shaped shrubbery lining the sidewalks and bordering the large picture windows. A few prefab homes from the '60s stood steadfast, clapboard wonders that had withstood the test of time, unsold and unchanged. Spencer hated them, calling them tacky and cheap, but he hated anything that brought down property values.

"Have you seen what Douglas did to his front yard? The willow is gone. People love willow trees. Now everyone can see that shitty woodshed that he's never re-painted. I mean, did he even stop to think what that would mean for us?"

Jenna waved at one of her neighbors who stepped out of the house in a bathrobe to pick up the morning paper. Did they care about the shrubs, and the sheds? Probably.

She picked up the pace.

Spencer's tirades popped up over dinner, before dinner, after dinner as she loaded the dishwasher and he finished another glass of Scotch. Their time together was bookended by his odes to well-groomed hedges and fresh coats of paint.

Common decency, he called it. She called it meddling and suburban fascism. When she said this out loud, he had glared at her and stormed out of the room.

When he returned in time for the beginning of Monday Night Football he just said, "This is our bread-and-butter, Jenna." Then he turned on the flat screen TV he had insisted upon and sat on the leather sofa he had insisted upon. The stack of For Sale signs with his bleached smile and photoshopped hairline gave her a thumbs up from the other side of the living room. People had given up trying to sell their homes. People had given up on calling Spencer. He had talked all his clients into expensive additions and renovations that were supposed to drive up home prices.

Then the market crashed.

Jenna had sat in her upstairs study staring at their backyard—the gazebo bordered by a real koi pond, the path leading to a hot tub under a willow tree. She didn't even like the koi fish, or the study. She didn't need it, driving 35 minutes to the city every morning. What she wanted in her backyard was a sandbox or an inflatable pool, not a *fountain*.

She stopped listening to Spencer so much from then on.

That was also around the time that she'd cancelled her gym membership and started running. At first she could only manage ten minutes without wanting to stop, then fifteen, then a magnificent thirty. It wasn't so much about the physical exertion—it was that running was boring. At least until she started daydreaming.

She ran past the few unkempt lawns in her neighborhood and saw the trigger that had set her off months ago: a toddler's three-wheeled bicycle and its hollow, plastic parts in their primary colors. Another house had a set of plastic buckets and shovels in red and yellow. At the next one there was a swing set/slide combo that was blue and yellow, with a slide in bright, McDonald's red. This was the only kind of mess that was allowed in Crescent Knoll.

Because she had to imagine to keep running, Jenna pictured her life as a Crescent Knoll mother. Maybe she was tired of being a career woman, of showing up to work every day in shoes that hurt and blazers that itched. Maybe she could imagine a change to her days of invoices and budget reports. She wanted to be a tired mom in mismatched sweatpants covered in stains, wearing the same flat tennis shoes as nurses and elementary school teachers. Spencer would come home from work, take a look at the mess in the house, Jenna's dirty hair caught in a loose braid over one shoulder. "You look beautiful," he'd say, and pull her into his arms.

With time, the daydreams grew. She ran for ages, dreaming of writing the self-help book for working women that Oprah herself would page through and exclaim, "So that's how you can have it all." Jenna ran and thought about press conferences and morning show appearances, bookstore readings and, of course, the inevitable screenplay for *How to Have Everything*, a story about a beautiful, successful young woman who just can't seem to find love or be taken seriously at her job: but then she does! And then she is! It would be a box office hit and as the opening credits rolled on screen, she would see it there in the bottom left corner: *Based on the bestselling book* How to Have Everything *by Jenna Newman*. Never mind that movies didn't start like that. When she was running they did. The colorful book cover would stare at her from imaginary bookstore displays, stacked in pyramids shouting that she, Jenna Newman, had it all. Love. Children.

At Christmas, when they went to see Spencer's family, his two brothers and one sister brought their brood. "The army of Newmans," her mother-in-law joked, then glanced at Jenna's stomach with a less than subtle implication. Last year, she'd just come out and said it. "You're 33, aren't you? You don't have forever."

Spencer didn't get any comments, and he didn't even want children yet. Maybe not at all. Maybe not ever. On the early runs, she tried to remember if they had talked it over while they dated, or since they'd been married. They must have talked about it. She wouldn't have *assumed*.

Jenna turned onto the sidewalk of the main avenue and started jogging against traffic, sliding her eyes away from the blank faces of the 6 a.m. drivers beginning to crowd their way toward the city. Her music, all Top 40 hits suggested by her young assistant, drowned out the traffic, with singers calling for everyone to put their hands up, or get out on the dance floor, live like there's no tomorrow.

Jenna slipped back into her daydream. The economy saw a miraculous surge and people who had previously been shy about purchasing a new home all rushed into Spencer's office at once. "We want homes! We want them big! We want them now!" they chanted. Money poured into the house, and one night when Jenna came home Spencer was waiting for her.

"I'm ready, honey," he said. "Let's have kids." Jenna flung her arms around him; they made love in a way they hadn't in a very long time.

Jenna had named them already, her two girls. The first was Alana. She would be smart and sarcastic and a giant pain in the ass, in the way that smart, confident girls always were. The younger one, Sophia, would be funny and brave—a complete tomboy who would drive her older sister crazy. Jenna was going to fry them pancakes in funny shapes and make their Halloween costumes by hand. She knew the colors she would paint their bedrooms (neither would be Spanish Olive). She knew how she was going to explain sex and God and politics and why girls were mean to each other and why boys seemed so stupid. She was going to watch them fall in love and be heartbroken, and she was going to watch them get married and have their own kids.

Jenna was winded. She had a stitch in her side and stopped running at the bridge that crossed over the highway. On the horizon she could see the faint outline of the city's skyscrapers. Spencer was in one of those, staying at his friend Mark's bachelor pad. He was sitting on the sofa watching QVC. That was all he did nowadays. Before the economy crashed his body had almost hummed with his competitive need, his high-octane energy. He'd met her at the end of the day and talked to her about what was happening in his life. They had gone out on the weekends and they had talked about their future. It wasn't that they had no budget for children. They had savings. It was possible.

Jenna started running again, pushing through the tightness in her ribs. She wanted to leave the view of the city behind. She wanted to leave her home. She had finally talked to Spencer earlier that week, telling him everything. She told him what she saw when she ran. She told him about Alana's long, straight hair, and the gap between Sophia's two front teeth. She saw him holding them for the first time; she saw him teaching them to ride their bicycles. She saw him teaching Sophia how to hold her own the first time a group of boys tried to tell her she couldn't do something as well as they could. She cried and smiled, believing that she could get Spencer to get off the couch, that he would get up and hold her and tell her, "Yes," that he would believe, say, "Yes, Jenna, that is what we need. That's what I want. I want us to be happy. I want us to be more."

Instead, he had scoffed. "Really, Jenna? This isn't the time to have kids. I don't even know if we can keep our house." He looked at her like she was delusional.

Jenna left the room—she had poured out her heart, every dream she'd built over miles and miles of asphalt. She filled a duffel bag with his clothes and dumped it at his feet.

"I want you to leave," she said.

He had stared at her. "You have got to be kidding."

She had hidden in their bedroom after that. When she heard the door close and his car back out of the driveway, she felt every tightly knotted muscle in her body unravel in relief. So, she started to cry.

Jenna ran. She imagined a divorce. She saw Spencer still sitting on Mark's couch, signing the papers she sent over in a manila envelope. She saw herself selling the house; it would sell, what did Spencer know? She would move to another city, transferring within her company to Denver or Albuquerque, somewhere with mountains or a desert, a place where the concept of extreme meant more than an oversized meal at Denny's. She saw herself finally getting a haircut with bangs, maybe slightly asymmetrical. She looked like a movie star. She would start running, by a tacit understanding, with an attractive man who lived in her apartment complex. He invited her over to dinner on Thanksgiving. She saw herself buying him a new tie for Christmas. He took her hiking in the mountains, or the desert. They went skiing in the Rockies or went on a road trip to the Grand Canyon. He had a stable job as an accountant, which would have been dull if he didn't care about it in a way that made it bearable, almost charming. He only did it so that he could go outside on the weekends, so that he could go swimming or skiing or just spend the day reading somewhere in the shadow of a tree. He had no television.

He asked her to marry him. Her second wedding ceremony was better than the first. There were fewer mistakes. It cost less money. He was a better kisser than Spencer. They would have Alana and Sophia or Robert and Amy or Jack and Evan. She didn't care about their names. He could pick.

She kept running, every day, before work, and after work. She kept imagining. Spencer didn't call and she didn't miss him. She listened as the singers told her to lift her hands up and get out onto the floor. They sang that her tie was coming, that she had only one life, that the moment was now. She pictured it all, the entire world stretching before her as the miles rolled by, her feet striking the pavement.

COWG ANTHOLOGY CONTRIBUTORS

Suzan Hixson lives with her two cats in Bend, Or. Retired from the US Forest Service after 30 years as hydrologist and Program Manager, she now spends her time working on her novel and her garden, hiking, and volunteering for the American Red Cross.

Marina Richie is a nature writer and environmentalist living in Bend and the author of the award-winning 2022 book, *Halcyon Journey: In Search of the Belted Kingfisher* as well as two children's books *(Bird Feats of Montana* and *Bug Feats of Montana)*. Her bi-monthly nature and poetry blog is featured on her website: www.marinarichie.com.

Karen Spear Zacharias is an Appalachian writer, and author of numerous works, both fiction and non-fiction. She holds a MA in Appalachian Studies from Shepherd University, Shepherdstown, West Virginia, and MA in Creative Media Practice from the University of West Scotland, Ayr, Scotland. She lives at the foot of the Cascade Mountains in Deschutes County, Oregon. Zacharias taught First-Amendment Rights at Central Washington University, Ellensburg, Washington, and continues to teach at writing workshops around the country. For more information see karenzach.com.

Hannah Love is a woman with a laptop from Portland, Oregon. When she is not working, she is practicing creative writing and befriending cats. Her fiction and poetry appear or are forthcoming in *Crow & Cross Keys, 34th Parallel, Across the Margin,* and *Audience Askew Literary Journal*.

Irene Cooper is the author of the novels *Found & Committal*, & the poetry collection spare change, finalist for the 2022 Stafford/Hall Award. Writings appear in *Denver Quarterly, The Feminist Wire, The Rumpus, Witness, Beloit,* & elsewhere. Irene teaches in community, & lives in Bend with her people & Maggie.

Christine Bell is enjoying retirement after twenty five years working in the tech industry. Now, she keeps busy with books and spends a lot of time outdoors. She is currently working on a memoir about her years of living in Italy with her family.

Arlite West (aka Barbara SilverSmith) was encouraged to continue writing poetry when she won the Newton Falls, Ohio contest. She aspires to be another Erma Bombeck, writing about life's mishaps and merriments. Meanwhile, she thinks in Haiku while kayaking. A native of Indiana, she has lived in 17 different places!

Ginny Contento grew up in Palo Alto, California and later lived in Venezuela and Spain. Retired from teaching Spanish and the mother of one grown son, she and her husband live in Bend. She works as a healthcare interpreter and walks their dog. She walks the dog a lot.

Minda DeBudge is an author of children's literature short stories. Her latest award-winning children's story appears in the *2023 Central Oregon Writer's Guild Anthology*. The first time she received a call notifying her of a win in a competition she thought it must be a prank and almost hung up the phone. Luckily, the competition representative was able to convince her the award was legitimate.

Cecelia Granger sprouted in Indiana and discovered Oregon in 1995 after sampling several other states. She alternates between painting with words and revealing stories with paint or pencil. A former Human Resources professional, she can often be found planning her next trip abroad with her husband.

William Barry is a professor emeritus in classics from the University of Puget Sound. He likes writing academic satire and has recently completed a novel titled *Swaddling U*. He is currently working on its sequel.

Andrew J. Smiley is a middle school Language Arts teacher and resident of Central Oregon for the last thirteen years with his wife and three children. He is usually pounding away at the anvil of his craft creating YA fantasy worlds, but in his downtime he can be found watching anime, playing video games, exploring dark corners, and tinkering with Gundam models at the dining room table.

Carol Barrett has been writing poetry for over forty years. She teaches Poetry and Healing courses, is a former NEA Fellow in Poetry, and has published two collections plus one of creative nonfiction. Her poems appear in *JAMA, The Women's Review of Books, Poetry International,* and in over fifty anthologies.

Mary Krakow is a retired educator, a member of COWG, SCBWI, and E-Z Writers Critique group. She writes flash, children's fiction, and letters to her elected officials. Mary's work has been published in various anthologies, as well as in print and online sites. Visit her blog for writers at www.findyourwritingnerd.com.

Gerald Reponen grew up in Minnesota. He entered the Air Force as a pilot. He has been writing for 80 years on his life of travels and adventures. His book, *The Vietnam War, My Life in the Air and on the Ground,* covered his four tours in Vietnam.

Marc Wagner is a science fiction and fantasy writer who has penned visionary tales and poetry since age 12. His novel, *Thin Places,* releases in 2024. He lives in Central Oregon with his wife, Janine, two children, Levi and Cortney, and an oversized Labradoodle, Theo, The Floor Wookiee.

Donna D'Orio, a five generation Colorado native, is an artist, mentor and evolving poet living in Bend Oregon to be near her family. She holds a BA in Art, Culture and Religious Studies. Her focus is poetry, painting, mystical interpretation/exploration, and indigenous clay process. She is inspired by remote places and village culture and always excited by the creative work of others.

Erik Frank has been herding words together since he learned the pen was mightier than the sword. His fictions explore our sundry encounters with truth, beauty, and transformation. He roams this territory with a poet's eyes, a comic's ear, and a child's wonder. To learn more, go to www.wordfevercircus.com.

Kendall Brown left her corporate job without a plan, seeking something more fulfilling. She writes about rejecting the default script in favor of creating your own. She lives in Bend with her husband and golden retriever, Penny. You can follow her work on her blog, "Still Small."

Lynda Sather lived and played all over Alaska while managing public relations for the Fairbanks school district and later, Alyeska Pipeline Service Company. Now retired, she splits her time between Fairbanks and Central Oregon, a.k.a. Alaska Lite. She is thankful to the Central Oregon Writers Guild for encouraging and supporting her writing addiction.

Matthew James Friday is a British born writer and teacher. He has had many poems in US and international journals. His first chapbook *The Residents* will be published by Finishing Line Press in 2024. He has numerous micro-chapbooks published by the Origami Poems Project. Matthew is a Pushcart Prize nominated poet.

Kiyomi Appleton Gaines writes fairy tales and other fantastical things. She was a contributor to the 2023 collection *Unquiet Spirits: Essays by Asian Women in Horror*. Her work has appeared in *Nightmare Magazine, Mad Scientist Journal,* and *Enchanted Conversation,* among others. She lives in Bend, OR.

Mike Cooper holds an MFA from Oregon State University. He is president of the Central Oregon Writers Guild and teaches writing at Central Oregon Community College and Oregon State University Cascades as well as creative writing workshops through The Forge and offers coaching and editing through Blank Pages Workshops.

Barbara Cole's book *Gifts: Reflections on Giving and Receiving* helps readers reconsider their giving and receiving experiences. A longtime Sisters cabin owner, she divides her writing time between Monterey, California and San Miguel de Allende, Mexico.

Samantha Reynolds is an aspiring novelist, marketing manager, and CrossFit athlete. She reads at least 50 books per year usually while sipping a honey cinnamon latte. When she's not reading she loves exploring the beauty of Central Oregon where she lives with her husband, cat, and golden retriever.

Dani Nichols is an award-winning writer, a cowgirl, and a mom of three. Her book for children, *Buzz the Not-So-Brave,* released summer 2022, and her work has been published in *The Other Journal, Oregon Humanities, Reckon Review,* and others. Follow her writing at www.wranglerdani.com or IG: @wranglerdani @buzzthenotsobrave

Kristine Thomas was inspired to be a writer after reading *Harriet the Spy* in the third grade. For more than 35 years, she worked as a newspaper reporter and editor, receiving several awards for her stories. She's currently working on a mystery novel. She enjoys hiking, reading, running, and exploring Central Oregon sites with her dog.

Jennifer Forbess has a Master's Degree in English from Northern Arizona University. By day, she plans Community Education classes for Central Oregon Community College, and by night, she writes literary fiction by candlelight. She lives in Bend, Oregon, where she enjoys reading, going for walks with friends, and agonizing over her writing.

Pam Tucker has been published in *Trestle Creek Review, Encore: Prize Poems 2018, 2020 and 2023*, and is the author of the picture book, *Paper Monsters*. Currently, she is working on her forthcoming chapbook, *Oftentimes, The Bird Still Calls*. She summers in Oregon and migrates south when the snow flies.

Maureen Heim an upcoming writer working on her first novel recently left the bustling metropolis of the Washington D.C. area to settle in Oregon. An avid reader, Heim writes heart-driven stories about families and the flaws that define them.

Cameron Prow's poetry has appeared in *PoetsWest Literary Journals, Fishtrap Anthology V,* and Central Oregon Writers Guild anthologies. "Elmer's Miracles" earned Honorable Mention for Children's Literature in Central Oregon Writers Guild's 2020 contest and was featured in an art education project in 2021.

Dan Murnan is an entrepreneur, second degree Aikido Black Belt, and golf coach living in Bend, Oregon. Being new to writing, Dan draws from his diverse background to create fast paced interesting stories. Dan's main genre is mystery short stories. His most recent series is the "Father Tim Chronicles," a series of philosophical action mysteries.

Jeffrey W. Kramer is a retired Los Angeles trial lawyer. He is also a former resident and Mayor of the City of Malibu, whose twenty-seven miles of scenic coastline and unique history and culture continue to inspire his writing. He now makes his home in Bend, Oregon.

Ted Virts is not a numbers guy. He ponders numbers he can't understand. Speed of light: 186,282 miles per second. Stars in our galaxy: 100 billion. Estimate of total galaxies in the universe:

2 trillion. Years in Bend: 10. Years Married: 40. Age in December: 75. Words in this bio: 51.

Janet Best Dart co-authored a technical manual for Oregon State University Extension. She now writes articles for Synanon.com, a compilation of stories about Synanon. Retired, she lives in Bend, Oregon with her husband and their mischievous Schipperke. When not writing, Janet can be found replacing her lawn with native plants. For more information, please visit www.janetbestdart.com.

Evelyn Moser studied English Literature at University of Nevada, Reno. She enjoys reading anything about history and politics. She lives in Redmond, OR.

Joan Gordon's loss of her identical twin started her writing endeavors in Bend. By weaving emotions into words, she artistically journeys through grief and creates a tapestry of hope. As a wife, mom, grandma and textile creator, Joan weaves love into her family and all she accomplishes.

Ted Haynes is the author of six books set in Central Oregon—most recently *Pole Pedal Murder,* the fourth book in his Northwest Murder Mystery series. He is a founding board member of the Waterston Prize for Desert Writing. www.tedhaynes.com

Diane McClelland is an award-winning entrepreneur and nonprofit leader who continues to work for 40 years creating economic opportunities for adult and young women entrepreneurs. She co-founded the Girls STEAM Institute® in her 70's to include girls from many countries who use global collaborative innovation™ to make a difference.

Anna Marie Garcia is a fiction writer who embraces the Central Oregon Lifestyle. Many of her characters are created while hiking trails and avoiding mosquitos. A world traveler, with a long ago journalism degree, she's recently returned to penning creatively.

Corbett Gottfried is the author of Voices From the Soul and he is currently working on his second book of poetry entitled Raven Speaks. He is retired after a long career in college administration and teaching. Corbett and his wife, Sally, live in Central Oregon.

Karista Bennett is a writer and author of two cookbooks, *For The Love Of Seafood* (2023), and *The Oregon Farm Table Cookbook* (2020), published by Countryman Press. She resides in Bend with her husband, and Australian Cattle Dog, Gus.

Eric Moser's stories have appeared previously in the COWG Anthology. He is retired from the US Forest Service and resides in Terrebonne, Oregon

David Cook, PhD, retired from university teaching, research, and administration, now writes poems and short stories about the real world and fiction, often from an unexpected perspective. He tends to probe the present and the future with a touch of irony and humor.

Kathryn Mattingly is the author of *Benjamin, Journey, Olivia's Ghost, The Tutor, Katya,* and *Fractured Hearts*. She has won multiple awards for her fiction novels and short stories. Kat teaches novel, memoir, and short story writing at her local college. She especially enjoys helping new writers achieve their goals.

Nikki Rainwater is a daughter, mother, friend, and kindergarten teacher whose writing has appeared in *Encounters: People of Asian Descent in the Americas,* and *The Butterfly Journal.* She recently indie published two children's picture books with her friend, illustrator Taylor Blacklock. By night, Niki is an imaginary guitarist for the Foo Fighters.

Nadra Mlynarczyk, a former native of Santa Rosa, CA, now resides in Bend, OR. She graduated from Santa Rosa Junior College with certifications in Early Childhood Education and Dental Assisting. Following a career in dentistry, she hopes to pursue writing. She is published in Dominican College & SRJC anthologies, and on Poetry.com.

Patti Lopez has lived in Central Oregon for 26 years. She has a B.A. in Sociology. Patti retired from the City of La Pine and in addition has worked as an editor for a customer service company. Patti has bred, trained, shown and trail ridden Arabian horses for several decades.

Bob Sizoo mostly wrote with and for students through the 90s. In 2001, Scholastic published his *Teaching Powerful Writing.* He has mostly rested on his laurels since then, though he takes seriously the notions of audience, voice, and purpose in every email he writes.

Pamela Mitchell is a native of upstate New York. She is an alumnus of SUNY Upstate Medical Center School of Nursing, and Goddard College where she earned her MFA. Her chapbook Finding Lost Pond won 2nd place in the American Journal of Nursing Book of the Year Award for Creativity. She has published in various anthologies.

Neal Lulofs has published short stories in *Ascent, Other Voices, Willow Review* and *Rambunctious Review,* winning the latter two magazine's annual fiction contests. He is a graduate of the MFA Program for Writers at Warren Wilson College. He is currently working on a novel from which "A Place Called Normal" is excerpted. Born and raised in Illinois, he resides in Bend, Oregon, with his wife and two golden retrievers.

Kore Koubourlis enjoys observing humans and listening deeply to them. Sometimes she writes about what she learns along the way. She is a leadership coach. She has served as an attorney and executive and holds a JD from Harvard Law School and a BA from Washington State University.

Anastasia Lugo Mendez is a writer based in Oregon. Her work has also appeared in *JMWW, Placed: An Encyclopedia of Central Oregon,* and *Sink Hollow.*

Made in the USA
Columbia, SC
07 November 2023